Shakedown Lifestyle

Shakedown Lifestyle

rapelling memory mountain

by

Patrick R. Penland

toExcel
San Jose New York Lincoln Shanghai

Shakedown Lifestyle
rapelling memory mountain

Published by toExcel

For information address:
toExcel
165 West 95th Street, Suite B-N
New York, NY 10025
www.toExcel.com

ISBN: 1-58348-290-3

LCCN: 99-62740

Printed in the United States of America

Contents

Personages of the Novel

As main character Bill Scolan struggles with a convoluted mental life and the laundered morality of a bankrupt humanistic world order. Behavioral poverty has been aggravated by attempts at self-aggrandizement during later adolescence in an incestuous liaison with half sister Julie and as a bawdy house program manager.

Intensely aware of personal limitations suffered since early childhood in a middle class family, he escapes domicile in a liberated Catholic Church. With strengthened acumen, he learns to outwit handicaps and take a measured advance towards lifestyle renewal as a career track counselor on Mary Bulinsky's professional staff.

Mary Bulinsky and Ann Patterson have been active mentors during Bill Scolan's personal development. In both actuality and manifest simulation, Ann and Mary share that virtual reality in his head with remnants of the older childhood gang of seven whose judgmental influecne has long been the bane of Bill's regressive pessimism.

Mary, taking the place of her own deceased mother, has served Bill's need for a surrogate maternal resource. Ann, though only recently coming to that realization, has accommodated Bill as a platonic Julie-mediator in Bill's life affairs.

Edna Masterson is the protagonist of the second part of the novel. Out of an unfortunate early life as an abused child-bride, a divorced adolescent mother of two daughters and yet a female priestess, she concerts to Catholicism. A sometime acquaintance of both Mary and Ann, Edna is hired, unknown to Bill Scolan, as a professional counselor. In the third section, Edna's appreciation of Bill's renewable patience in tolerating professional humiliation is evident.

To Bill's surprise and unexpected compensation, Edna expresses support and shares roles with him as a co antagonist or alter ego in the interpersonal negotiations encountered. Further empathy is awakened in Bill by quickened interests and scarcely suppressed mating instincts. Together the value of downsized expectations heightens reciprocal attrition and builds mutual respect. Bill starts to reclaim his mind excised of the porno images that have sexually inflamed his male imagination.

Section 1

Outwitting Liberation

1

"You may wonder what Catholic religious do when they leave the ministry and particularly after they apostatize. They go into work with militant Protestants, especially those groups whose mission it is to convert Catholics to their own manufactured brand of Christianity."

There was an angry undertone to the speaker's voice which jarred awareness as he continued. "Along with Muslims and Jews, Catholics are considered to be damned if they do not condemn the Church of Rome. They must be saved. It is up to 'real Christians' to take the gospel to them or else they will go to hell. Any 'pious' actions on the part of Catholics will not save them in the least."

Listening, Bill Scolan could not help feeling critical about the lambasting of Catholics to the very audience being addressed. Yet, the fellow's verbiage was understandable since Bill too, stemming from parental heritage, had been anti-Catholic for many years as a nominal member of the heretical Yoofnas Catholic Church.

Still, in back-of-mind, suspicions wondered whether such a mouthpiece might not be a mole planted by the ministry of civic religion in the United Federation of North American States (UFNAS, commonly pronounced "Yoofnas"). Propaganda in this relatively new government had fragmented the Church of Rome into a liberalized schismatic version of religion from which he himself had but recently been rescued by amazing grace.

Nevertheless, Bill remained seated in this duty assignment while the comrade persisted. "Some of these former priests and nuns are attached to mega-church organizations. They guide those of similar persuasions on their way, escaping from Rome. Others are traveling consultants to smaller congregations. They may drop in for a day or two, giving instruction and helping members set up a local committee whose job it is to coordinate efforts toward proselytizing Catholics.

"They all seem to have plenty of literature and audio tapes to distribute or sell in large quantities inexpensively. All of these tracts have a familiar sameness. The content seems to be sententiously repetitive. In fact, most of them are direct excerpts from, but unattributed to some major anti-Catholic sourcebook of which two or three are well known.

"Usually, the diatribes against Catholic positions are based on passages in scripture, either fragmented or taken out of context, and screwed around to support a premeditated point of view. Then again, they may force their opponent back to 'original' sources—to what the Greek says, for example. They neglect to point out that the first gospels were composed mainly in Aramaic, the language Jesus spoke. They get away with Greek-based arguments because even though they know little if any Greek themselves, Catholics are embarrassed with even less knowledge.

"Some of the sacrilegious dissenters may come to congregations with a travelling case of expropriated Catholic artifacts which they set up at an exhibit. This display could be presided over by an ex-nun, explaining the idolatrous use of such items as holy cards, rosaries, scapulars, medals, and crucifixes. To the greater titillation of 'customers' there may be a chalice filled with small hosts—brittle with age, but quite serviceable as 'cookie Christ's'!

"Of course, these promoters and pampheteers profess to be person centered. Their work, they claim, is being done out of love for individual Catholics trapped in the snares of a pagan Roman Church. However, it should also be remembered that much anti-Catholic concern loses a lot of credibility because zealots so often stoop to the most unfair of tactics. All too often, they'll use any weapon at hand, no matter how foul. They become then religious of a different ilk—Christians with little compassion and less wit.

"The content of many of their materials feature a couple of standard approaches to the attack. On the one hand, there is a tract on supposedly 'doctrinal errors' in the Catholic position on faith, morals or church government. Frequently this is coupled with an expose of dark 'secrets' deeply buried in the protective machinery of Church bureaucracy. Pedophilia and homosexuality have been perennial topics.

"On the other hand, the pamphlet may feature 'conversion' from Catholicism to whatever Protestant fission is sponsoring the tract. Testimonials are taken from women and men, young and old, under some such title as 'another ex-Catholic opts for biblical Christianity'. Typically, these conversions are quickies—a sudden born-again experience. Perhaps not as dramatic as Paul on the Damascus road, still they are nothing like the humanly developmental process of converts to Catholicism,"

The jawsmith droned on and on from a protected position behind the podium instead of orchestrating a discussion which anyone would have expected in attending a "seminar". Seated in an observational position near the front of the room, Bill could see that the fellow was reading from a prepared text.

Bill's eyes drooped and mind drifted away, trying to avoid the underlying anger of the speaker bouncing off his eardrums. It was a wonder that the Institute, even though just established, could get suckered in by such people!

Bill had been asked by the newly appointed director, Father Thompson, to attend this seminar which unfortunately had turned into a lecture dominated by a talking head. The impresario was all too reminiscent of the ego-massaging ministerial heretics who controlled the Yoofnas liberated catholic church.

Abruptly, Bill was startled alert. At this point the speaker had been interrupted, apparently, by somebody in the audience who had taken seriously the seminar intent, which the jawsmith seemed to be doing his best to subvert.

At least it was a different voice asking the question. "How can you say one conversion is superficial and the other significantly relevant?"

The speaker answered in continuation almost as if he had not been interrupted. "The use of the word 'conversion' is at the root of the problem. The term is used so often it can refer to something that is but a momentary change in point of view, all the way over to an extensively deep revision of one's lifestyle both secular and religious. 'Ex's' are all around—ex-fundamentalists, ex-Catholics, ex-priests, etc. Ironically, many ex-evangelists depict fundamentalism as a cult complete with brainwashing. However, it is difficult to locate ex-Catholics who consider Catholicism as a cult in the same sense."

"Come again! I don't understand." The badgering one was persistent.

Again, the preacher pressed on, you'd wonder if he had heard anything. "Few ex-Catholics stick very long with reverse conversions. They soon drift into agnosticism. Others however, in emotional revolt, out-fundamentalist the sectarians in the viciousness of their attacks on former Catholic beliefs. In other words, there is no substitute for Catholicism deep down in the human psyche. Unfortunately, it is part of human nature."

At this point, the intonation of the speaker's voice aroused a certain something deep down inside Bill, as of a thousand doubts squirming in suspicion. He could not shake the apprehension. A degree of insincerity had begun to color the fellow's words.

Somehow the denotation picked up by Bill's ears did not match the connotation which reverberated in awareness. It seemed as the talking head was doing his best to look like a faithful Catholic while poking tongue into cheek. If this continued, Bill would have a hard time of it, making a recommendation to Father Thompson.

"Almost nothing thrown at you by a bible thumper can be taken at face value. Anything appearing to be on the up-and-up should be suspect. Facts are bent to the snapping point. Nearly every word requires an exhaustive investigation—all deliberately contrived to weary the victim, break the spirit, and set them up for the shill of friendly fellowship once inveigled into an audience with other born-agains shallying around in assembly.

"The most charitable thing to be said is that their minds lack subtlety. To them, it is incomprehensible that anyone, even other denominations, could have any conclusion different from theirs. For the fundamentalist 'true believer', any other persuasion has to be necessarily erroneous. For them, this obsession becomes so intoxicating, it is a substitute addiction that freezes their attention into a locked-in perspective.

"Of course, the Catholic Church can be criticized for an ostensibly similar bias, even though in its world view other religions are weakened by varying degrees of error. The Church willingly acknowledges the greater or lesser degree of truth in them, depending on how much they mirror Catholicism. But, for the self-righteous, fundamentalism is fundamentalism. Anything else is a cult.

"The self-sufficiency of the fundamentalist is astonishing and so self-justifying as to border on the abnormal. Such a fascination with fixed diatribe such as slander, lies, half-truths and bizarre elliptical statements is as scurrilous as the fixation of many a homosexual with the literate of that perversion. The effort required to respond to such screed is so disproportionate as to be overwhelming. The temptation is to do nothing, to make no response, allowing the dog-biting thersites to suckle his contempt by default.

"The worst Catholic-baiters differ little from avid homosexuals fondling the scrum handed down from one attic to another through a thousand flea markets—cherished in repetitious passing—the more it can arouse their need for a fix the better. The fix for the fundamentalist is the look of discomfort, the hurt in the eyes, or the turning of a head in disdain which their deliberately contrived diatribe has aroused in another human being. Instead of jacking off like a homo, they thrust their heads in the air, stirring up the wine of conceit for brain effervescence.

"Needless to say, the fix is addictive. Once having tasted heady conceit they scurry around, nibbling at this pretext or another, saddling their intelligence to whatever grunts they can distort again. The most deliberately unfounded and most bizarre claims are ripped out of context and pirated from previous anti-Catholic diatribe materials. Their slight of hand is prodigious, dropping one phrase, adding specially placed emphasis words, or changing a sentence for slanting towards their personal addiction."

"Aren't you being pretty hard on fellow Christians?" This time the interruption came from a heavy set female.

"A Christian in fellowship is to me greatly different from an addiction to bias calling itself the truth. Such disturbers of the peace use a deliberate cover-up to stir up attacks on fellow citizens called Catholics. The prince of this world eagerly eggs on such satanic covenanters."

"Can't more be won by charity than enmity?" she probed.

"Ours is not hatred and strife, but a forbearance in humility. Christ made us aware of such ilk. And Paul was quite forceful against them. Today however the synagogue of Satan has been joined by the Christianity of Satan. The paganistic witchcraft of Satan is in a global war on the Catholic Church."

"Isn't that kinda overstating the matter, even to the point of becoming an alarmist?" It seemed like the issue bothered her like a bull raging away at a red flag.

"Christ was pretty direct and 'alarmist', if you want to use the word, in commanding us to watch for the signs of the times. One major sign of the times, is the ever widening collapse of other religions as well as humanistic liberalism and the coercive power of political reality, all directed into anti-Catholicism.

"Some of the television ministries got caught up in their own come-uppances several years ago. However, their success legitimized anti-Catholicism and emboldened all too many worldwide to take on the Church. A major chink in the wall as to ridicule the Catholic way to salvation and to redefine the word religion in a secular sense.

"The redefinition of religion, not now so new certainly but worldwide, means a complex, rule-laden, man-made scheme for effecting salvation on one's own. Of course, the rules have largely been discarded which made up a common morality. In America, the practices were coupled with individualism in a peculiar way of doing one's own thing. It became a subjective experiential thrust towards ego gratification exposed to the hazards of specious rationalism and casuistical tactics of self-justification.

"There has been a tendency to accept more and more scientific evidence and less and less bible revelation. Those, however, who accept Christ and his church do have a frame of reference for which to understand bible knowledge and wisdom.

"We do not have to start out with the conclusion that the bible is inspired, searching it for passages to be taken out and laid on others. The bible has to be considered as any other ancient work. The authenticity of text is traced back to early times. There are manuscripts to work from away back."

Bill had heard all his ears would hold. He got up from the unobtrusive seat and walked out, not attempting to appear apologetic about departure.

His mind seethed with the recall of judges-in-the-head, especially the speaker's alter ego reminding him of Judy and Gorkos—that malign pair whose "assistance" had given him so much trouble in the past. What little gained had been more than polluted with evil consequences.

Perhaps the memory was telling him something. But the information was inchoate. In some nonverbal way, the message remained global yet suffusing a sensation of foreboding entrapment, as if that jawsmith were planted for destructive malignance.

*   *   *

As Bill was about to round a corner out of the building, Father Thompson appeared with a bombshell of questions. "Where's the audience? Has Ariel Baker finished already?"

"Oh, is that the guy's name?" Then chagrined at being denied escape from the unpleasant task, Bill could only mumble defensively. "My hearing gave out. I couldn't listen any more."

"Is that the impression I'm to get from you?" the priest demanded.

"I'm surprised the audience stayed," Bill began apologetically. "They were all pretty edgy. But, more than that, there's something twisted about that fellow I can't put my finger on."

"You sound kinda turned off?"

"You can say that again!" Bill emphasized.

"I can't believe he'd do that badly. He's always been a likeable fellow. Perhaps it's his lack of experience."

"It's more than what meets the eye. I'm sure he's a good toady when needed. But he's got a hanger-on manner I don't trust, no way!"

"Well, I've gotta have more than that before even considering dismissal," the priest protested and then added weakly. "It's all so frustrating when nobody at all's interested in the deaconate!"

The note of dismay in the voice of a man of God got to Bill. His thoughts shuffled and backtracked into reversal. "I'm sorry, Father. I'll go back in and try to make something more of it."

"No, that's not necessary. I asked for a candid appraisal; and first impressions like this are more often telling than reconsidered hashment."

Bill could hardly believe his ears. A response tumbled from his lips. "I'm sure God'll take care of the matter in due time."

The religious minister smiled. "You, indeed, Bill Scolan have come a long way since the days of your own checkered past!"

"Father," Bill quipped, "you don't have to rub it in! I have enough problems going to confession as it is."

The priest uttered a chuckle as he turned to leave. Unwilling to tempt fate any further, Bill for his part made good an escape from possibly other scrutiny.

He could not help being a trifle nonplussed with himself. In previous days, any ill-perceived imposition of a thwarting experience imposed on an authority figure would have been nearly impossible.

Repercussions had always been immediate, making him cringe with shame as unfounded guilt and remorse depleted psychic energy and undermined courage. But in those times, the sacraments had been avoided like the plague they were in a heretical church.

Or if inadvertently partaken, Eucharistic reception would have saddled him with increased despondency and completed a mounting despair of salvation. However, staving off the possibility of impending doom, at least two of the judges-in-the-head and remnants of the juvenile gang of seven had helped him escape eternal damnation.

*   *   *

Bill had come a long way in the past five years. He would never have thought it possible to be on friendly terms, at least in a quasi-sort-of-way, with any priest before whom one had confessed sins.

Nevertheless, two of the previous mentors-in-his-head, Mary and Ann had been instrumental in behavior modification. Though technically his employer,

Mary's professional expertise and sage humanity had been to advantage, jump-starting a personality development that bordered on the good news of Jesus Christ.

Like the winged creatures of another world, those two women had stood beside him, figuratively, whenever the going was rougher than usual. Far be it from him to claim to have completely crawled out of an inner cave. Yet he no longer yearned to gaze in the reflecting pool, a craving that had for years dominated his escape from intimacy.

The void had not so much been empty but that it was a perversion, an entanglement with Julie where each of them seemed to have leaked into each other without any discrimination at all. In complete turn-around, neither Mary nor Ann would tolerate such dependency and put up with the feverish delusions that, for the lust-addicted, were self-debilitating.

In this regard, part of the problem was in learning how to separate love from power—how to love without controlling the one loved, and let something or other just happen. Could he put imagination to sleep long enough for some special person—whomever that may eventually be—to exercise her liberation?

Yet, once having hazarded growth with such a one in a long-term mutual relationship, could he then forestall an unleashed and still unrestrained imagination? Who then would take responsibility and save him and her from himself?

Far be it from him to claim an entire release from unnatural cravings. But he could at least work side by side either of his female associates without figuratively tearing off their clothing.

Once in awhile, he may have feasted illicit cravings on their imaginary naked flesh. But not for long. Their female objectivity had immediately brought him around in a way that had never been an available feature of earlier youth development.

Perhaps the greatest learning of all was that female bodies were simply female bodies, wondrously resourceful, if not provoking sexually overloaded and wild images, and the porno gymnastics manufactured in the factory of addictive imagination. In fact he had had a hard time forgiving, let alone praying for those in the past who, if not directly involved with the porno industry, were habitues of the prosthetics mass produced by various cults in cahoots with mob distributors.

One other former teenage judge-in-his-head, Mary's husband, had unwittingly served as a belated mentor in Bill's regard. Once an associate in a mob's virtual porno enterprise, Terry had been able to reorient himself and make a major contribution to the development of an interactive electronic diorama—a Christendom reconstituted on the post-apocalyptic good news of the gospel.

To his own surprise, and that of influential others, the externally validated simulation had become an experimental learning environment. In the holograms, policy makers could grapple with social reconstruction after a century, for the most part, turned over to the ravages of anti-Christ's last fling in destroying the Catholic Church.

In actuality, instead of being suckered in by the so-called "Christian" henchmen of the "reformation", Christ's persecuted, martyred, and bleeding sacramental openness was still available to all. True to the Church's Christ-ordained mission, and despite massive clerical defections and porno-related miscarriages of ministerial function, a priestly remnant had kept faith in solidarity with humanity.

To build upon these spiritual resources, earned in such pitiless, heart-rending savagery, work on a simulated Christendom was being dedicated in a manner reminiscent of cathedral building in the Middle Ages. If only the pharisaical excesses of those times could now be avoided.

2

The two of them had been sitting across the desk in Bill's office at Leland House, going over some notes towards a proposal for refunding on-going research. The day had been long. He dozed off momentarily.

Abruptly some dimensional change had occurred. Startled awake, he found himself recovering from a salacious dream, as if the woman across from him were naked and alive with passion.

Bill came to full awareness with a start.

His mouth opened to hastily apologize for anything he could have mumbled which might be taken for coworker sexual harassment. Any words that could have come were quickly doused by her immediate interruption.

"Bill, I can feel your lust!" she exclaimed. "I'm not a prostitute. It's more'va a burden than I can bear! I'm not gonna bimbo-up to the syncopated wiggles in your inflamed imagination, porno-queening my way into following all the weirdo shimmies of your self-infatuation—trying to sashay up to the gambol of an infectious mind! Why d'ya bother with human females when the slave-economic holographs can easily outpace every whim you could ever have?"

The cutting edge of her words reverberated in his own sharp intonation. "Computers will never match the human mind!"

"Not if you maintain moral integrity. But weaken it with porno-diseased liberalese and it'll soon fall prey to super computing powers."

The intensity of her outburst still bothered him. After all, he could have flubbed off in a wet dream. Reluctant, it seemed as if he were being disciplined by some "parental" reprimand.

The prospect of having to now pick up on the conversation left him perplexed. A deep-seated sense of remorse held him to whimper under breath. "Could he be expected to be sorry for feelings?"

Out louder, all he seemed able to mutter, nearly below hearing was, "Well, I got needs you know."

"Is that what I heard you say?" Ann demanded.

He really was stuck on that one! He shrugged a shoulder before realizing impact implications. But apparently, she was not bothered by any impending significance.

Though still attracted to each other, the prospect of any deeper commitment between them had never materialized. Bill had told himself that Ann did not want to jeopardize Lucy's future by allowing any possibility of stepfather intimacy with her daughter.

Nor could his reputation be considered of much worth to a growing teenage female. No doubt he was still handicapped by an incestuous affair with half-sister Julie.

Surely Ann's reluctance and lack of closure on any proposal for a marital pledge could not be due to the fact of his being ten years of age his senior. The cause, he suspected, must lay deeper in the sinister make-up of his previous lifestyle. Apparently he had been more deeply corrupted than some others of the childhood gang-in-his-head.

Bill's momentary reverie was cut short as Ann charged into awareness. "You may be a 'roman' Catholic now, but fornication's still the hang-up no normal woman can every rectify on her own. You can't fight fire with fire! You gotta purge it first."

Bill was not ready psychologically to handle his "fornication" so openly. Instead his mind closed in on the deflecting issue of church allegiance.

Her emphasis on the word "roman" was in recognition of his regularized transition for a church of liberalized catholic heretics. Conversion had been facilitated on discovery that his baptism and confirmation had been ministered under intact residual sacramental powers.

Bill had not changed external religious affiliation simply because of employment by the Catholic Archdiocese. The spontaneously restrained convictions of Mary and Ann over their years of professional association had been an important factor.

Nor had the conversion been the result of some magical séance. Indeed, he still suffered from the aftermath ravages of previously unrestrained addictive inclinations. Nevertheless, rebound time had decreased and consolation from the struggles of inner endurance was stronger.

Of considerably additional weight in his conversion had been the example offered by many individuals whom he had interviewed or treated as clients in counseling. Their recovery under sacramental providence had been a compelling influence, unable to be ignored.

Ann tossed her head, obviously indignant. "You better get over to your old porno house and work it off with Terry's holograms. They can snuckle under your skin like I never will!"

"Whyn't I just take a shower!" he quipped, glad that the strength of their social solidarity had seen him through yet another interpersonal boo-boo!

"That's hardly enough!" she protested. "You oughta know better. You're the psychologist supposedly an expert in addiction therapy."

"You sound like a nagging wife. Is that the way you'n Tom got along?" He let the audacious words out before regret surged up to silence his tongue momentarily.

Abruptly though, a natural even uncouth shrewdness crowded back into thought. "I'll bet you'n Tom were into a thwarting experience the night before he was mugged to death!"

Then exploiting the nonverbal impact he supposed was upon the woman, he charged back in for the bully-kill. "You been all froze up ever since!"

Surprisingly, nothing in her appeared to cringe nor rebuke what others would have called an unfair condemnation. She looked at him with an open face. Eyes brimmed with a candid solace as if she considered him to be a child waiting approval from an adult.

Instead, she observed flatly. "Bill, we long ago decided neither of us is helped if I become a pleaser, tolerating if not sucking up to every whim you could demand of me." Then, turning the shive, she added ironically. "I still have too great a respect for your potential."

"That's what Mary'n her mother've always said'n I never asked them to marry me!"

"How much Mary has suffered over your continuing escapement—indeed, prayed for you as I have too! What more could I have done as your wife?"

"Well, I'm here, aren't I, trying to build a professional career and enable client maturity by lifestyle counseling."

"True enough! But you still have new age hang-ups."

"The new age's defaulted," Bill objected. "We're working our way beyond moral laundering."

"Maybe so, in external behavior. But the roots of the disease still send weeds sprouting, infesting the blind leading the blind. Virtual reality's virtually nerded the entire population."

"'Forsooth' croaked the raven evermore!"

"Seriously Bill! You're yet one've them who figure on professional excellence while refusing, or at least ignoring the dependency trickling into all of private life everywhere."

"That's being a luddite!" he reacted, feeling the sting of criticism directed at his reluctance—even though declining—to condemn all of contemporary life.

"The effect is not as noticeable in technology. There, mistakes are readily evident. If not corrected, the impact of nature is directly unforgiving. It's in the humanities where decay is insidious, devastating the entire range of socio-political life."

"Are you referring to that reformation antichrist and the apocalyptic fallout through the renaissance, age of reason and industrialization? Didn't deTocqueville indicate that the American experiment was the antidote to all those Old World hang-overs?"

"He was blinded by a side-winder interpretation of evangelical good news. Averse to the truth, his anti-roman fundamentalism favored a simplistic constitutional interpretation."

"Not its originally stated principles?" he queried.

"No document is secure from subsequent massaging by dirty hands. Look at the bible—how many countless revisions has it spawned when the living presence of its Referent is ignored? Worse still, it is denied, and now deliberately countermanded in legalized aberrations."

Bill looked at Ann thoughtfully. From the familiarity of their long history together, he observed. "You seem to have lost whatever train of thought you started with."

"Succinctly," she began informatively, "Goedel's theorem has been ignored; no system can be evaluated from within. Yoofnas society has gone all hog-wild, deliberately escaping into what's been called 'living measurement'. Continuous polling tracks the continuous re-polling of previous poll findings. Concatenation completely subjectifies investigative science and enslaves itself. Homogenous concensi evolve on and on, steamrollering any minority as politically incorrect, rendering independent thinking impotent if not dangerous and unpatriotic."

"If I remember right," Bill recalled, "deTocqueville did warn about opinionated tyranny."

"The effect is codified in the ideology of inclusive pluralism for nerds going blind over electronic screens. Your own liberated Yoofnas Catholics have become unwitting dupes, politically correct mouths spouting species purification, genetic experimentation and artificial population control—all thinly coated with the Teflon of inclusive license."

"Ann, don't tar'n feather me with my parent's predilections. I may not be completely roman yet, but give me credit for some progress."

She smiled, Bill observed to himself, as if tolerating a child who had talked back out of ignorance. "Bill, you've come a long way under Mary's good work and my prayers, I hope! But I can't cut off all the strings that're puppetting your dependency."

He protested. "You're still hung up about my goof over lusty thoughts!"

"That's only part of it—just the squirmy crust of deep oozing sores infecting so many others today—especially those who crave what are supposed to be charismatic highs in the decayed spirituality of the day."

"Are you referring to the alternate thesis in my much neglected doctoral research—compensating for the limitations of stimulus-response motivation?"

"Either you didn't fully realize the significance of results or were not able to make applications in your own personal thoughts and behavioral development."

"What've I missed?" he wondered.

"You've bought into an apocalyptic ideology of progress. That trap has replaced the freedom of the moment in Christ's anthropology. Evaluation, there may be, but it's only the apparent result of ever recurring cycles of challenge and observant obedience."

"You make it sound so patriarchal!" he objected.

"Only because of your outmoded humanistic rebellion—refusing the creative humility through which spiritual intuition flows. Without it, psychological boundary development lies dormant. No protective restraints are available to support individual convictions to the contrary. Few, even roman clergy remain able to name a spade, or call people to account for the murderous complicity of infant cannibalism in their hearts."

"If Christ's vineyard is so ravished, what avenues have we got or even hope for conversion?"

"A few seminaries thrive who seek the Virgin's protection," she explained.

"I've never had any inclination to become a priest," he countered. "You oughta know that!"

"The deaconate is open to any male, married or single. In fact, married men are preferred. Experiments with preaching have made that ordination fruitful."

"I'm surprised. You cotton to female denial?" he asked provocatively.

"Unfortunately, that's a feminist bias which subverts women's real strengths—counseling and homily-izing episodic enlightenment."

"Homily? Sermons? What's the difference?"

"Men are good at sermons with principled conviction and logical persuasion. But they're dupes at existential sharing. Actually, a husband'n wife deaconate team may be the very instrument of the Lord's visitation before the end of the world."

For what could have been an embarrassing length of moment, Bill gazed at the woman. The intensity of his intuition dissipated all inhibitive fumbling.

The absence of any subjective backlash whatsoever was guaranteed by his perceptive probe. "What was the burden of your thwarting experience with Tom?"

With unexpected vehemence the woman broke down, yielding to an anguished sobbing. Instantly, Bill's heart went out to this female, detached as he was of all emotionally chauvinistic and smothering affection.

For this woman, the end of probably a youthful aspiration had come, possibly never ever to be fulfilled in the cards of life. Still, to make her expectations viable seemed less than a valid reason for an otherwise honorable marriage proposal.

Bill got up from the chair and moved across to sit beside his distraught associate, deliberately placing an arm around her shoulder in a constrained masculine hug. Nothing coyly submissive was evident as she gently leaned into the protective support of the other half of her human entity.

For the first time in his life, or as far back as memory could be taxed, Bill was able to offer a dimension of being never tapped before. A sexless gesture, platonic gift if you will, shored up the presence of one psyche with another— no strings attached, whatsoever!

Nobody would have believed such a happening possible. Wait a moment! Why did he seem to see in mind's eye a surrogate mother smiling and a grown daughter nodding heads in accord?

*   *   *

The lack of psychological boundaries between him and half-sister Julie had been a major dependency problem from the early stages of his young life. Even so, now that he was out of adolescence, the influence of her associates whether beneficial or for ill—like the other judges in his head—still clung to him, hovering in addictive awareness.

The struggle had been horrendous, the perpetual bane of his existence—an infestation that even yet visited him. The images of molestation waned and waxed with the strength of those lunar searching's for wholeness through a relationship with anything at all.

Seldom had he ever found the peaceful nourishment of beauty and happiness than as a child coddled by a surrogate mother. Since those ancient days of his own near prehistory, the evidence had more often been pilfered away, leaving him saddened and vulnerable.

Then would his psyche fling itself around in wounded innocence, unable to avoid the irrevocable cycle, or even soften critical defeat? No wisdom would come in time to suffer through mood swings and deny the wild urges to suckle on the intoxicating behavior of acting out.

Laying his mind on whatever came along for addictive arousal would corrupt attention by delusion, eager to copulate in fanciful ecstasy. But suddenly at the brink of tumescent omnipotence, power ejaculated, abruptly draining away any remnant of long gone sublimation.

Alarmed by that devastating loss of vitality, he would cram around—like a rat in joy-response machine—for whatever levers of greater fulfillment could be triggered. But the near instantaneous insult of fright always reared up, erupting in despair.

An unwanted sense of complicity somehow wormed into awareness, snuffing out any embers of the smoldering candle. Doom and gloom blackened expectations with a merciless guilt dancing on remorse.

Swamped in fear, the cycle devolved lest anybody else discover the abject weakness of his individual persona, but never the critics in head. Those demons would be upon him, tearing at resolve until some other satiation experience came to the "rescue".

Relief had ever been questionable, tempered by uncertainty until partition occurred separating him from the surroundings. Dimensional removal was always pleasurable, however virtual that state might be.

No matter the skilled maintenance, simulation eventually floundered on the dialectic of its inevitable thwarting experience. Vain attempts to escape connecting with the source of his being only furthered alienation.

Nor were the youthful experiences of stepfather's emancipated denominational life of much help either. Adherents of the liberated Yoofnas

Catholic Church had nearly perfected their heretical methods of Trojan-horsing Rome while outwardly professing membership in the world body.

Working on the addictive qualities of change for its own sake, a nameless horror of the same-old-thing in traditional ritual had stirred up widespread resentment. Instead of downsizing, instigators had mediated all manner of celebrations to mold every parish into a group-sensitive reflection of its members and their opinions. Thus, power was shifted from the hierarchy to the laity where it could be controlled for vested interest purposes.

Once the priestly sacrifice was emasculated, ministerial power would flow from men to women. In this regard, feminist agitators playing Svengali troubadours had exploited the "needs" of itchy camp followers for a more scenic mass-journey.

The heady flow of progress and the orgiastic kaleidoscope of happenings were mediated towards something more titillating in seeking sensual "enlightenment" through addictive substances and behaviors. No longer was the spirit welcomed in moving across the waters to alleviate stress, or rekindle freedom and reconnect with self-healing and charitable compassion.

Instead, the charisma of bear hugs, handshakes and liturgical kissing were employed to mask the effect of bedroom killings. Soothing music and hymnal singing at the adulterated services disguised the murder of senior, and other citizens in the elimination centers. Then will the inclusive liturgy of a nutbread mass pacify the infantile couples as they find "god in themselves", and repair to the parish hall for a communal ice cream sundae or an afterward shopping trip to the mall to be good to themselves after the abortion!

Far be it from him to wave a hand or toss his head in a pharisee pomp. Though denied any possibility of prevention, he had been there when his own child had been murdered.

The infant may have emerged deformed from half-sister's body, or incestuously disfigured internally; but infanticide it had been! Nor could the killing be condoned as the rotten fruit of a tabooed abandonment.

The murder, instigated on his own killing bed, had almost traumatized any thought of female relationships. Nearly all female smile, which now seemed common on women's faces even when encountering male strangers, had for him turned into giocondan leers.

The natural urge upon a woman for male insemination—or, "the desire for your husband" as the bible would have it—had been polluted by lascivious gymnastics. Here was another "she" ready and eager to seduce him on another killing bed while swallowing the abortifacent that would curdle his semen!

The very thought of such intersexual carcinogens was enough of a thwarting experience to compost nearly all heterosexual inclinations. Any push to a rebound on the contrary was unpalatable. It had never been his thing to seek a mood change while browsing in an adult head shop, or in cruising shrouded tree-lined streets.

3

Somewhat longer than a month later, Bill was in the presence of the minister he'd had to disappoint with a candid speaker appraisal. They were sitting across from one another in the Yoofnas-ized version of a confessional that, for better or worse, was currently being offered as the common penitential mode for Roman Catholics.

On this particular occasion Bill found himself absorbed in a peculiar manner, or thought pattern. Of course nobody could escape remorse for sin either by confessing the guilt or in hardening the heart.

Harden our spirits, not our hearts,
Let us pray to the Lord.
May compunction soften the murder in our
Hearts, Let us pray to the Lord.

Try as he might to deny it, his culpability was darkened by another dimension. The evil of his devising had been more agnostic, a straddling of the dividing line between permissibility and sin.

It was all too easy to let his mind be dissuaded by extenuating circumstances—counting intentions on the pinhead of explanation, of excuses over which responsibility remained a clouded issue, as if the deciduous trees of memory had been replaced by evergreens.

Could he take credence and explain to himself an excusable justification for such divided mental patterns—unless the falling leaves were a more contrite manifestation than the rigid skirts of the puritan spruce hardly bending at all in the wind?

Could such behavior be excusable, a reeling with the punches in the interests of arbitration? Or, were such timid replies but the mark of quisling, a chickening-out of any allegiance to principles and conviction?

But no! How could the ordinary fix of psychological support and everyday bodily energy be enough? Only frequent, if not daily sacramental reception would compensate for the anthropological dead weight of common humanity everywhere in desolate evidence.

However, unfortunately having neglected the Bread of Life, his psyche suffered from the absence of supernatural vitality and continued to mope. He had allowed the depressive aftermath of an incestuous affair with half-sister Julie to fester, and get the better of him.

The reverie over those remembrances was disturbing and may have aggravated Ann's continued reluctance to accept mutual commitment. As for himself, Bill was convinced there had been opportunity enough.

But for Ann, the rancor was apparently deep-seated—scarcely to be talked about, he suspected, in the intimacy of one-on-one female conversation regarding the bodily repercussions of abortifacents demanded by the unbridled imagination of male lust.

Nevertheless a halt must be called somehow on former tendencies, or rather addiction towards the mumbo-fumbling in mind so common to himself before his days at Leland House. He had to get on with life, even though sisterly sex may have spoiled any chances for a normal marital engagement in his own life.

No longer could he afford to mope over what seemed to be a lingering inconclusiveness. It was difficult to put a finger on any other reason for Ann's lack of movement toward enduring commitment. Surely it could not be some underlying feminist resentment.

Still the hang-up persisted, even though he had spent many hours not only in mentoring example but in training Ann for development as a helping practitioner. She had been successfully weaned of enabler limitations and was on her way towards fulfillment as a catechetical exergist complementing his role as researcher and professional consultant.

Young in years and perhaps because of it, he could not be relieved of the nagging suspicion that his own maturation lacked something or other. But the inchoate remained inexpressible. To fill the persistent void, he had picked up on preliminary research in order to write a book as an alternate to the thesis for professional recognition.

For him, the changed situation had become familiar because he too had abandoned active association with the heretical liberated Catholic Church. Yet despite repudiation teenage memories persisted, reminding him of the mental horrors he'd suffered when forced by stepfather into compliance.

His mind-drift was short lived. The gentle words of Father Thompson soon brought him back from distraction.

"Well, Bill, there used to be a lotta talk about decision making at one time during the new age. Imaging and channeling especially were in vogue. The trend was a rebellion, for the so-called liberation from typical methods used by everybody for centuries."

The priest looked distracted for a moment, but then returned in focus. "Nevertheless, the more new ideas were supposed to change, the more the applications in everyday behavior held onto the scientific formula of controlled investigation—you know the routine: survey the situation, analyze opportunities and constraints before identifying the advantages and liabilities."

"I don't know how any professional could live without it in daily research."

"By the way, how is your book coming?" the priest asked in passing.

"Slowly! I still got more interview records to analyze and codify," Bill replied and then added. "I don't mean to complain, but it's all Ann'n I can do to keep up with the growing caseload."

"I got somebody in mind that's undergoing an early mid-life crisis…"

"Father," Bill interrupted hastily, "we got enough people who're psycho-spiritually impaired. Misfits trying to help other misfits'll only screw things up."

The priest smiled broadly. "You're tripping it again, Bill. Your faith and trust have a ways to go."

"Yeah, I guess. Anyway that's one sin I gotta confess."

"Wait a minute! Before we get into the confession part, let me finish the orienting we starting with. It'll help you take on more personal responsibility for opening up to the Lord in humility and intimacy."

"Interpersonal candor has been my problem, I'm told, more than once."

"Relationships with others do help offset ingrown addictions. To gain a foothold in the realm of the spirit, persons have got to free themselves of prevailing trends in action."

"How well do I know that!" Bill exclaimed.

"Well anyway, the new agers superimposed visualizing and mirroring onto the problem solving method everybody has used. Nearly totally impatient, they couldn't stand waiting and hungered after the gimmies. Their motto was, 'wishing will make it so when crowded under the synchronicity of cosmic serendipity'."

"Well do I remember Julie's bouts with the infernal and my complicity!"

"Forget it Bill. You've confessed the past in a general confession. Let it go in God's mercy; otherwise remorse can be suicidal."

After a brief pause, the priest picked up his thought pattern again. "Actually, that's where the 'Jesus-people' and the born-agains got into the act of redefining problem solving. Instead of selecting the least interesting and non ego-massaging option, they sought the alternative considered in a biblical sense the most pleasing to Jesus—that is, according to the version of Christ manufactured in imagination."

"That," Bill reflected, "is kinda parallel to the psycho-psychic experience of choosing the least ego-massaging among any two or more options of equal expectation. Our clients are encouraged to use it as a counter-addictive measure. Once habituated, it becomes a foundation for whatever extension is followed such as twelve-stepping, or the indwelling of ignatian virtue enhancement, or any other method of spiritual development that may be employed."

The confessor looked upon the penitent before him with appreciation. "As I've said before, Bill, I hope you pray to the Lord in humility and obeisance…"

"You mean," Bill interrupted, "become a genuflect-bunny!"

"You've sure a way with words," the priest laughed. "No. Thank God for release from slavery to the heresies of the Yoofnas Catholic Church. There's scarcely anything worse than half-truths and lies in clouding one's thinking."

"You've hit it again, Father! My thinking's been addle-brained all too long."

"You could try expressing appreciation for the grace begun in your conversion. Any effective apostolate has to be grounded on the interior life where Jesus dwells."

Bill's ears picked up what suspiciously sounded like a challenge in the cleric's voice. "You suggesting some re-tooling of my work at Leland House is needed?"

"Not at all," the priest stated flatly. "But I am wondering if you've got the potential to rise beyond the ordinary."

"You mean with the spiritual approach to problem solving you've not got around to telling me yet?"

The other smiled at the unrealized candor of the recruit sitting across from him in the penitential room. "In part, yes," he responded. "What I had in mind though was the assignment the Cardinal's just given me."

Bill looked more closely at the cleric, but did not interrupt the possibility of an informative continuation.

"One aftermath of the apocalyptic age we've just escaped has been the fall out of priestly vocations and the defection of so many others. The diocesan seminary is practically vacant. The few recruits trickling through take many years of preparation."

"Is the Cardinal preparing another stopgap measure to back-fire and end up to the triumph of the feminist agenda?"

"Get thee behind me, Satan!" the priest exclaimed and then added. "Women have an unharnessed potential for the good of the Church. But until those policy implications can be worked out, the Cardinal has taken a newly insightful approach to the apostolate. Even if there were no ministerial shortages, the function of the deacon has been underutilized. Unfortunately, in need of correction, its role has become vestiginal, if not defunct."

"I know the word 'deacon', but have no ideal of entailment or opportunity."

"The cardinal reasons that priests can only become the apostolic mentors they're ordained for, if deacons take on many of the sub-powers which priests are now saddled with. He envisions a mixed deaconate of married and some celibates. A matrimonial team approach to the role would raise the consciousness of holy family life. Both women and men would be offered the spiritual fulfillment already becoming so widely desired in this era of the good news. As a result, he's about to announce a deacon training program and appoint me in charge of it as co-rector."

"Congratulations!" Bill dutifully enthused and added. "You're just the person to get the job done."

"May be, God willing," the cleric responded with serious mien. "Bill, I'd like you to come on board."

There was a moment of silence before Bill almost shouted, "What!", while the shrapnel of the bombshell exploded in awareness.

"I'd like you to continue working out in the field for a while. You could take on the odd homily—gaining some experience in preaching before taking a few theology courses at the seminary, as well as training in public speaking. Eventually, I think, you'd make a suitable faculty member."

"I don't have a doctorate." Bill hung back from further comment, feeling the rise of near uncontrollable fear.

"Given time and an extension of earned credentials, something could be worked out."

"It sounds preposterous!" he burst out in rising panic. "My lurid background…"

"Bill," the good father interrupted, "have you forgotten Magdalene, or St. Augustine? Both of them suffered the pangs of lust and the chill of recuperation. Your convoluted way of thinking is the disastrous aftermath of sin. We all suffer from the wages of evil in one way or another. But those thick-tongued ideas will eventually pass. Remember Christ's words to the apostles. 'Have no fear of what to say. I will send the Holy Spirit to enliven your minds'."

"Yeah, I know Father," Bill hastened to add. "My sins are forgiven and I'm routed born-again. But I got no prospect of marriage, let alone the kind of family life you'd expect."

"Bill…"

"Father, hear me out! What about research and publication? What about client services at Leland House, and the in-service training of para-professionals?"

"My, my!" the priest wedged in. "All I hear is the New Ager gimmies—hanging onto mine possessions. How addictive have you become!"

That cool appraisal undercut Bill's headstrong assault. He lowered eyes briefly, but adamantly rejected any hangdog submission.

In a moment the priest observed. "You've been hit with a kind of 'thwarting experience'. That is so typically needed by all who seek a spiritual mode for problem solving. In the old days of Christendom, before antichrist was unchained in the reformation, problem solving was not recognized under that name. For a millennium and a half it was known as discernment and obedience to the Holy Spirit. So today we've got to bridge that devil-imposed hiatus and call upon the Lord to rescue our heritage and build it up under his guidance for the good of all peoples."

"Father," Bill began, now having reestablished a more objective control of emotion. "I got no quarrel with the proposal. Actually, it's needed. What I can't cotton to's any role in it for me."

"Well, the seed's planted. Let the Lord of the harvest bring it under cultivation. Maybe in time, something will come of it."

"Okay."

This time, Bill did bow his head under compunction, finally willing to accept the priest for what he was—the ordained representative, directly appointed by Jesus Christ to release him from bondage.

Though he had come a long way in recognizing the load of guilt provoking false humility, Bill had not made enough individual confession to feel entirely comfortable. Regretfully, his emotions preferred the penitential services where general absolution is administered to all those in the assembly who had silently identified sins in the privacy of their own thoughts.

Though he'd been fingering a sinner's aid card—handily provided for the occasion—he by-passed whatever pertinent suggestions were presented. Instead he began to list in mind subjective impressions of inner psychic movement. He considered it a preliminary venture to get the ball rolling, so to speak, like his own counseling clients.

"Father, it has been several months since individual confession. I'm often irritable. I sweat—my hands get clammy and my heart beats funny. It's hard to swallow with a dry mouth. My mind goes blank and I can't concentrate."

Without individual address, the priest spoke. "These are psychological symptoms of predisposing sinful conditions. If you would try to confess more often, it would be easier to recognize personal disobedience, indifference to God's spiritual resources and the damaging effects on others."

"Yes father," Bill agreed, finally pushing himself to make the penitential effort. "I been angry and resentful…suspicious of other's intentions… uncharitable and envious…impatient and fearful. I been lazy and wasted time, even rambling in self-pity and lack trust in past forgiveness."

Again came the calm assurance of spiritual awareness. "Can you place a number on these transgressions?"

"No, but they have been often," he admitted and then with rising courage added. "Sometimes the brooding goes on for hours when I should be working."

Carefully but dispassionately, the pastor concluded with a question. "Is there anything else to confess?"

"Probably a lot. The sins of my past life…"

"If confessed, don't scruplize. Have confidence in God's mercy. Now, make an act of contrition."

Bill threw attention to the leaflet in hand and read aloud. "Oh my God, I am really sorry for all my sins. I hate and detest them with all my heart, because they displease you, oh my God. I firmly resolve, by your help, never to offend you again!"

"Through the merits of Jesus Christ, I absolve you of these sins and those of your past life. For a penance, say an Our Father, Glory be, and Hail Mary in that order."

"Yes father."

"Now go in peace, and pray for me."

*   *   *

After leaving the rectory and the presence of the priest in the confessional, Bill's mind was preoccupied. On the one hand he was aware that it is impossible to return to a life past except in memory. That mental faculty however could be confused—focused at one time in recalling the wonders of God's amazing grace or, at another, be clouded with regret over the insensibility of lost opportunity.

Who but himself was to blame? He could of course rebuke the devil for conniving around in his own inner daemonics—impossible but for consensual volition. On the contrary, the wheel of judgement had stopped head-on—the pointer aimed directly at his own weakened omissions.

It was no wonder that his psyche still had not warmed up to the living Flame. Only recently had he bothered to take the time and begin to study the will of God. Thus, no one else was responsible for a cluttered memory, too crowded for any share in God's power by recalling the Divine goodness, beauty and truth.

Unfortunately, it was easy to lapse into a sense of remorse over inadequacy and bitter recall in the innumerable instances of neglect beginning wit the inevitable concomitant phrase of, "If only..." But then, even scarcely before the smile could vanish from the presentation images in his head, the mask of appearance would vanish, leaving the bone of a cranial skeleton exposed in sepulchral stare.

On the other hand, with only a modicum of effort, it was possible to revamp one's attention and allow a proactive comprehension to enlighten the past with reference to the present moment. Of course those events had taken place in the sequence of human time. But to the Divinity one day is as a thousand years; and an eon of age is but a moment in the presence of God.

Despite such initial philosophical reflections, Bill's thoughts turned back to the sequencing of individual human events. Almost before realization, his mind was engaged by happenings of a darker nature—parental neglect, demise of an infant brother, and the longing for intimacy misplaced on Julie.

Where, oh where in that desert of interpersonal relations would he ever find the culture of family life he felt the need to have bolstered? Were these mummified remnants of thought the ghoulish mockery he could expect instead of the adequate mentoring influence so essential to the development of a wholesome marital culture in his own lifetime?

Could he afford the support of confidence proffered by Christ's representative, vicar Thompson? Or, were his aspirations to remain forever down in shakedown mode? Perhaps by taking matters in hand, a more proactive approach might emerge based on trust in divine providence and the vitality offered by the amazing strength of sacramental grace.

In the absence of any other assurance to the contrary could he deny, or at least ignore, the family of Christendom characterized by a spiritual emancipation during two millennia from the slavery of paganism? Why not enjoy to his eternal satisfaction, the heritage offered by the communion of saints and the substantial foundation established by Jesus Christ? The spiritual benefits of that "city of God" have resourced all the actual multitudes that have become holy during the eons of years since the mercy of god has been manifest in human creation.

In light of these realities manifest in Christian hope and faithful trust which "eye has not seen nor ear heard", could he still afford to play it loose with the phantasmagoria of virtual reality, kaleidoscoped in the hyped-up guise of socially correct fashions and dehumanized mannerisms channeled into popular humanoids from the synchronicity of cosmic forces by messengers of serendip?

Worst of all perhaps, he might still be on the edge of the unknown in life and yet unable to realize opportunities. Maybe he was suspended in a prelude stage, having been thoroughly exposed to the effects of thwarting experiences.

The uncomfortable dissatisfaction persisted. He was doomed, it seemed, to always be on the razor's edge, constantly engaged in the process of becoming. The future, he surmised, had perpetually been just around the corner, beckoning with the smile of a giocondan pay-off.

Had he ever not been frustrated, flirting with that come-hither look which just as soon would shade off into a Mona Lisa ogle. That leer as quickly evaporated, leaving a skeletal head to glare at him from hollow eye-sockets.

Then, in such a condition, the thwarting experience would turn into an awful silence over the hyped-up promises of a virtual morality. Even the question of psychic survival would emerge, so stark had his days become!

The yearning for personal authenticity had remained hung-up all too long on the pursuit of heroes within. This lack of an externally validated sense of self-definition had surely precluded the search for individual purpose. Thus had he wasted vitality searching for advantage among the megalithic sons of gods!

In hindsight, such musings as these seemed all too often like a mixed blessing in the dynamics of an inner psychic movement. They but served as a prelude to lower level ramifications set in motion and processed in reverie. Instead of being formulated in meditative sequence, his output of verbal phraseology groupings resembled more a stumbling over words that, in note taking, would strike any eventual reader as inchoate ramblings.

In a way, he thought, these summaries of personal experience by himself resembled Tom Patterson's notebooks. However, the tenor of reflection was surely never as dark and foreboding! Or, could it! Perhaps there was some hope for himself in time, whenever that pay-off might possibly come.

On the other hand, while characteristic of his own inner wrestling, the recorded mental aberrations appeared to be stretched at verbal expression. Were his intuitive urges denatured and creative insights handicapped by desperate efforts to get anything at all down on paper?

4

Despite whatever difficulty might be endemic of his ability at compositional expression, the encounter with Father Thompson followed by an individual penitential rite, had been the occasion of a personal high. Yet the exhilaration could be considered but an unintended emotional by-product at initiation to spiritual transformation.

While he had fulfilled the minimal penance imposed, preparation for the subsequent bridal enhancement had not immediately been followed up. In fact it had been some time since last reception of the actual body and blood of Jesus Christ.

There was really no excuse for that guilt-addicted reluctance commonly exhibited by members of the heretical Yoofnas liberated Catholic Church. Even though sympathetically remorseful over the same omission, his eyes were open to the liabilities incurred.

He had fulfilled the letter of the opportunity, but had cold shouldered the Spirit. He was suffering the consequences of a regression that could as easily have been overcome had his own prescriptions for withdrawal been followed.

There had to be more to it than that, more of a positive dependency upon the providence of God whose mercy is as boundless as his justice. Somewhere along the lines of his life there must have been critical thwarting moments, even if only brief intervals however much buried in the forgetfulness of implications. Somewhere on the scales of existence, the limitless love of the Creator must have tipped the balance enough for his own redemption, just a squeeze in the direction of salvation.

The difference was awesome. At that time he must have acceded to be impulse intuitively provided when affirming dependency on the divine and agreeing, if only to agree. What a minimum on his part, but with what untold consequences for his own spirit flooding in gratitude for the favor of a possibility in God's own good time.

*   *   *

All at once, Bill looked up from the swivel chair in which he was sitting. A reflection from the big mirror mounted on the wall of his apartment on the top floor of Leland House arrested awareness. Attention was held by the imagery streaming onto the glass from the outside environment.

From the many times of lounging, the chair had never before been pivoted at quite this angle. His eyes too in the reflected panorama stretching northward of Port City's harbor, examining broad features of the mountain-backed landscape he'd hardly paid much attention to previously.

How nice it was to let his body-relaxed head lean back on the neck rest and sink his shoulders into the velvety pile! Who would not want the surcease of such a physical position where the mind can roam free, unencumbered by any humiliating sweat and muscular activity?

Thus, with constraints removed from reality, Bill could let serendipity take over and drift inward. Anything inhibiting reverie, he felt, could be banished from the realm of self-perception. Sloughed off in the centripetal effects of fantasy, the inner core of his being wanted to indulge itself.

A nirvana of mind rose within as he tried to prolong the luxuriated escape from reality, favoring the illusions of simulated thinking, divesting himself from the presence of actuality and other troublesome details of existence. How much more comfortable it was to revel in the synchronicity of magical inversion than face up to the proactive!

He could remain withdrawn into the slogans of mock culturation, allowing himself and everyone else the inclusiveness of pluralism. No one was around who might dare to fetter the negligence of roaming, of meandering in the delusion of anything else going down with impunity.

Then did the demonic forces rejoice, worsening the narcissistic insides of reflection with all manner of idle distraction catching at thoughts. Like a snake mesmerizing victim birds, sensations fluttered, unable to break loose—betrayed by the daemonics of himself and trapped in the compulsion of random images.

Of a sudden, a happening was upon him. Whether real or virtual, Bill Scolan could feel it. Through mind's eye, the scenario was being screened by the kaleidoscope of imagination.

He could see her, pre-madam Judy and friends, chanting. Scantily clothed, the provocative figures danced lithely around the recumbent body of his half-sister.

"Praised be you, oh great mother and father god! You have given up the power of choice. We are saddened over life circumstances where Julie had to make a termination choice. We affirm and support her in that decision!"

Then in unison, the seductive waifs began to reify to plaintive threnody while sprinkling dried flower petals that all but crackled in chorus. Still absorbed in illusion against a backsound of soothing memories, each struck a match and lighted a candle.

Abruptly, striking a tremor in his eardrums, the shutter of the kaleidoscope blinked and fluttered from the impact of another sequence of images. Madam was in charge, all gussied up, brandishing in one hand a nutbread cake and in the other a grape-juiced glass before a female coven.

"We redeem the symbols which slaved us by ex-communication. Inclusive liturgy celebrates a community life free of patriarchy and curiarchy. Let the semen rot! Women are empowered dreams in the dark night are reincarnated in the rising moon."

Suddenly, with nonverbal violence, she smashed down the nutbread and grape juice glass, splattering the lectern before her. With the resounding cry of a jungle-Jane, she screamed aloud.

"Blow-up, you emasculated ones; we've trojaned your stables. Blow-down your triumphs; we've co-papacyed Rome. We've voted in the women-abled, plural inclusives, the siblings of Saturn and all other four-cardinaled feelies.

"We've seasoned the liturgy, honored the harvests and welcomed in all the traumatics and victims of foreign religions. We've promogated Gaia's theagenesis and celebrated her progression in the saints' assembly."

With that, the image of Madam blipped unexpectedly, virtually splashed by some liquid—as if her water had broken, sending a treacherous signal to the unspeakable vulture that had swooped down to scavenger the leg-opened vagina!

Bill's mind flip-flopped, whirling around on itself like a dog hounding its tail. Scarcely able to believe the fall-out downpouring awareness, sensations started to shiver in the clammy haze engulfing attention.

How many strings were attached to his psyche that slouched, retrenched wooden-like at the mercy of the puppeteer! Why had the guts of him become gullivered by the pluralistic ropes of a thousand Lilliputians shouting in his ears, egged on by a troubadour pied piper- the media in an insane chant? "We all are one, as you are one in us!"

In desperation, Bill glanced up from his position, cowering in an easy chair. Awareness abruptly fled, to be captured by the reflection in the mirror hanging across from his head. In relief, he felt the bridled muscles-in-arms relax. The strings in attention shifted as his mind began to feed on the virtual symbiosis reproduced in apparent reality by the glass on the wall.

He yanked himself away from the simulated observations and walked to the western end of the apartment and looked out over the afternoon environment. But the satisfaction of escaping the glass visage seemed premature, even capricious in taking advantage of any rudimentary position for the advent of another evening.

It was one thing to be released from the addictive necessity of gazing at life through a mirror. It was quite another to completely sever the threads sewn into him by a thousand attachments being needled into the flesh of compulsions. Nothing less than a thwarting experience would cool down his inflamed taste buds.

Purgation would not come from anything less than the obstruction of inclinations doused by the actual transition through an evening advent. To back up from this western panorama now, walk back across the apartment and luxuriate in a chair would only extend the mirror of virtuality and con him into delaying accountability.

He could not retreat. Once again, in imagination, Bill found himself in a balloon, hot air-lifted far above the old hotel and the city below. He looked out of the gondola, letting the western atmosphere absorb attention. Awareness flicked around like a pollinating insect absorbing the nectar of so many manifestations. Everywhere hovered the works of God within which the efforts of humans were embedded like huts among the poppy fields.

From this height, the contrast in scenic purview was remarkable. It was like riding a breeze, slowly drifting between earth and sky, free of constraint imposed by the pavements below and released of compulsion racked up over the years in the fretting of his days.

The Lilliputian wires that had held him trapped in the brothels below were snapped away. The chariot of his psyche soared aloft on the thermals of buoyancy. He had been freed of earthly confinement, at a distance from the guilt and remorse that cluttered attention on the downside.

Worry and fear fell away from the casement of his body. The muscles of back and legs relaxed as the astringent tensions evaporated. He could stand erect on the floating floor and stretch out his arms, feeling the pain drain out of his neck.

The balloon lofted, and was kept under control by variations in energy wasted by earth-made contrivances. The gaseous effervescence allowed him to hover at a reasonable height between the mundane practical and a premature death in the rarified atmosphere of utopian cosmoscopia where the one-in-all was supposed to dwell in beckoning nirvana.

This view from above put a new slant on things. For once in his life, the perspective lifted thoughts beyond the delusions of a mediated maze, and the power of a virtual existence where it was too easy to always feel important, power sufficient and safetied-up by habit.

At this elevation he should be on a level with St. Mary's mount in the eastern distance if his surveying sight line were accurate. Anyway off in the distance stood the ancient Church-on-the-Mount, one of those sacred places where the mind can most readily be released from the gullilver ropes of attachment.

At the thought, he glanced below. But it was difficult to pinpoint the little Church-on-the-Square where Christ in the sacrament was continuously exposed to view. It had been placed there in commemoration of the first Catholic martyr in the region murdered by hit-and-run hired hands.

Despite the soft air aloft, he shuddered at a premonition of thought. Would the apocalyptic aftermath, now being endured by people of faith, have run its course before another of Christ's lambs be martyred by vigilante hoodlums available to wealthy anti-Christians for contract hits.

Of course in God's memory no death goes unrecorded. But hidden from the eyes of humans are so many others who have been snuffed out in bedroom privacy, elimination centers, and in the rat holes of isolated oblivion, or in the gross magnitude of new age savagery. Surely, no longer would anyone he knew be in jeopardy!

With a force of resolve, he steadied himself, comforted to be available and standing firmly upright. The psychological change was heady, even swaggering in a bluster of self-expansion. Who was he not, but someone who could take it or leave it on his own spontaneity?

The euphoria was short-lived. Suddenly, arm muscles shivered involuntarily as a spasm reverberated throughout the entity of his presence standing there like a homolith on a hill braced against the sky, boasting in self-preparation to face down anything whatsoever.

But then who was he to even think of bodily sufficiency or mental endeavor? Did he suppose that one humanoid-cum-potential was capable of such an affront to the landscape before him, let alone the universe edging towards him through the castellations of clouds and atmospheric enormities over which even the best scientific enterprise had pittance strength?

Who was he to strain the synapses of thought and reach for an environmental control that would place his psyche at rest? Why butt trophisms against natural events whose random occurrences oscillated around the invariant law of their Creator?

Or would he succumb once more and escape into the prosthetic womb of holographic space which simulated the serendipitous mirror of inner fantasy? Nor could the temptation be gainsaid to lapse into the whimsy-aided and quirk abetted mirror images on the wall?

Then again his muscular frame convulsed, tremor waves shocking the autonomous nervous system. Resolve was challenged. No longer would he be suckered by the instincts of inner space and sleepwalk through providential experience!

*   *   *

Abruptly, awareness was shifted downward. He had been returned to floor level again, finding his body standing at the other end of the apartment, facing eastward towards the sky from whence the evening moon would soon be coming. Rather than let himself solidify in lithic rigidity he crowded over, elbows propped down on the windowsill.

His mind took up the task of confronting the sensations now streaming over him from the wide-open casement. Thus were his thoughts released to begin testing the stimuli impinging on consciousness.

The vista overlooking the surroundings extended outward towards the east. In the direct distance of eyesight appeared once again the steeple of the Church-on-the-Mount. Beyond that edifice, behind the remnant of its forested land grant, lay River City and the enormous valley of the waterway which drained the hinterland of this recently federated state.

His eyes were lifted up from the horizon in scanning lofty slopes in the far distance. In the slight-northeast, far past the inner harbor lying below Mount St. Mary, ranged the crenellated peaks of the coastal mountains held at bay by the Great River. Its water-race surged to the sea through gorges carved out eons ago.

Even before awareness had a chance to appropriate movement in the atmosphere, let alone process occurrences deliberately, thoughts settled into studious perusal as the sense examined the epiphenomena that accompanied consciousness. In fact, attention teetered between reverie arousal and the verbalizing of perceptually connected nominal description.

The pull on reflection wandered over the atmospheric reality beyond this sill threshold upon which he had slouched, arms akimbo. Presence of mind felt so small, crowded in skull bones that existed in such an insignificant way within a universe hurtling since the big bang had exploded with omniscient power.

So what! Matter had evolved in benign unfolding as the leaven of vitality worked through the cosmos. What was he compared to the totality of supposed subjects and phenomena that were available to the cognitive observation? Would he ever follow his mind in capillary through universal space as promised by the pronouncements of such diverse sources as empirical savants and religious mystics?

No doubt he would have to wait beyond death until after the final judgement. Then was it supposed that bodies will be raptured up to join the countless souls who have ever been created. Onward, Christian soldiers! Reconstituted humans will inhabit, for infinity, whatever place they've been judged to merit.

Still it bugged him to have to curtail anticipation and temporarily fit limited ventures proposed by investigators plodding along from moon extrapolation to the teeny-bop advances being made towards other celestial bodies. If and whenever space travel were available he and mega-trillions of others once living would long be gone.

And to think of all those yet to come before the miniscule efforts of experts were ever realized, let alone the infinite finitey of humans denied the possibility of having such an opportunity. What was fair in that expectation which stemmed from the mind's capacity to wander a universe and drink in the order of the cosmos?

Surely a god, if there was a Creator, would never have endowed the human mind with the powers of possibility were the potential of the species not able to evolve into actual realization. For him, this conviction had off-and-on been a troublesome likelihood shrouded more often than not by the self-imposed impediments of hooded thinking.

From a crouched position on elbows, Bill stood up—not like a dog dangling front paws in obedient submission, but erect and straightforward. His eyes leveled outward again, focused on detecting a pattern behind the random surroundings in the atmosphere.

Far be it from him to expect naked eyesight to pick up any semblance of other dimensions. Even a heritage of religious agreements was not able to produce such evidence were he not willing to accept the proffered helpmeet of belief.

Yet what did it profit him to tolerate the eve-like quality of faith and suffer the vicissitudes of relationships not of his own doing? Why this finicky hesitation when all around him were forces and spirits upon whose reliance no confidence could be placed?

Bill backed down from that snag, an impending awareness threatening to embalm attention in convoluted thought patterns guaranteeing reincarnation as the channeler for cultic behavior. He'd had enough of that remorse crowding emotions forever troubled over with fear and guilt enactments.

No! If the courage of reliance was a necessity, what more profit would impend from the imminence of the beyond? Of these, why not prefer good spirits over evil ones, and especially the Lord of all from whom omnipotent energy flowed?

Would he let his ears itch for the pandering exuberance of the Marseilles, or eschew the pied piper, and harken to Gregorian Ave Marias? Was one doomed to rub Flintstones in the night; while the other absorbed the dew of a glorious morning?

Section 2

Shaking the Dust

5

It was a beautiful Sunday morning when nature can be at its best in the Pacific Northwest. Although still low in the ascendancy of its arc, the sun was in full shine. Radiating its heat as strongly as it could, the warmth enlivened the lusciously green grass and border flowers along the walkway to the church.

Edna Masterson walked towards the open outer threshold of the edifice, and stood to one side, waiting as the effluent parishioners crowded out after the fairly early morning mass. Although a visitor, the people like similar to what she suspected were comparable to other Catholic Christians in this area.

The snatches of conversation she was able to hear revealed comparable interests, overlapping needs and aspirations. Some people did linger, as so often had been the case in her own previous evangelical experience.

She could have felt right at home. But here, something new was added. Along both side of the broad cement walkway, out in front of the church vestibule she observed interlopers and obviously proselytizing born-again fundamentalists.

How well she knew the type, having recruited many examples in her own years of ministry—giving them such an apprenticeship as they would need in "soul-winning" tactics. She smiled, thinking how they were trained, at least initially, to recite a fixed patter. This preparation was enough. It was based on the assumption that the people met in their salvation walks would know little if anything about the Christianity they "professed".

Well, here "they" were, out in front of a Catholic Christian church. She easily recognized their leader, down in the thick of things while the neophytes fanned out to the fringes. Obviously, this congregation had been targeted for the day, at least this mass. All Catholics must be the same everywhere else because she, and her trainees had always found them woefully ignorant about their Christianity.

She could not help being amused at the reactions of the accosted parishioners. Obviously they were uneasy, not knowing quite how to react. Their front door was not handy enough to be slammed shut in exasperation. Here they were with acquaintances, exposed directly face-to-face to questions thrown at them over which they had no control.

These recipients of such frontal attacks reacted so typically—squirming, thoughts in disarray, little if any back up information for ready retrieval. Obviously, they were caught off-guard, little expecting to be "unfairly" attacked, as they would see it, on their own church grounds.

But was it really so unfair, so gauche, so unneighborly to be "attacked" on one's own church grounds. Perhaps that was the problem—to consider one's church private. Ought not a Christian church, if only little else by definition, be considered a public place—obviously supported by parishioners—but open and available to all.

After all, this was the plenipotentiary year for born agains to win over souls for Christ. All across the nation, they had been preparing and accelerating their efforts over the last four years. Now in an all-out thrust they would celebrate the maturity of American evangelism, highlighting the differences with European counterparts.

On her part, Edna had done an exhaustive study of the history behind the movement. As far as she was concerned, it had had to be an historical probing as far back as possible, certainly long beyond the "great awakening" in the new world. For her, it had been the personal awakening which led to her individual conversion, or "downfall" at least in the eyes of her own congregation.

That phase of her life was over. As painful as some aspects of the transition had been, she had few regrets. She had always been given to prayer, a practice that stood her in good stead, bringing acceptance of the fullness of God's word and a never-ending source of abundance of divine grace.

She continued to wait, her attention once more focusing on the mini-encounters taking place directly in her presence. So close was the nearest confrontation she could hardly avoid hearing. Apparently the over zealous former co-religious denominational worker had trapped a victim by thrusting on him a leaflet about the mass.

"Here's the truth about the idolatry of your 'mass'," as he spun the words. "Read it!"

"No thanks. Not interested."

But the victim had been netted, kept backing away towards the flower bed border of the sidewalk. Retreat was cut short and futile attempts at a semblance of brusque defense were ignored.

"This mass is just a jumble of medieval superstition. Christ died once for all. It says right here in the bible. Therefore there cannot be any continuing offering for sin."

"But, but'a…" the defenseless one hesitated. "Christ said this is my body, given for you."

"That's only a figure of speech," the proselyte hammered out. "Jesus Christ had to do the best he could with the Aramaic word 'is'. They had no word for 'represents' which is really what he meant."

"'Is? 'Represent'? What's the difference?" expostulated the badgered one. "It's Christ's body and blood."

"You mean Christ dies over and over again?"

The tempter was at it again, hammering in a wedge that would soon split the victim's equilibrium wide open.

"Well'a…Yes."

"Paul says, 'Having died once for all, Christ dies now no more!"

"I don't believe it."

"It's right there."

The bible thumper pushed the passage right up under the other's nose.

"See, 'once for all'! Not a daily sacrifice on your altars that've only been erected in Rome."

The badgered one tried to slip away sideways, hoping to avoid backing into the flowerbed. He was only partially successful. As one heel sunk into the soft soil, he was turned by the attacker into facing her.

"Here it is right in Hebrews 7, 9 and `10. Any pretence of a continuing offering for sin is worse than vanity. It is blasphemy, don't you see!"

The proselytizer was only doing what he had been taught to do. But there was no mistaking the matter at issue. She knew it only too well.

Fundamentalists do not like the mass. It is the anathema to end all abhorrence!—the worst possible defilement they could consider.

Talk about the Jungian shadow ego! It was sure evident in this matter. It had only been by the grace of God that she herself had been able to transcend the hurdle.

Catholics were a prime target for this kind of attack. They know so little, either about the mass or most other aspects of their confession. Like babes lost, they were never able to identify whether quotations had been taken out of context, as these young evangelicals were certainly doing right before her eyes.

Here, so obviously clumsy if not stupid, was a typical Catholic who did not have the vaguest notion of an answer. Probably he was even troubled by a nagging suspicion that maybe the opponent was onto something truer than what he had been taught as his deposit of faith.

The poor fellow looked like he could have held his own in other matters. But as for religious belief, it was all too often so confused as to have become a foot-in-mouth embarrassment. Such types took too much for granted and then could be doubly offended were someone to allude to their over-dependence on priests.

It was painful to watch the victim's confusion and hopeless efforts to extricate himself. So rattled was he that escape seemed beyond his efforts alone. In fact, it was not until a friend came over, grabbed him by the arm, that he was assisted in pulling himself away.

Culpable as the weakling loser was, it was not half so debasing as the look of hubric triumph on the tormentor's face. The smug look of satisfaction suffusing his cheeks was insufferably depraved. Looking her way, the conceit in his eye was unbearably high handed.

She could have sworn that the tempter was about to make a move on her own self. But he must have caught the utter disdain in her eye and the fixed rejection of her glance. In any event, he backed off, without a word, and went snaking after some other victim of more easier prey.

To think that she had had a hand in training such street types as these, oriented and poised to tear away the religious convictions of others. But what else could she have done before the assurances of her own tenets were transferred over denominationally towards a strength she had never known before!

Could she be held any more responsible for previous conduct than Paul was before he so suddenly was unhorsed? How could self-pity be of any use in God's kingdom of the living? Better to put remorse aside and get on with the business at hand.

Then abruptly, apparently out of nowhere, a somewhat older woman appeared who looked familiar. Edna stopped forward, making her was to establish contact with a now recognized former acquaintance.

"Ann, how nice to see you again!"

"My, oh my! It's you, Edna. How long has it been?"

"Years, I guess you'd say. How's Lucy?"

"She's quite the young lady—nearly out on her own by now. How's Trudy and Tamar?"

"You remembered! How nice you are! Oh'a they're doing fine. Trudy's kinda settled in New England. Tamar's doing final student teaching, before coming back with me for parochial school employment."

"That's odd! I thought they were about Lucy's age. But then Tom'n I were married later in life."

"Oh, that's okay!" Edna commented with a smile. "It's just…I was a child bride."

"Well whatever! We're all so glad you're here for the workshop."

"Is Mary'n your boss gonna be here?"

"Mary's already busy with affairs. Bill Scolan will make it later, if assignments will allow."

"What's that fellow, Scolan, like anyway?"

"Are you interested in a liaison again?" Ann replied with a provocative question.

"God forbid," Edna exclaimed. "Anyway, you know Mary. She wants me working with you over at Leland House. I just thought, since he's head of the department, I oughta know something more about people I'll be working with."

"He's moved from where Tom and I used to live into an apartment on the top floor of Leland House. He does research. He's got a heavy client load, which changes as they get better. He's writing a book. So…I guess you'd say he's a workaholic."

"That doesn't tell me much about the person."

"Well, he's from a middle class family, from around where Mary'n I grew up. He had a thing for Mary's mother—a puppy sort've love, I guess. He always hung around us older kids—but being a ten year senior's a big gap, at least it was then. Ever since he's sorta had it in for us, like we forever were ganging up in his head!"

"That's kinda weird, isn't it—he carrying around a shoulder chip all that time?"

"Not exactly," Ann differed. "I'd say those hang-overs from a dysfunctional family are mostly over. However, his own past's been sordid."

"None've us're perfect. You oughta remember what kind of childhood I had, if any!"

"Sure was a shocker to me, then—you being a child bride at ten with two kids by twelve. Anyway, you've turned into a lovely young woman."

"Well, God is provident," Edna agreed, backing off ego entrapment. Then she added. "Anyway, what's he like, now?"

"Well, Mary'n I've worked to bring him out of depression. I think he's over the worst of it." Ann paused, then continued almost apologetically. "Maybe he has taken a little advantage. You know Mary; she can be pretty enabling at times."

"Yeah, I'd'a guessed that. But why worry; she's been so wonderful with her work."

In near doleful reluctance to let the matter drop, Ann went on. "In fact, I thought he'n I had a thing going together. But maybe it's because I'm so much older than you'n him."

"You saying you want him to get more committed?" Edna exclaimed, looking at Ann carefully. "Don't worry. I've had my hands more'n full enough with husband problems! Life's too precious for any more tanglements like that."

"Edna, don't get me wrong. I've just been cautious about him. The only intimate relations he's ever had's been with his sister. I've just been waiting to see how more interpersonal association would turn out for him. Maybe I've waited too long."

"Is he looking around with somebody else?"

"Not that I know of; it's his life, not mine! Anyway you'll be meeting him if you're gonna take up Mary's offer."

"That'll have to wait. I've got to take care of some unfinished business in the interior—that is, if I ever get back from up there."

"Why do you say that?" Ann asked anxiously. "Sounds like you're expecting something terrible to happen."

"It could! That cult I grew up with in's been sending out enforcers to recapture backsliders. Some they even hush up, permanently."

"Really? Not this far away from the old South!"

"You don't know how cruel they are on dissenters! They got memories like Ganesh, the elephant."

"Surely father'd protect you. When I was down there on furlough he was the leading church-planter in southern religions."

"He's been more of a circuit rider—ministering to people, not in consolidating power. That's where the firebrand came in who forced father to marry me off as a child. He kept right on raping me like a slave owner. Father was cruelly deceived and his pastoral work with people exploited. Mother helped me escape and raised my two girls in protective custody."

"What about mother? As I remember, she was pretty independently fixed."

"She wouldn't kow-tow to the henchman. The enforcers ran her off once when father was away. When he got back, they broke him down for having married a woman out of the cult."

"I heard she went back to Episcopalian roots in New England."

"Yeah, the family took her back in—being an only child," Edna explained. "Her influence and money was able to get me out. Actually, she raised my girls while I was on the run, so to speak, getting educated as a minister in various seminaries. Each place took me in until the long arm of some enforcer got to them. Anyway, it was long enough to get a degree."

"How does all that go on in what's called the Christian church?"

"Being a Catholic you don't know half of what's been taking pace since the reformation with the agents of antichrist! Indeed, you better think twice if you've got any ideas of taking on that Yoofnas liberated Catholicism."

"I think that heresy's nearly worked out. I hear nobody's seen any pregnant women or even found children at all around their congregations."

"What about Bill Scolan?"

"He was raised a liberated catholic. But he's now been regularized in the sacraments. In fact, believe it or not, he's being considered as a deacon."

"Whatta ya mean, deacon-acting?"

"Father Thomson's been working with him. Deacon's minister to group catechetical work, not the apostolic prophetic role—at least not yet."

"What's holding him back?" Edna asked.

"We've discussed the matter. He's more'n more convinced. But with his past, he needs an intimate sexual relationship to maintain integrity and solidarity with the congregations."

"You must be pretty close together, having discussions like that. Still, what's the big deal. Neither Paul or the apostles had it, once ministry in Jesus began.

"Ask him," Ann reacted huffily. "Let him explain his own self!"

"Not me!" Edna exclaimed. "I don't want to become a deaconess, let alone a Roman priest. The pastoral work I've done's been the counseling ministry. I'm good at it and Mary thinks she can find me a place to live close by once I get my life tidied up a bit."

"The girls going to live with you?"

"Not Trudy. But Tamar wants to live out on her own once the parochial school's put her on staff."

"They are close in years, aren't they?"

"Scarcely more'n nine months apart. Anyhow, the way Mother raised them, they could'a been twins all along."

*   *   *

Seeming not to listen to Edna's response, Ann looked away over the young woman's shoulder and greeted the approaching priest. "Hello Father! Edna'n I were just getting reacquainted again."

"Oh, you know each other?"

"From way back in our lives," Edna responded for both of them.

"Well, me too then," the priest quipped with a smile. "Ann, would you like to join us. We're going over a few things before Edna's lecture."

"Oh no, Father! You two have a go at it. I've some things to do too, so's to get her welcome talk."

"Father, proselytizers are not my friends anymore!"

"I know it. But it sure brings up the point again."

"What's that?"

"That fact of your God-sent presence. Most Catholics are such babes-in-the-woods when it comes to explaining their religion."

"It seems so."

"Come on. I've held you back long enough. Let's get some coffee-and to hold us over until a late lunch."

The priest led her back towards the newly established adult education building.

"Please don't apologize," Edna proffered. "I wanted to go to mass anyway."

"Your phraseology is interesting. Most Catholics would have said, 'had to go to mass'. But no, you 'wanted to go."

"Isn't that the same thing, nearly?" she asked.

"Not at all. Catholics take Sunday mass as an obligation. To you it's an opportunity."

"Indeed it is. We 'johnny-come-lately's' have got to make up time, I guess."

"Not really. One sacrifice is infinite in its benefits. Admittedly however humans have lost the capacity to appreciate a single occurrence. Their limitation makes it necessary to hear mass over and over again."

"You're right, Father. That was a poor choice of words. Anyway, it's been divine grace working through my uncle, the Monsignor, and that angel of God, the bishop."

"By the way, how is your uncle—on your mother's side, I presume?"

"Yes, it wasn't such a big step from Episcopalian to Rome—but not the way you'd hear it from Mother's family."

"I can imagine."

"Uncle and my Bishop have had a living martyrdom. Up there in the interior of the state, anti-Catholic forces are still entrenched. No 'quarter' is given anybody, except quislings and sycophants."

"Down here, in the metropolitan area, they're none the less rabid. However, the pluralism of the City has kinda held them at bay."

Together, they passed back through the church, and outside again, skirting the rectory down a cement path leading into the new all-purpose building. It was obvious form the bustle of activity that some event of importance was about to take place.

The priest waved to one person, said "hello" to another almost continuously as they made their way to the cafeteria line. It was all so familiar—the presence of the pastor—to her, for she had been an ordained minister for years and in charge of her own congregation.

Enroute, the priest turned his head to ask. "How do you like our new adult education center?"

"It seems very functional."

"We're only now starting to get these into the outlying parishes. Almost too late for the changing demographics."

"Oh?" Edna queried. "Has the Catholic population give up birth control and abortion for natural family planning?"

"Demographics would seem to indicate that. But religious training doesn't stick that long. Yet in some mysterious way—like your uncle and the bishop believe—God is able to transmute all the media garbage into a longing for religious experience."

"What about homiletics?"

"Preaching's not enough, at least not in the way it's been done today. It's gotta be more cathechetical—not a pep-talk which makes little impression on the plethora of influences crowding in, saturated with blipped information and multi-mediated images. Then perhaps a celebration of the liturgy can stop the kaleidoscope of virtual reality."

"It'll take some follow-up. Something's gotta get through so more'n more of them will come back."

Momentarily, conversation ceased, interrupted by a change in venue. Together, they passed down the food distribution line in the cafeteria, picking up a light repast. After selection was made, they carried the trays over to the sunny sidewall and sat down at a convenient table where conversation could be resumed.

6

As the priest and his guest finished coffee, it became increasingly evident that more and more people were coming together. Cars were slotting up spaces in the parking lot. More individuals and family members seemed to be assembling in the auditorium next to the cafeteria or drifting in for coffee and a light snack before the program started.

"It looks like we're gonna have a good attendance," the priest mused.

"I hope so for your sake."

"We have spent a lot of time preparing for this series."

"Why is this so important to you?"

"For them really. The area's been hit by so many different fundamentalists lately. People're confused, wondering how to answer their questions."

"They even come up to the church's doors after mass."

"It's disconcerting."

"I can imagine," Edna agreed. "But something must remain from childhood and the weekly sermons."

"It does. But indifference sets in. The ways've the world jostle them around. Continual media bombardment leeches most everything spiritual out of them. They're left without foundation and hardly any backbone to bristle up at all."

"Is it hopeless?" she asked.

"Nothing is hopeless with the Holy Spirit. But once they're challenged, doubt eats into them. Too often enough, they're prone to drift away—caught by the fundamentalists' fervor, liveliness and conviction."

"And I have contributed so much to that!"

"You can't let remorse eat into you for what your conscience told you then and the training you'd come up through. You were making the best faith efforts you could. God the Father knows every heart and builds on that."

"You are so charitable, Father."

"We can only emulate Jesus Christ in the ways revealed to us individually. Little is gained by confrontation, recrimination, or self-vindication for that matter. We have the Lord's words for it, work as actively as you can while the times still there."

"That is true. There seems no better way for it."

"To come back to our point, the Church has found that adult training has been absolutely essential. We've got to involve men and women in a continuing process of self-development and activity learning by themselves and their children—meanwhile praying desperately to the immaculate heart of Jesus' Mother."

"Is that the focus of what I hear is your outstanding leadership?" Edna asked, deliberately suppressing any trace of subjectivity that might be misconstrued as flattery.

"Yes," the priest replied in a matter-of-fact voice. "The cardinal's made me responsible for two areas of proactive advance—getting the deaconate going again after centuries of neglect as well as the development of adult-child educational programs."

"How feasible can that be—adults and children in the same classroom?"

"The children have their 'classrooms' during the usual, but redistributed school hours. Then later in the afternoon, there are two periods a week in a 'sharing' room with parents. After that, comes the adult learning sessions."

"Sure sounds mechanical to me!" Edna replied with a wry smile.

"That's the whole point of why we're so glad you're here—and other women, hopefully!"

"Wait a minute!" Edna came back at him in a suspicious hint. "I thought I was being considered for a counseling position, not teaching."

"Perhaps part of the time; but it's not 'teaching' in the old sense. We think you and your daughter can pioneer a new way of communicating with children and adults together."

"Thanks a lot!" Edna retorted. "Now, you're telling me! Does Tamar know what she's getting into?"

"It's been discussed. She's kinda excited, I think," the priest assured her. "Anyway, the teacher training she's got'll give her the background. Have faith, Edna!"

"I'll need it," she replied in a half-wry, half-mollified tone of voice.

"Pluralistic interpersonal relations," the priest began in what seemed a dodge from confrontation, "are essential in the affairs of everyday life. In this regard, the proselytizing efforts of the fundamentalists play a necessary role. Often confrontational, and even obnoxious, they bring an awareness of God's presence into consciousness in a way that's more frequently hard to ignore."

"Indeed, I know."

"You've had experience," the priest observed wryly. "Are you gonna find it hard not to be accepted into the Catholic priesthood?"

Edna burst out laughing, not uproariously, but of a mildly calculating kind. "You're a sly one, Father! You putting me on—testing whether I'll promote another Catholic feminist uprising?"

"Well, a...No! I was just wondering in passing. You've had so many years with your own congregation."

"My bishop, up in the Interior, has twice asked me the same question. My reply is as then. Jesus led me to his Church, not mine. Whatever that church says is his voice. I accept the responsibility of new-won liberation and freedom. In addition, historical research helped me understand Christ's position. Anyway, a person with my talents will not be wanting for a profession. I've had another offer or two already."

Edna paused, caught by her own reflexive overtone. She had not wanted to sound like a tit-for-tat; but the words were out, and she'd have to live with it!

"Well spoken and of considerable maturity. That's what we need, especially grown-up women with training and experience, an education and perspective in particular."

"My education's more Christian than it is Catholic. Training and experience's been mostly in street polemics, the direct challenge and the 'patois' to keep the victim's attention confused."

"That's all to the good in the participatory training sessions. But the priest who gave you Christian instruction and the bishop who brought you into the Church were particularly impressed how close your views then matched and have now matured."

"That, I cherish. He's like the bishop of Smyrna waiting to overcome. He shares the poverty of his people. He's borne the hatred of his enemies, patiently suffering all the persecutions we'd been handing out to his congregation."

"I understand your area was a test site for the fundamentalists in this whole region?" the priest asked.

"We were it. We were able to 'convert' over fifty percent of all Catholics in that diocese."

"That is remarkable from one viewpoint, and tragic from another. But, thank God, many of those came back to the sacraments and mass, especially when the media got wind of it. As usual, I understand, they ballyhooed it all out of proportion.”

“Yes, unfortunately,” she agreed, provisionally.

“How did you achieve that? Usually, they’re so liberal, anything honest and truthful gets buried in an active indifference.”

“You wouldn’t believe it. Only God knows how. The owner of the local newspaper and television station returned to Rome.”

“Returned?”

“To my eternal shame, I’d enticed them away in the first place. As it was, we couldn’t have succeeded so well without them.”

“Oh?”

“He’d have his staff invite the bishop over on a program. Then at the last minute, on his instructions, they would switch arrangements to make the bishop look as stupid as possible.”

“Did it backfire?” the priest wondered.

“Eventually, yes. I told the owner it would. He persisted. The bishop continued to respond in as gentle and Christ-informed manner as possible. His knowledge is fantastic. But his blessings were always the same, ‘Heavenly Father, forgive them. They don’t know what they’re doing.’”

“I’ve never talked much to that bishop. But I’ve seen him in religious ceremonies. He has a commanding presence.”

“It exudes from him, like Christ were inside.”

“I’m sure He is,” the cleric agreed.

“Anyway, afterwards, the media owners told me that he had been carefully watched every broadcast. The bishop’s example was what brought one owner back. Actually, he confessed to, and was admitted back to the sacraments by the same bishop. Only later, after my conversion, did I find out.”

“What jubilation in the Lord!” the priest exclaimed.

“So, if I have anything at all, it is from the Lord.”

“No better source to be used to other’s benefits, actually! That bishop must be something like those ‘angels’ of the Lord, referred to in the latter chapters of the Apocalypse.”

“Come again, Father?” Edna questioned in puzzlement.

“The description from the middle of the Apocalypse onwards seems to fit post-modern and new age remnants. In many episodes and scenes the word ‘angel’, whether holy or fallen-away, is used for bishops who help or hinder the cause of Christ in the sacraments and his Church.”

"Like Luther, you mean?" Edna surmised.

"Well, he was more aptly called a fallen star—one whose influence deluded many nations, peoples, congregations—making it possible for governments to get away with anything in their assault on the sacred. The secular city of the moderns has now become the sacrilegious environment where films, communications and commerce have made Jesus and his Church as a laughing-stock. These fallen angels are the authors of devilishly clever ideas and the makers of the pagan idols that seduce the masses."

"You mean pornography?" she wondered.

"Especially the video kind where bodies act out the inner depravity, bestiality and cruelty. Business interests and enterprises are so debased that it is difficult to get protective legislation past their lobbying flunkeys."

"What's the 'message' I'm supposed to get from what you're saying?"

"New agers think they have too much going on for themselves to let go except in paroxysms of violent coercion. The antichrist nations, and institutions, and satanic societies are not going to give up anything with less than a cataclysmic wrench."

"You saying something I'm not getting?" Edna concluded.

"The only force that has withstood the attack has been the Catholic Church. In the world's eyes, it is being whittled down to size by the moderns who've done everything possible to make it look stupid and ineffective. That the Protestants have added to the attack is to be expected. But the Trojan horse has been filled with dissenting bishops and priests. Religious've have used her doctrines to aid and abet worldly interests."

"'New' Catholics, like the Yoofnas liberated ones?" she asked.

"They too'n many others've been baiting the faithful from within, not wanting to leave or else their false doctrines would get little attention."

"Why're they not kicked out?" she asked.

"Excommunication's a last resort. The Church would rather try to win them back to Christ with patience and love."

"Meanwhile they backbite the hand that blesses them."

"That's ever been God's way—repentance, not the death of the sinner. You see it in the Apocalypse. God seems to bend over backwards again and again letting sinners inflict punishments on themselves so they'll repent and the Catholic'll be confirmed in faith, even martyred perhaps."

"That's my secret fear," Edna confessed. "I've had to fight that over'n over since converting."

"Your courage must give you the strength to persist as Paul said, 'When persecuted, then am I strong in Christ'!"

"He was a saint, Father!" she protested.

"Not when he said it. He was only in process, like us."

Edna shrugged, not knowing what else to add.

The priest picked up on the hesitation and asked. "Do you need some time to yourself before we start?"

"I'd appreciate that."

"Well, I've a couple things to do. Why don't you come with me? I'll find you a space beside the office."

They got up, the priest leading the way through the cafeteria and out in to the auditorium, skirting along the nearest wall back around into the office area. Edna was left alone to collect her thoughts, make some final notes before the delivery of her presentation.

She was only dimly aware of subdued voices and human movements outside somewhere that served as a background to her recollections. Not long thereafter, the sound of music drifted into awareness, probably indicating a parish ensemble calling the audience to assembly.

In a few moments, there was a knock on her door. In answer, she was met by a younger woman calling to escort her to the low stage facing the assembling crowd of parishioners.

She was led to the end of a table just off center facing the assembly. The escort introduced her to a woman religious who was principal of the high school and to a man as the coordinator of the adult education program.

The priest was out in the audience, glad-handing as many participants as possible in the short time available. When the small musical group off to the side had signaled finale, the priest turned and quickly made his way to the low platform.

Obviously the other two platform participants beside her at the table needed no formal introduction. Each, in turn and in place, made a few remarks on the general theme of the assembly.

Then, the priest introduced Edna to the larger group, commenting on a few general observations about the guest speaker. Mercifully, the remarks were brief. Edna soon found herself facing the large group.

So many people, everyone an individual, each with a concern, a problem or an interest of particularly weighty import. She was impressed with the youthfulness of the audience. Some were obviously married, others not.

They seemed so vigorous in the subdued attention of their intensity. Maybe some of them could be moved to release their participation and ask some questions. Hopefully, she could hit upon some topics that would arouse them to interrogate and pose some problems.

From years of experience, she knew the power of a gracious appearance and the pull towards interaction with an immediately practical experience. With a smile of acceptance, she started.

"After mass this morning, I was standing at the church door for a few moments, waiting. Out front, several parishioners were in friendly conversation with one another, renewing remembrances and reactions to the passing of events. Nothing unusual about that, you would say! But they were unaware of the four strangers looking on, waiting to strike. When confrontation occurred, it was too late. Some of you were caught off guard, cornered by one of those agents."

With scarcely a pause, Edna continued. "I noticed how clever the operators were. Intruders captured the attention of couples. One of them backed an individual almost off the sidewalk, nearly into the flowerbed. The rest of the parishioners hastily found they had something else to do and left—probably thankful for not having been the caught-ones."

A low ripple of a sniggle shot through the assembly. And Edna knew she had their interest, and least initially.

"I won't recount the skirmishes, word for word, as I heard them. In fact, I'm sure most everyone here can remember personal encounter of a similar nature— probably all too graphically and painfully. You answer a knock on your front door always it seems at an inconvenient time. There in front of you is a woman with a wide smile, an open bible and awkward questions. Most likely she began with a strongly worded affront, 'Have you been saved, friend?'"

Again, a little sound of suppressed laughter rippled over the audience.

"Of course, you say! You're a Catholic, hoping to frighten her away. But woe and behold! That, you instantly find, is only a come-on. She reaches into her bag for a 'catholic' bible and says, 'You can't prove it'!

"Challenged, you talk for what seems like hours. No effect! In fact, you find you've been talking at, not with each other. Finally, the woman stranger leaves with an air of triumph. You close the door with a sore throat. Exaggerated? Maybe. You feel taken advantage of. The net effect is defeat. You're especially uncomfortable that her worst suspicions of you are confirmed. You've put your foot in your mouth. You know she's taken things out of context. Worse still, you didn't know where to look in the bible, or even whether there was any support for your beliefs."

The interest of the audience was evident. Edna capitalized on it. "You've lost on two counts—content and process. Maybe it seems unfair. The proof must be there somewhere. But they can, and do pick apart the bible simply to dispute you—and, it seems just to get under your skin! You know that you did try hard to be pleasant. But conversational technique is not good enough. She deliberately set out to provoke you, to twist you up with half-truths contrived to make you lose your cool."

She noticed a hand raised tentatively back in the audience. Edna nodded her head with a brief verbal acknowledgement.

"Can I ask you a question? Or, should I wait to the end?"

"Very much so. Please go ahead," Edna invited.

"Just about every bible thumper you come across has a different interpretation of the bible. That's very confusing—especially when you also gotta deal with atheists and the secular world as well," admitted the questioner.

"It is that, until you realize the bottom line for all Christians is the birth, life, death and resurrection of Jesus Christ. If you focus on who Jesus Christ was, and come to the conclusion that Jesus is God, then you have an entirely different way of looking at the Old Testament. You look at the different things there the way Jesus did. It becomes an integrated whole with the New Testament."

Another person felt compelled to comment and ask. "Galileo is said to have said the bible tells us how to go to heaven, not how the heavens go. There's always a war between science and religion. Facts are facts. Belief is subjective myth."

"That was certainly the established position in a new age world. Now it's become the fashionable thing to believe. Mythological signs, symbols and rites have become the in-thing of the New Age movement. To an extent, the evangelicals are caught up in the same demonic mysticism. Everywhere it's heard—in humanistic universities, the mass media, and governmental institutions. In these violent times, it's becoming absurd to see science touted as a religion with universal explanations for everything. It replaces God for political purposes, and everything else, as sole source and provider of human happiness on earth. There are now fewer discrepancies between itself and religion. The metaphor of warfare is misleading because the temple of God has finally been occupied by the technocrat's stormtroopers. Still, if science is science and not mysticism, it is more appropriate to say that there are areas of disagreement and matters for further discussion. And, I might add, learning. The intruders at your door spend hours every week studying and praying. Yes, praying indeed. They are very sincere in what they are doing. They really believe that Catholics are long gone after the devil."

This time, the person interacting was of a more challenging and provocative frame of mind.

"Why do you ignore the facts in dispute? Everybody knows that the Genesis account of creation and of the flood are just myths. Nothing else!"

"Well, on the contrary, science—at least unindoctrinated science—has discovered evidence for the creation of the universe explained by a 'big bang' theory. This has been substantiated by mathematical models. Now, astrophysics has discovered the eleven essential steps in any solar system formation. The Genesis story has these eleven steps, and only those, in right order and with all the requisite conditions. No other creation story can match its accuracy, not even the Babylonian one."

Edna could feel their attention. The effect was a palpable sensation that would eventually compromise her own objectivity were she not to break the impending mesmerization. However, a related thought was needed before any respite however short lived that might be. "During this period of billions of years, God either created millions of miracles—to bring about all the happenings so briefly summarized in Genesis, all the way up to when he rested on the seventh day—or he left it to evolutionary mutation and random chance after the big bang. I believe that God was directly involved, creating and controlling everything happening over those billions of years. That's a viewpoint seldom heard among secular 'Christians'."

With that, Edna paused briefly to make a show of rearranging her notes on the lectern. She took a drink of water, having sensed that the audience was in a momentary holding mood.

7

Apparently, Edna's timing had been accurate enough to generate the question seemingly required to dampen her subjectivity.

"What about cave men and the dinosaurs?"

The question was raised by the same person earlier. Edna shrugged off the latent premonition that threatened to bump into attention and distract concentration. She picked up the theme and continued.

"Those apparently were secondary phenomena, not of first level importance, fitting in place into the eleven major dimensions of creation. Mathematician friends of mine tell me it's one chance in 6 billion that the bible could have only 'guessed' correctly. Such fantastic probabilities would almost guarantee that the author of Genesis had first hand knowledge of the truth of what he wrote down. Where else would that 'certainty' have come from but from God? As to the Flood in chapters six through nine, I believe, science has found that to be not a global flood but a universal flood. A study of the actual Hebrew words reveals an area flood covering all the humans at that time together with their animals—that is the mammals and the birds, not the insects and the reptiles, apparently."

"You make it sound like a local drizzle you could avoid by putting on galoshes," sung out another voice.

Edna was amused at the audience's merriment and deliberately made no effort to hide it. When the people's attention had quieted down, she continued.

"There is a danger in looking for science to corroborate everything in the bible. When science goes wrong—and it is frequently corrected, as you know—then there is a negative spillover undermining the bibles credibility. People are prone to suspect the worst about biblical truth. Wherever possible—at least for atheists and other worldly people—the benefit of doubt is given science, not the bible. It is held to higher critical standards, a backhanded compliment which'll convince no one like a made-up minded person. Atheists are atheists. They won't even accept established scientific evidence when it's not convenient. Take the 'truth' of the second law of thermodynamics, for example. In fact, this law is almost more than truth with a little 't'. That law says it takes energy in a closed system to keep it from becoming useless. To an atheist, the universe has to have been around forever since there is no God or creation. If so, it and everything else under the sun would have had plenty of time to run down, completely exhausted by now. So, how come he himself's still got enough energy to talk about it? The contradiction is so blatantly evident! The ultimate appeal is always to God who set a finite universe in motion. You can never have complete certainty—which so many people say they need—before making an act of belief. In fact, the only real certainty is a belief in God. Any other 'certainty' is always a probability."

Off to the left side of the assembly, back up in the audience, she noticed a young woman who seemed agitated in her attempt to stand. Edna paused to give her an assist.

"Do you have a problem?"

"Yes," she replied nervously, stumbling for words, "...theory's not practical for us. I'a..."

"Take your time. Obviously, you have an important question."

This added prompt appeared to be all the assistance she needed.

"You were introduced as a converted Protestant minister—say a priest in the Catholic Church. Why'd you let yourself come in as a second class Catholic, not an ordained priest?"

Edna felt the tension shoot through the crowd and the ripple of voices threatening to rise above a murmur.

"Yes, I was an ordained minister in a non-Catholic church. I was a successful pastor of a large parish. I trained and led many young people to badger Catholics and others about their religion. If they had none, we tried to convert them to evangelical Christianity. I was raised in another church down south and gave my life to Jesus as a young girl. My father and mother were a ministerial team—an innovation in those parts in those days—itinerant bible thumpers as they were called. As an only child, I wanted to be like my parents. So I became a minister like them. Recently I converted to Catholicism up there in the interior where my former parish still is. It is very anti-Catholic and needs work. However—the facts of my conversion can be discussed at another time. Right now, your question wants to know why I didn't become a Catholic priest. Nobody should come to any Christian religion on a bargaining basis, least of all to Christ's church. It is a surrender of yourself to Jesus and his Church, and nobody else, so that you can worship Jesus in fellowship and to better spiritual advantage. For, believe me, I thought about the matter you propose very seriously. But in reading, praying and talking to others, I soon was disabused of that notion, even though at first I was somewhat resentful. But then, I thought about Jesus and what he wanted for His church."

"How could you be minister in one Christian church and not in another?" came another question closeby the first. "You could at least become a deacon!"

"And wedge my foot into the ecclestical doorway like the religious salespersons so many individuals have become to their financial profit—and, loss of their immortal souls, perhaps."

This aside drew some laughter from the audience and a mild applause. Edna half –smiled in acknowledgement and went on with her pattern of thought.

"If you understand what Jesus did, and really taught, you can only find one true Catholic Church which he established. Just because people call themselves Christians is not the only true mark of identity. Jesus himself said you'll find many saying this or saying that, 'But of me they do not speak'. So you have to find out what he did say. You all know that the present pope is alive and in direct descent from Jesus Christ."

"Aren't your talents being wasted by dictates long out of date? What else could Jesus do but have only men back then? Today, women are liberated."

"Yes, liberated to function in their own nature. To take on the nature of another is usurpation. You can only go so far with that until things break down. Then you very being becomes debased, enfeebled, strung out on the appearances of reality, not on any substance. My talents were never used as a priest. I could not, and never would be able to minister the sacraments. No one anywhere is ever like a priest. Christ commissioned priests and bishops to renew the Eucharist every day on the altar of sacrifice. Only a priest can administer the basic five of seven sacraments. Then, they are to preach the gospel as Jesus wanted. Perhaps deacons could relieve clergy from heavy burdens of sacramental counseling. But sermons should never exhibit individualistic logorrhea."

"Isn't that authoritarian, patristic and chauvinistic?"

Once again Edna had to suppress an uneasy feeling. She could not now tolerate any sensation that might bring on paranoia. "Perhaps, it may be—from any point of view except that of Jesus Christ. He is the one who said, 'Either you are for me or you are against me. The lukewarm I spew out of my mouth'. It is not easy to be for Jesus Christ. Nor is it easy, for that matter, to be against him. That's where we've long been in the Protestant world. It's one thing to read your own thoughts and wishes into the bible—then thump your way out, jabbing at others, driving them to distraction with superciliously derived fancies. It's a whole other matter to weigh the facts discovered over two thousand years. Innumerable holy women and men by study and discipline have developed the deposit of faith without changing any of it since Jesus Christ gave it to us, least of all trying to fashion something new to suit people's fantasies. It is only the Catholic Church that's been able to keep the essence of what Christ taught.

"That in itself has been a stupendous miracle—nay, a whole series of miracles that cannot be explained by science. Science and technology do not work in the same mode. Science has only the creative universe to work with in order to beautify and make the physical world productive. Theology has the deposit of faith in order to help human beings save their souls and be happy with Jesus in heaven.

"Unfortunately, science wants to be the master, non-servient, vaunting its meager discoveries in the face of theology, scurrying up the dust of its facts to confuse and to control. Since it is not God-centered, it serves the cause of antichrist who's way is being prepared more and more obviously every day. Even the best of science is being subverted, perverted to unholy uses of bestiality, satanic worship and hedonistic dalliances.

"But to come back to the problem of our differences and denominational disputes with one another! The 'great awakening' around about two hundred and fifty years ago made Americans consciously religious and thus overtly argumentative from the viewpoint of other countries. We were so often seen to be frontier individualists—crude, loud-mouthed and undisciplined to royalty and people of 'quality'. Dispensationalism preoccupied American Protestants. They felt compelled to divide the 'word of truth'—deciding which parts of the bible referred to Israel and which to the 'Christian' church. This led to a rapid fissioning into all kinds of fundamentalists, born-agains and evangelicals.

"Millenialism has continued to be a hot topic of speculation as to the end of the world and the imminent return of Jesus, alive and well, as they say! As a result, there is not a topic more hotly and consistently, even relentlessly debated by evangelicals. Religion in other countries of the world is just religion for the individual even among Catholics, it seems. Catholics, I've found, are reluctant to discuss, let alone argue. It's not surprising they are not very good at it, either in content or in process.

"To being, we must come back to dispensationalism and the partitioning of bible utterances about Israel and the Christian church. It is those about the church which are the bone of contention. Protestants reject tradition utterly—all that magnificent work done over the centuries by Catholic holy men and women elaborating the deposit of faith under the guidance of the Holy Spirit in Christ's Catholic Church.

"The Protestant rejects the whole of it as monkey business. He can find no literal, explicit or verbatim biblical justification for any such on-going tradition. To him or her, it is at best 'inventions' and at worst 'fabrications'. Since Protestants have rejected any papal authority, tradition is hugely suspect. They are left with only a weary literalness that all too often ends up in agnosticism.

"We really need to pray for our separated brothers. They are sentimental, immature and babes in the woods. They become easy prey to the devil whispering at their addictive personalities, either enticingly or doubtfully. However, the Catholic has to be wary, alert and ready to explain the fundamental 'proof' behind it all. Jesus said, 'All power to forgive or retain is given to you on earth and in heaven'.

"That means of course Jesus endowed the Church under the Pope to be the source of spiritual blessing for all mankind. Nobody else has the sacraments as Christ instituted them and continues to preserve their integrity for our benefit. Such references to the authority of the Catholic Church are completely glossed over. Large groups of our countrymen have even out-protestanted themselves. Fundamentalists and evangelicals attack both European antecedents and the Catholic Church as outmoded patriarchal relics.

"They act as if all developments since the death of Christ can be swept under the rug of history. Two hundred and fifty years ago there was a new awakening and a great beginning in America. Everyman's bible was the source of study and re-interpretation as to what Christ had wanted his church to be. Everyone was in the religious business, proliferating new sects based on novel interpretations of scripture. As these illuminations wore thin, and boredom set in, other sets of intuitions were discovered and expounded.

"On and on, the process went until today it is considered an affront to the individual to speak of authority, let alone insist on it! The new religious humanism that has taken over, is a warmed over 'con-con' of all the heracies that have plagued the conceits of modernism into a secular religion of sentimentality and liberation that is being used by the state to control the masses.

"On the individual level, where it hurts and stings one's ego the worst, this has denigrated into the social 'simpleton' who is all things to all people, for all purposes at all times. Anyone with personal convictions is highly suspect, shunned as a boor and rejected from any in-group. Anyone with religious conviction is a psychological leper who cannot possibly be tolerated, let alone admitted to any social benefits or entitlements of his hard-earned taxes. In fact, double taxation is more often the case than not.

"The problem, and a practical one at that, is to so muster the evidence of the bible about the Church which substantiates the basic position created by Jesus Christ. From that perspective, all their other attacks—in fact, they themselves skirt that basic premise—are largely smoke screens to throw you off-center, badger you and self-justify themselves in ignorance.

"You all know those smoke-screens, or should do, such as: 'Catholic tradition like any tradition is only the work of humans'; 'Doctrine was pristine and pure at Christ's time and needs not further development'; 'Every born-again is automatically saved, almost predestined to be in heaven'. Then, all those other bones of contention such as baptism, purgatory, forgiveness of sins, papal infallibility, Eucharist, mass, saints worship, Marian beliefs and the inquisition— on the inquisition and Galelio!

"Catholics have a double burden—to be so steeped in God's bible and in God's tradition as to be able to explain cogently, and make sense such that if God's grace moves them we're not the stumbling block in their conversion they make us out to be. For me there was a remarkable Catholic bishop of the diocese where my former church was. Like the bishop of Smyrna in the Apocalypse, he was a true 'incarnation' of Jesus Christ for me.

"In this regard, Catholics have another area of concern—the direct confrontation with hedonists, atheists and militant anti-Christians. They categorically deny that Jesus Christ is alive today and particularly that the Catholic Church is directly guided by him. Protestants may be of some help in limited ways as we try to Christianize society. But they too deny the real presence in the Eucharist. Their Christianity without Christ is tolerable to anti-Christian forces. When the chips are down, you'll have to go it alone. Nobody can tolerate a Christianity with a living Christ continuously available at the center of the present moment.

"The insidious thing is the desire for certainty, for a factual basis of belief that bypasses the obedience of faith. That is a contradiction in terms. Belief is the acceptance of truth on the basis of the reliability of Him who says so. That him is God who cannot lie or deceive. Contraposed is the anti-god who does deceive and does lie. So often are the lies repeated by the propaganda media that the very repetition is commonly accepted by the gullible. So much is this the case that the credulous have become the norm in society at large.

"The quest for certainty is an illusion fostered by the humanist emperors—too many little Caesar's of local, state and federal governments. It is so easy for them to have their way by exploiting this common motive. They substitute the 'certainty' of a public opinion which can be manipulated for the certainty of Jesus' truth. If we do not have the courage of Jesus, we do not have the backbone to be free and liberated in his cause.

"I thought scientific knowledge is developed to give us reliable information," someone called out from center audience.

"Scientific truth is always provisional. New empirical findings call into question all the previous truths that have been quantitatively established. Even mathematics is constantly open to new schemes. In fact, one textbook in the field was recently titled: "Mathematics: the Loss of Certainty"—if my recall is that accurate. Few scientists are that arrogant any more!

"Neither can Catholic Christians afford to be arrogant, exploiting the certainty of God's word for the belittlement of others. Even though we have the certainty of God's promise, no one can count on a predestined salvation. It is so easy to sin not only by pride of certainty and the disparagement of those in error but especially by the saturation of addiction that permeates every aspect of the culture we live in. It is better to experience failure in any encounter over biblical interpretation than to walk away with a feeling of unseemly triumph.

"Let the other have his day! No words of yours can ever replace the grace of God, which alone enlightens others. Suffice it to know in yourself release from heresy and apostasy, and that you have presented Catholic belief as fairly and 'objectively' as possible. Be accountable in God's love and peace lest the guilt of your conscience grip you to disadvantage.

"In all things, my friends, remember and count on the words of Jesus Christ that you love one another—not in the sentimentality and good buddyism of the secular humanist—but in the wily fortitude of a badgered Savior.

"Now, I think I've said enough for awhile. Thank you for your attention."

*   *   *

Edna Masterson paused at the end of her speech. For a moment, the audience seemed to be caught by surprise. A sense of unsettlement appeared to gravitate across their faces. One looked at another in God knows what kind of wonderment.

Then, from away back, seemingly the last row in the assembly came the sudden clapping of one pair of hands, enthusiastic in its insistence. Almost instantly, the sound spread like wildfire across the entire audience.

Someone stood up close by in the front row. Others followed in spontaneous undulation like a tsunami boring over the ocean deep. Someone whistled, concatenated by others up and down, over and across the assembly.

Edna hesitated no longer. She waved her hand, smiled in gracious appreciation and stepped away from the plasti-kleer podium, to return to the end of the platform table.

The priest followed here in reverse transit, clapping loudly as he stepped in behind her to the podium. He motioned for her to stand up again, in place, in response to their insistent applause. The clapping roar accelerated again.

She stood up with a smile, bowed slightly in acknowledgement and then returned to her seat. The two others at the table turned towards her, each with a word of appreciation. She smiled again in turn and voiced her thanks to them.

The priest held up his arms for an end to the applause. Gradually the audience ceased clapping and settled down again in their seats. Once attention was restored, the priest pulled them back to the agenda of the day.

"Few words of mine could add to the great appreciation you've given our keynote speaker. Her experience is substantial. Her wisdom excels like so many noble women in the bible and Church history.

"I know all of you will pray for her pilgrimage as she continues to work through the Catholic lifestyle you and I were born with. We are the inheritors and beneficiaries of the great work of the Holy Spirit begun in her development.

"You too have responded so well—far beyond our expectations. In fact," motioning towards the two others seated at the table beside Edna, "we had a panel all prepared to react to the speaker's message. Due to your response, and the lengthy significance of this major address, the schedule has been somewhat revised.

"It is almost noon time. We are now going to break for lunch. Our morning speaker, the panel members and our afternoon resource persons will each position themselves at a lunch table where those of you can sit who want to follow up on any topic of your interest.

"Since we've got such a good start this morning, the afternoon sessions are advanced one-half hour. We will reconvene at one o'clock. Those of you with children back at home may find it convenient to get away a half hour earlier this afternoon. Thank you for your attention."

The audience regressed back into the constituent sub-group units from which it had originally assembled. Individuals, couples and functionally small groups stood up, exercised their limbs and started to eddy in rippled movements in the cafeteria direction.

Having expressed themselves as a group, any immediate follow-uppers seemed to have satisfied their interests. Only two individuals came up to her from separate locations out on the floor. They were the afternoon resource persons expressing their thanks for the "excellent" introduction to the workshop seminar.

Then, Edna was left alone with her thoughts as the two panel members and the priest were off to one side in conference. As always, she felt a sense of let-down after having thrown herself so heartily into a commanding presentation.

It was the kind of deprived feeling any mother could sympathize with on being rebuffed by her children. Surely unintentional, children are often so unaware of adult need to be appreciated that they appear callused and even distant. So much so at times that her heart went out to Mary experiencing similar rejection by her own Son.

8

A brief moment of separation from speech presentation—although possibly considered by some as a respite—did not arouse in her any feeling of loss of control. In her own various congregations, she had so very often been required to be speaker, master of ceremonies and resource person all rolled up in one that the change, albeit penitential even impoverishing in one way could in another be considered maturative.

But who was she that it not be done unto her as the necessity of changed circumstances required. In any event, she pretended to be busy with her own follow-up—sorting her lecture cards back into order again and recording a few notes for remembrance.

"Well, Edna," came the priest's voice over her right shoulder. "You were a smash!"

"Smash?" she smiled in reply.

"I hope all of our 'friendly' women agitators were here to take note."

"I doubt anything I could say would impress them!"

"It's not so much your words, as your presence of spirit and maturity of lifestyle."

"Well, I really didn't want to get much into that."

"How about another time?"

"Could do. But not in this seminar, I hope?"

"No. The afternoon is scheduled. I feel a responsibility to our other resource persons."

"Good! They deserve a hearing."

"I hope you can stay?"

"I'd like to. There's so much to learn about Catholic affairs. And I'm so new."

"You've advanced rapidly, open to the grace of God."

"I hope to be. But I need so many prayers."

"We will remember you on the altar of God."

"Thank you," she replied as humbly as was consistent with this great promise.

"Come on! Let's get you joined to the group before I have to leave." The priest led her towards the cafeteria. As they entered, he spied a table full except for one seat.

"Here we are," he offered, "is a table set for you!"

He held the chair back for her to enter the circle and then snugged it up around her buttocks as she sat down.

"This is a catered lunch," he explained. "They'll be serving you seated in a few moments."

Then, noticing that some wine had already been poured at this table, he turned to a young man across from her. "Ariel, I have to leave. Will you bring our speaker a glass of wine?"

"Sure," the fellow replied, getting up to execute the errand.

His acquiescence to the priest's request was ostensibly gracious. Still there was a certain shrouded something about the fellow that Edna was not able to put a finger on.

Perhaps her antipathy was stirred up by the resemblance to the still deep-rooted hatred of her abusive, erstwhile husband. Both of them had the bodily frame of a savage bully who raped her to advantage within reach of fist.

"Now," concluded the priest as he finally turned to leave. "Why don't you all introduce yourselves to Ms. Masterson while I attend to some other things."

"Just call me, Edna," she hastened to soften the formality of the introduction as she turned to the group.

The round of introductions was made. Each person had on a tag more or less prominently displaying first names. Mentally, Edna noted five younger women and three young men who, all but one, flanked her on each side—all of them probably not that long out of adolescence.

One of these girlish women—the furthest from her on the left—was the same person who earlier had asked whether she resented not being able to become a priest in the Catholic Church. Edna paused in brief observation. Certainly her appearance belied the seeming belligerence of her previous question.

Cautiously, Edna shifted her glance around the table past two obviously mature individuals—self-introduced as a wife and husband—to the younger single "woman-out" seated directly across from Edna beside Ariel's empty space. It seemed she had no relationship with him. While perhaps younger than Ariel, there was a certain precocious "maturity" about her that troubled Edna's first impression.

Was she another group "leader" type to be watched surreptitiously, but gently in order to bring the best out of her for the good of the whole group? It was too early yet to tell, so she remained alert, with hands comfortably resting on her lap.

In any event, this odd twosome—probably placed together by the vagaries of "random" seating—were themselves flanked by two married couples of early middle aged vintage. What a build-in demographic disparity! And those two couples? Each could be a semi-center of vested interest.

Instantaneously, a protesting thought silently flashed through her mind. "Why, oh why could she not have been more appropriately seated!"

Was this to be her penance for having let the adulation of the morning's session touch the quick of appreciation too deeply? Whatever weight that might have had, she was brought back to attention by Ariel returning with the wine.

"It's champagne, Ms. Masterson!" His voice sounded mockingly as he deposited the glassful on the table beside her right hand, and returned to his seat.

"Call me Edna, won't you. I've asked the others to." She felt compelled to make the offer even if his charm had the evil fascination of a snake.

"Okay, Edna."

His deep-throated suggestivity drew her attention to the quick. But perhaps she was imagining things.

Ariel seemed of a middling age between the two couples and the other younger adult singles. Yet so condescendingly sure of himself did he appear that Edna moved to diffuse a sudden temptation to provoke him into revealing subversive intentions.

"Don't you like champagne?" she asked.

"French champagne, yes. American, by sufferance."

He turned and winked at the young woman beside him. Then, with the innuendo of double-entendre, he again faced Edna in what appeared was an attempt at a direct affront.

"The French may be behind in science and technology," he started sententiously. "But they are undisputed leaders in the pleasures of the table."

"Oh?" the young woman beside him responded.

"Included among these are eating, drinking and thinking about seduction. Wine is the stimulus. The better the video, the better the talk."

"Oh, those vintage champagne conversations," the nouveau female beside him echoed in mock flirtation.

Leaning his head close to hers, Ariel picked up on the invitation. "You know, a young woman executive recently confided that she would like to know more about champagne."

"What did you 'advise' her?" the flirting female asked.

"Well, I took one hand like this." Ariel pontificated, deliberately placing one hand over hers on the table, then continuing. "How could you survive even one day without wine? My father's advice to me for a long life was to drink wine and make love every day."

"In France," she countered, "is sex the favorite table topic of conversation?"

"I'm Quebecois. Our approach to sex is different from Americans, especially apostate Canadians."

"There're no more Canadians, or Americans—only Yoofnaseans, " she shot back provocatively.

"I know, unfortunately! Anyway, we feel different about life, about marriage."

"How?" she asked.

"Marriage's a long drawn out meal that begins with dessert. If marriage is boring, one makes adjustments."

"Oh, I'm divorced," she informed him.

"Divorce is a failure. It's better to have found a lover—like me—or a friend like a psychiatrist or a counselor. They can listen, solace and give comfort without any strings attached."

"Listen, you? Never! Give 'solace', yes. If only I'd known you then, I could have been the friend you wanted."

"What're you thinking?" he asked in "plaintive" mockery.

"I'm wondering if I should ask you to come home with me tonight for a 'friendly' get together!"

She threw back her eyes in mock seduction.

Ariel was not startled; the two couples seemed to be. Two of the young females off to Edna's left suppressed a giggle. The young man next on her right squirmed in his chair.

However, no flicker or dismay showed in Ariel's eyes, just like any brat she had ever found in juvenile confrontation. Rather than any embarrassment or flustering, he fronted up in bravado. In fact, he placed a second hand over hers on the table.

"If only we had known one another then!" Ariel gloated, turning in full face to confront Edna across the table in mock exultation.

Edna's eyes met his in bland patience, as she had done so often with her husband. Though somewhat younger, there was something about Ariel that was similar. If only she could have put a finger on such a troublesome thought!

For a moment her eyes held his, not glaring but so rested in calm deliberation that he all to suddenly had to drop his. Without self-recrimination, she had to face recognizing how wrong she had been to have even appeared to give the conversational lead to this creature.

She remained calm. Not for a moment did she think there was any seriousness to the encounter. For that matter, Ariel may have thought this was the way to get some hospitable interchange in the group. He may even be experiencing some care for the unfortunate divorcee, but probably not much more than he could for a chair and table.

It was just not the nature of this type to be taken seriously. Be that as charitable as it may, she could not help but coolly observe that his behavior was patently satanic. She must think of some way to diffuse the damage already done.

The others around the table shuffled their mannerisms nervously. Edna would have to do something to redeem this interpersonal event and move the conversation around to a more productive avenue of discourse. Otherwise, the evil which hung ever so odiously in the air over them might enter and solidify in every individual. And, they would begin to point the finger of their eyes at her.

Surely, it was an inspiration of the Holy Spirit, hovering over the depth of consciousness, that brought a possible tactic to mind. She was calmly in control and at peace with herself, and could do it!

The deep modulation of her voice drew all eyes around the table to focus on her invitation to the disrupting tormentor. "Now that we've been served. Ariel, I wonder if you'd say the blessing."

"I'a…!" the brute jerked in hesitation as if his devil's chain had been yanked by some concealed hand.

"Oh, come now! I'm sure your old Quebecois mother's praying for you—wherever she is right now—with all the intensity of a Monica."

Edna could feel the strain ease out of the others around the table. Their bodies seemed to naturally relax as each of them placed their hands together and bowed their heads in expectation.

"I'a, don't know…"

"Oh, come on Ariel. Put up or shut up!" his flirting companion challenged.

"Okay, okay!" he sounded piqued, but continued stumbling. "Bless us…Lord? Thank you for food. Don't get indigestion!"

The incongruity of the spontaneity brought a chuckle all around the table. As each fell too, eating, the normal expectation of conversation was momentarily suspended.

So like her own home table, Edna ruefully reminisced on the spur of the moment. Then it struck her with startling suddenness. How like her cherished daughters these two people seemed. Fortunately, back-home antics had not burst out in such festering venery as these two seemed to be doing—at least, God forbid, she might have to keep her fingers crossed.

Edna knew the momentary lull could not last without the danger of someone else again leading the group astray. But then, one of the young women on her left opened up—the one who had challenged her on the female priesthood.

"Edna," she asked in anything but an inimical voice. "You said you were raised in the south?"

"Yes indeed! The 'deep south' they used to call it."

"Do you find it much different from up here?"

"There are certainly more Catholics. We hardly knew a Catholic back home. None of my friends ever were."

"How'd you become a minister?" asked a young man on her right.

"My parents were clergy with a messianic bent. I wanted to be like them."

"Women ministers aren't all that common down there, are they?" chimed in another.

"No, they are not. But I'm an only child. And father really wanted a child to carry on, since everybody in the family had been a minister before. I was out mid-west, and elsewhere—the only woman in any seminary."

"It must have been difficult?" the married woman, named Betty, on her right joined in.

"It could have been worse. But my mother's family were influential people. I guess a way was found."

"Did your father have a large congregation?" asked another young woman on her left.

"No. He was a wondering type. To mother's distress, he was always on call as an itinerant preacher."

"What brought you up here?" asked the married man on her left, clearing his throat.

"A large group of southern evangelicals had moved up to the interior city I just came from. They wanted one of their own, from deep south—even if she were a female," she added with a wry smile.

"Was there a lot of resistance?" asked the young woman next to her on the left.

"That's kinda like the question Betty asked."

After glancing her way, Edna looked outward into the group, well aware of how easy it would have been to get locked into a small eddy adjacent to herself.

"At first, they felt affronted that a young annulled female minister cold be taken for real," she paused amused at the knowing glances between three of the young women.

"Just like chauvinist males!" Ariel's companion exploded, looking sideways at him.

"Perhaps," Edna replied. "But there's always been something suspicious about female priestesses. I have felt it over the years in my weaker moments. I think both men and women have at least some reservations."

"Are you an anti-feminist?"

The question, surprisingly, came from one of the young men on her right.

"No, if you're referring to the militant feminists. Yes, if you mean a cooperating one—in both sexuality and personality."

Some quizzical expressions appeared on several faces. But she preferred to let that jell some more rather than acerbating the edges of any raw nerves.

"I can only say that the Holy Spirit's been leading me. It's been the Lord's blessing all the days of my life."

"Are you Jewish?" came the preposterous question from another voice.

"Not at all. Just baptism-steeped in the bible."

"I don't want to be prying," called another. "But was your husband a minister?"

"In God's mercy, yes," Edna replied, momentarily hesitating. Then, immediately, a disarming thought came to protect her from further embarrassment. "When you're married young, not many young fellows are ever sent courting."

"Sent?" someone gasped.

"Yes. By God, of course," Edna replied, letting a twinkle remain in her eye. "We believe in the spiritual privilege of marriage, almost like troubadours in the middle ages."

At that, Ariel nearly croaked out a violent protest. "What...ever!"

Edna suspected he would love to remain the devil's advocate. But what held him back remained uncertain.

A second middle aged man opened up to Edna in an apparent concern for diffusing the mysteriously shrouded protest. "You recently converted?"

"I was received into the Church by our bishop just at the end of Advent so I could receive the Christmas Eucharist."

"How touching?" exclaimed the man's wife. "Did you go to midnight mass?"

"No, early Christmas morning. The bishop said a special mass for me and my family."

"A special mass!" exclaimed Ariel.

Edna was sure of a note of envy, revealing the essentially crippling vice of his nature.

"I don't see anything to be jealous about that!" retorted his companion.

"Much is expected to whom much is given," mused the married man on her left.

"Yes indeed, Harry," Edna responded. "You've put your finger on it. It kinda scares me. But I can't let others' expectations override my own development under the Holy Spirit."

"You sound like a born-again," opined the young man next to Betty addressing himself to Edna.

"I hope so. But it's a continuing struggle. No one can presume to be saved once and for all. We gotta work at it continuously."

"What are you going to do now?" asked Betty's counterpart, Felice.

"I have experience and training as a personal consultant."

"You mean a counselor?"

"No. A counselor's either a lawyer or a clinical psychologist. I do have that kind of training. But a personal consultant is more positively developmental and humanly creative."

"Oh."

"Anyway, I'm good at it. So I'm sure the Lord'll find a place for me."

"Where do you get the wonderful self-assurance every woman should have?" Toni asked, who had challenged her previously.

"Yeah," added Ariel's companion. "So many of us have been raised in broken homes, sometimes with abusive parents.

"Parents are primary, of course. But community sets the climate. That's why your Cardinal is such a holy man of God."

"No wonder you are you," blurted a young man on her right. "Where're we ever gonna find women like you to marry?"

Two of the young women on her right again suppressed a giggle.

"The family's the main place to do it. We gotta educate women and men better than we've ever done before."

"It's like the chicken'n the egg," Betty's husband offered in resignation.

"You can't give up hope," Edna countered, "just because antichrist has been so devastating. We've got to pray and work as daughters and sons of our heavenly Father. You have made some significant developments in this diocese—space age financial homesteading supported by small family enterprise, supercomputer-based soft and hard technologies, and inclusive schools addressing self-help economic problems. Now, you need to address the religion-human problems of personal maturation that will counter the leftover caesero-hedonistic exploitation by state-controlled and entrenched socialistic overlords. I pray that training, like in this workshop today will be the making of ever so many everyday saints. Countering the individually personal attacks of your faith-baiters in confident humility will be a schooling for maturity unparalleled anywhere."

"Is that what you're gonna talk about this afternoon?"

"I'm not sure I'm talking at all. I have to see Father Thompson. Anyway, it'll be my chance to learn something."

9

When lunch had finished, Edna was accompanied back to the adjacent assembly hall by two of the young women. Hardly had they started than interruption appeared in the person of Father Thompson, the priest coordinator.

He motioned Edna to follow him, leading her to one side, out of the others' earshot. "Edna, I have a problem."

"Oh?"

"We have a group here of all senior high school students. I've deliberately scheduled a young man to give them a talk. I want him to have a try-out with, what could be a difficult audience."

"That's for sure!" she exclaimed. "Who is he?"

"He's on the staff at Leland House—probably not any older than you," the priest added slyly. "Mary Bulenski, the administrator, brought him on board several years ago as research coordinator and consultant for client services. He's worked closely with Ann Patterson in training paraprofessionals for catechetical instruction. It's all part of the Cardinal's enterprise to rejuvenate society and culture with the good news of the gospels. Mary's husband, Terry, has been developing an electronic environment in which the cultural resources of the Church are being hot-wired for individual access."

It seemed the priest would, if not interrupted, continue to wax enthusiastic. She pushed herself into his attention. "Father, what's the problem?"

"Oh yes, well, he's being considered for the deaconate and a place in the seminary. I'd like your appraisal of his potential."

"Potential, in what way?"

"As a speaker and other ways he'd be a mentor to seminarians."

"I thought deacons were older married men?"

"That's been the traditional way. But the Cardinal wants to revolutionize the role, recruiting young married so they and their families will be the models of spiritual development."

"Is he married?" she asked.

"No, but I think he's got something that'll inspire others to follow."

"What's that?"

"The potential to be a saint."

"A married one?" she wondered, surprised.

"Especially a married one. According to the Cardinal, that's the great need of the Church today."

"What are his prospects?"

"For what?" the priest asked, puzzled.

"For marriage!"

"I don't know; he's not made much headway in that respect. But the Lord willing, God will take care of that."

"God's gonna have his hands full, if you ask me! Sexual activity can be pretty hard on males to transcend. Pregnancy's the great stumbling block when their imaginations run wild in overweening fascination. The older they are, the worse the problem of abstention becomes with a galloping imagination like they were burning up with porno-fever. Then does violence build when male urges are thwarted by the higher duty of couvade protector."

"Well, I don't know about that. But the Lord's accommodation will surely overcome as it always has since Adam and Eve."

"Yeah? Look what it got her!" Edna retorted with a slight edge-in-voice. "Forever afterward condemned to the role of insemination seducer!"

"Edna, I'm surprised! You got a feminist problem?"

"Not at all, Father!" She hastened with wry assurance before adding with a tinge of resignation. "Let's get on with it! You got a room off to one side where I could hear without being observed?"

"Yes. He'll be with the principal. But just off-side is a one-way window for unobtrusive observation."

"Thanks."

The priest again led her, skirting the audience now rapidly assembling, back to the side of the hall. They entered a doorway and up a half flight of stairs into the technical support room, raised high enough for the equipment operators to see out of a glassed panel over the seated assembly.

"There you are! Piped in sound can be controlled with this rheostat. You can see, too, if you want," the priest offered, pointing to a lighted button. "When that red transducer is on, the glass becomes a one-way mirror."

"Thank you, Father. This is fine."

"Okay. I'll get you after this session."

Edna sat for a moment collecting her thoughts. Then inner attention soon shifted outward, eyes attracted to the images of an assembled audience coming through the one-way glass observation window.

To bolster her assurance of unobtrusive viewing she raised an arm and wiggled it a bit. Nobody noticed. She lifted up another arm and waved both of them vigorously.

Still, nobody glanced her way from over on the other side of the treated glass window-partition. Confident in her privacy was affirmed. She lowered arms and would have attended to her notepad.

All at once, the youthful audience stiffened. Heads turned towards the upper corner of the room immediately beyond her view. Then a figure appeared from that location, back towards her. Leaving the principal at the speaker table, the young man stepped up to the podium.

She could see the right profiled face of a young man as he stood momentarily looking out over the assembly. The fellow, not more than a year or two older than herself, seemed calm enough in appearance.

Shrewdly she observed the body language of the older adolescents in the audience. Minute twists of head and small hand movements revealed a certain sympathetic worry, emphasizing about how nervous the speaker might be before them.

For a moment, the young man continued to pause with a widening smile growing on his face. Surely, it could not be a fake!

Yet she was amused at the uncertainty of it all, of a young audience expecting him to leap into the space between them—hoping against hope that the fellow would not panic, nor desperately try to fill up the void with words, scary words, restless words of self-recrimination, self-justification—anything at all to fill up a frightened impatience.

But no! He paused just long enough to get their attention and quiet themselves down, especially the finger twisting and jerking of heads. Then gently, slowly in a clearly modulated voice the fellow let the words come, flowing from the patience and forbearance of careful, peaceful enunciation.

"The other day…in my practice…a young girl appeared. Like a ghost…she arrived in my counseling office… skin and bones…with a pasty white face, like a séance doll bobbing up out of a sack of old-rag clothes. I searched for her eyes…but they showed nothing. The orbs just lurked inside the head…sunk deep in the sockets…hiding from everything."

Edna watched, fascinated by the self-control. The charged emotional impact of the speaker's deliberate cadence got to her, compelling attention.

"Her body slumped forward…her spirit was already dead. Obviously marking time—maybe even lost to any passage—her body must surely be rotting away. If ever an individual was too late for help, this one had lost all personality."

For Edna, on the outside of a treated mirror, the angle of the sight was not as adequate as could be. But every once in awhile, the profile view was augmented as his head turned with perceived audience feedback.

The fellow was surprisingly adept and agile, and like herself of similar height. His body was lean, muscular and nimble—not dissipated at all as one might have expected.

She could see notes on the lectern before him. But they were little used except for an occasional prompt. He spoke emphatically without the dawdle which could bore an audience to distraction.

The more than occasional pause for emphasis in delivery seemed to enthrall the listeners. At least they appeared focused, not given to impatience tics, eyes closed and downcast heads.

The presentation style of speech he used, reminded her of the penitential rite in individual confession. Apparently, this male being had been frequently strengthened by the sacraments of Christ's living presence.

Watching the young man's poise and graceful mannerisms of effective delivery, Edna recalled an incident in her own seminary training. The professor had once organized a brief practicum to supplement lectures on the supposed communication style of Jesus Christ.

The faculty member had contended that Jesus used a gnomic style which featured short pithy sentences, almost injunctions, separated by somewhat lengthy pauses where the divine presence nonverbally projected almost telepathically into the psychic center of each listener, holding that person's attention singularly as if nobody else were around at all.

"To begin with…this child of the streets was not my friend…or anybody else's, for that matter. She wanted to end it all. She wanted to die…and I was the enemy…We found a place for her…at Youth Hostel where I understand some of you have done volunteer work."

Edna watched as several heads nodded agreement. Instead of rushing to mine the supposed capital of emotional support, the young speaker smiled and let the pause sink into momentary reflection before continuing.

"Several days later, the young girl was returned to me for an attempt at further enablement. But Betty—let's call her that—was not able to accept me. All the while, she kept her face hangdog. I refused to let my own head panic… Something inside me said a prayer…In a moment or so, the Holy Spirit lead me to say… 'I'll never know whether you're pretty or not if you keep your face covered…'" That took some little while to sink in. I stood by waiting. I don't know what happened inside her head. But after awhile one arm dropped a little…letting me see a sad, tear-stained part of her face…'You really are beautiful…' There didn't seem to be much effect, even when I repeated myself…'God knew how pretty you are all along. God loves you and believes in you…'" That brought a reaction. 'No, he don't. I wanna be dead…' 'Don't you know why God made you, Betty?' 'No, he don't care!' 'You really loved your mother?' But no answer came. 'Supposing your mother could have any girl in the world, who would she have picked? I waited as she thought about that…most other little girls would not have hesitated. But Betty had been deeply hurt and asked, 'Me…? With the hesitancy of someone facing an oral examination…she wasn't even certain of her own mother's love."

The speaker paused longer for a moment—apparently not out of necessity to glance at his notes. Those, he seemed to have well under control.

"Betty could have said her mother loved her. But she didn't feel it deep down. How many of us say the same thing, but don't feel it profoundly…I don't know who Betty's mother would have picked. But I do know who God picked…God made Betty and each one of us for the one and same reason. God needs you. God needs me…not a need like for food to live on, but a longing for love…God doesn't make anything he doesn't love. In all the universe, there is only one you. There has never been another you and never will be any other. God loves you in sadness, joy, peace, and pain…Once you realize God's love for you, and your love for him, no one can ever take it away from you, not even death. I told Betty that God knew how pretty she was all along. God needed her to love him back in the only way she could, or would. Apparently, Betty began to believe in herself. Some months later, I saw Betty again—a fine young teenager who now wants to help others believe in themselves."

At that moment, Edna let awareness drift. Attention to her own thoughts overrode the words of the speaker.

No! She paused to observe the words sink into the audience and to anticipate whatever reactions they may have. Teenagers always had reactions, mostly nonverbal, and were not really that good at concealing them, if only one knew just how to read the evidence.

On the other hand, they were not particularly effective at expressing themselves either. So, she divined it was time that the speaker now make it comfortable for them to do so.

"You know," the young professor started again, "I just became a Catholic not that long ago. When I was preparing for the Church, they said I had all the questions any teenager would have. Each one of you has some very good ideas. If you want to ask questions, please do so. That way I'll be able to talk more about what you want to hear."

Almost before his words were out, a hand was raised—it seemed tentative and in hesitation—over in the second row to his extreme left. It was a young female, somewhat more emboldened than others.

"Did you have a question?" the speaker asked.

"How can God love me when so many people are starving and suffering?"

"Are you referring to the destitute and homeless down where you volunteer?"

"Yes," came the reply.

"You know, Father Thompson took me down there one day for a visit. I talked to a young nun probably not that long out of high school. It seemed strange that a young, beautiful woman would be so happy living in all that filth. You know, she just looked at me and smiled at my question. Her smile and tone of voice were so gentle and powerful. I'll never forget. She said, 'How can you be happy living in your filth, the filth of your own selfishness. In God's eyes, your life may be worse than this place is to you!' I was taken aback. You know how self-righteous and downright rationalizing we all can be. 'Me filthy?' you might say. She was trying to show me that if I'm not part of the answer, then I'm part of the problem."

"Are you saying we all oughta go off'n live like nuns?"

Edna could almost hear what surely was the young person's rejoinder "Yuk" in her own mind! She smiled slightly as the speaker followed up.

"God wants us to follow whatever desire for life he's planted in each of us, way down deep under the boredom it's all too easy to feel. None of us like to think we're the cause of our own boredom. It's always their fault, not mine! Lost in a pity party we'll never find out what to do with ourselves. It was like me and the nun who found me out. It is social injustice. Negative thoughts could have easily led me to question God's love. I could have found someone to blame. The world belongs to him. It was his fault, nobody else. But the nun was too honest to let me off the hook. She would not let me hang loose in apostasy, with an excuse to ignore the church and disobey the commandments."

Then further back, towards the middle of the audience came another question from a bespectacled male youth.

"How come God put such a mess in the world? I don't like it hardly even me."

The words were out, Edna was sure, before he even realized the import of his own question. The other two, on each side of him, started to giggle.

"Poor God. He's so easy to blame for everything. He gave us a free will to obey. But commandments are so negative we think, not positive guides for living. Who cares? God does! 'Though all disown you, I never will'—always listening even when you run far away. Especially then, speak to God. Tell him how insecure, how inferior, how self-conscious you feel. Talk it over with God, how you need to be with others, dress alike, talk alike and even rebel alike."

"How do you know when God listens?" came another, almost challenging inquiry.

"You know, for years, that question used to bug me. I knew there was a wind even if I could never see that wind directly. I could feel it on my face. I could see flags flapping and the weather changing. Surely there had to be a God, if for no other reason than how wrong weather can be—yet surely guided through random events. But how to feel him was real tough, until I realized the power of silence and talking to myself. Silence is dreadful—very, very uncomfortable unless you talk to yourself. I had to. It was so silly until I started talking it out to God. He'd made me just like I was. I just couldn't be alone with my thoughts. They were too terrible—I'm no good, I'm rotten, I'm useless, I'm garbage, I'm too sexy for my own good. I can't do anything right. Everybody's against me. As I learned to talk all the garbage out, there'd come a time when I'd feel comfortable just being silent—wondering to myself, deep down inside, how good I could be in God. It just felt so good to think about good things. Not just enjoyment, but in a deep sense I knew I was right by God's commandments. Not that fake feeling, so easily come by always when everybody else is doing it, even though it may be a sin. Not a lax conscience that makes sin appear to be good. It's not just sex. How honest are you? Did you steal? What about jealousy? Or macho slinging like apes in the trees! God isn't hung up on sex. Some individuals are. Others on drugs, or whatever. What about the excuses you dream up when backed into a corner? Or fight to get even with someone, just for the devil of it. Not all sins are those we deliberately do. What about all of those times we have the power to make things right, but don't? How many times do we refuse a kindness, thinking we aren't with it, or care. So, you can know when God talks to you! When the fear of silence grows less. And you like yourself well enough to let God move deep down inside. God doesn't make junk. Quit knocking yourself down. God made you!"

"What's all this business about sin?" one person asked.

"Sin is a deliberate refusal to think like God does, nobody wants to use the word anymore these days. It is easier to call it something else, like teenager premarital sex sins against purity. No, they call it 'freedom of expression'. Women don't say they're murdering babies in abortion. Oh no, they're just liberating women. Rich people don't call it injustice ignoring the poor. No, that's just preserving one's security like we all do when rationalizing. In other words, what's it costing somebody else so we can have the big lies? Maybe even costing ourselves, shortening our own lives just to have something to do!"

"It takes so much energy to do all that! Nobody'd get anything else done!" a woman called out.

"You have the sacraments," interrupted another.

"Oh, they're just signs, like magic and the occult."

"Well, there are magic signs, and there are power signs. Magic signs are wish fulfilling like when I delude myself into believing something'll come true. The more I wish, the more I'm sucked dry—energy depleting, as you put it. Power signs do what they show, like a radio switch brings sound. A TV button brings a picture. A light switch brings light. Under a different sign that same switch could bring heat or cold. Signs power life regardless of wishful thinking. So, there are signs of God's power, switches which turn him on for us. When used, these signs make Jesus present in my life. The sacraments, especially the Eucharist, put us immediately in touch with Jesus. If you want to know when God talks, that's the time to do it."

"Why not T.M. it through?" asked someone else.

"Who needs a guru to repeat some meaningless words like 'oom' over and over again that have no reference to God or Jesus. Christians have been meditating for centuries like in the 'Jesus prayer' or the rosary. When we talk to ourselves and think about God and his mysteries, we are meditating. As we think, we begin to feel about the happenings. Feeling about holy things helps contemplation. All this is so natural to human beings, we do it all the time. If we're not thinking and feeling about holy things, then we're thinking and feeling about everyday things. Even if they may not be unholy, we become predisposed and overly inclined to do so. When the things we think and feel about are unholy, then we got sin. It is so easy to become addicted to thinking and feeling about anything at all other than God. Today, the media continuously 'force' us to think and feel about everything else so we can buy, or steal what's not lawful for us to have—all so business like—the commercial system where anything can be hyped in self-interest words of wishful thinking and feeling that is habit forming. All too easily the 'gimmie' urge becomes so powerful we gotta just do it. That's what the Apocalypse calls the great whore of Babylon—the lusting after anything and everything that'll make some big profits for someone else. But that feeling was proscribed when great Babylon was destroyed and media hype'd gone. Then the merchants wept and wrung their hands. There afterwards, people would only buy the bare necessities for downsized living."

All of a sudden, a teenager leaped up right under the speaker's nose, it seemed. The young woman's words were so excitedly agitated as hardly to make sense. "The Apocalypse'll not happen...? You mean the great destruction is already over...Antichrist has just withered away...?"

"Hold on a minute," the speaker cautioned. "Do you read the bible?"

"Yes, every day."

"Does anybody else do so?" the speaker asked, looking out beyond, back and forth, over the audience.

Several hands shot up in the air. "My word! Times have changed," the speaker exclaimed, before turning to the school principal still sitting at the platform table behind him. "I didn't realize so many Catholics read the bible."

"Well," the principal replied. "Adults still don't. But we have a project on in the school to get as many teenagers reading as possible."

"That is remarkable! May the Lord be praised for these results." Then turning back to the student, the speaker readied himself to continue. "In no way am I pretending to second guess the Catholic Church's substantiative interpretation of the Apocalypse. That is reserved to Rome and the bishops. My statements are more a result of the descriptive way I used to go about reading the bible. As you can see, personal reading unguided by the Church, all too readily leads to subjective interpretations."

*   *   *

At that point, Edna pulled herself together in reaction to observations of the speaker. Awareness was suddenly flooded with the conviction that she herself could give the same speech.

It was scary to think that another person anywhere in the world, but especially right here, could think similar thoughts. Shrugging off resentment, she got up from her seat and departed.

10

Edna had not waited for the speaker to finish. That could have provoked the possibility of being trapped in a confrontation. To observe the young fellow surreptitiously was one thing; but a direct interface was more than she was willing to endure.

She had turned off the sound and the switch. The one-way glass had darkened, releasing her from the compulsion of any further surveillance. In delayed reaction, Edna had suddenly found herself insecure from a peculiar feeling—a sensation of overwhelming powerment.

The young fellow was a compelling speaker. Suffused by appreciation overload, enough had been heard to last a lifetime! Edna could have become mesmerized were she have remained on the sidelines beyond the direct involvement of an audience placement.

She had turned away. But in departing, part of her remained in the room in empathetic response to the echoes resounding through short-term memory. The further the distance covered, the deeper the impression settled into a sort of mutual enclave within her psyche.

Further down the hallway of escape, Edna scarcely noticed a figure coming her way. Then precipitously, she recognized Father Thompson who greeted her cheerfully.

"Edna, why don't you come back. I'll introduce that speaker before he gets away."

"Father," she reacted, "you've put me in a very awkward position, having to observe that young man unobtrusively. He's really good at what he does. But right now, I just can't face him—maybe sometime in future, but not now!"

"I'm sorry to have imposed," the priest apologized.

"It's not a compromise. It's just—I can't!"

"That's okay, maybe even for the best. Anyway, he's got to get back on a schedule; and you need to get away. I understand."

*   *   *

A day later, Edna settled up some personal affairs prior to departure to the interior of the state. Principle in accomplishment had been to inspect the home where she would lodge on return from the brief trip upstate.

The house was still owned by her uncle, the monsignor, since the days before being transferred with the bishop of her conversion. That reassignment had been the beginning of a living martyrdom for both of them.

*   *   *

Next day, finally it seemed, Edna was in her car for the trip. On spur of the moment, she decided on a brief visit to an old historic landmark before mounting the interstate highway eastward out of Port City. She wanted to pray once again in the old mother church of another ancient colonial days, Our Lady of the Mount.

It was no longer the central church it once was. A more recent edifice, standing in the downtown area of Port City, had been designated as Cathedral of the diocese. This old superceded church was dilapidated and worn with age. But it had an especial atmosphere that, for Edna, carried a whole environment of meanings.

This particular old church provided continuity with the past, such a physical past as is available in the New World. But in spiritual matters, the unbroken progression reached back beyond two thousand years of Roman and European hegemony to other millennia, even to the Genesis accounts of happenings in the near Middle East.

Had someone asked why this visit to an ancient church, Edna would have been hard put to come up with an immediate answer. It was more a spur of the moment feeling or beckoning that had overshadowed her than a verbal rationalization.

All of a sudden she felt enervated, drained of her usual out-going vitality— as if she were a child again, reprimanded for some unintended demeanor. She had a new faith. But the old denomination and its institutional affiliation could still exert considerable lashback.

Having arrived at the Church of Our Lady, Edna parked on the street in front of the old edifice. In no time at all, a small mini-bus pulled around her car and pulled in right next to the steps into the church. A few mid-, to older women got out and made their way inside.

Edna waited until the small vehicle had turned around and departed from the area. Seeing no one else in the vicinity, she got out and closed the car door behind her.

Edna mounted the old stone steps that led up onto the outer porch underneath a covered balcony. That overhanging extension of the inner upper church was possibly an old fashioned choir loft.

For a moment, she paused, noticing to her left an outside stairway. That entrance may have been used by musicians in the past to come and go independent of congregational movement through the main church threshold.

Instead of proceeding through the front door, she took the side entrance as a double assurance of protection away from possibly others making a visit down below in the nave. Having gained entrance to the balcony through the portico, she crouched down on a seat at the railing.

Abruptly, the deeply suppressed motivation for this church visit burst out in a flood of pent-up emotion. She loosened thoughts in earnest acknowledgement of the guarded way her interactive behavior had had to be held in check during the brief interlude in Port City.

Edna had not only maintained rightful privacy but had also refused to serve up the enormously tragic and incestuous rape of Trudy by her father as a gossipy can-of-worms. Actually, young as she was, the misplaced guilt endured was none of their business, nor that she was a grandmother. That could be taken in stride, later.

She had deceived no one. But a troubled disjunction in psychic displacement was already beginning to ease. Though not requiring penitential forgiveness, equilibrium was being restored by coming here and reflecting without reservation before re-encountering what lay ahead up in the interior.

*   *   *

The entire inside of the church under its vaulted dome was in full view. Here was no great "plant" of a church, built primarily for meetings and activities, announcing to the world that some great Ministerial Doctorate was an enormously successful money-raiser. Here was no powerhouse of "religious" activity that served as a backdrop to the popularly mediated messages beamed from its broadcast location across the air and light waves to mass marketed audiences.

The atmosphere spoke clearly, simply and eloquently of the gospel mysteries in all of its ancient design and even somewhat dilapidated furnishings. It drew one's attention to the incarnation, death and resurrection of Jesus Christ, and little else. The frugal iconic accouterments tugged one's awareness outward beyond self-imposed limitations towards the wonderment of God's creation and continuing workings throughout the human and natural environments.

For a moment, on entering the pew, she hesitated wondering what position to take for prayer. Stance was not really that trivial a matter, not merely a taste of a whim. Stitting, as she was used to as the all too common preference, was often distracting and now, with clearer realization, could incline her sensibilities towards disembodiment.

Kneeling, on the other hand to which she had only recently been introduced, could overcome a certain shallowness in worship and add to her appreciation of the Incarnation. In fact, it was well known that an outward posture did help to create a more appropriate untrustworthy and wayward feelings and help trundle them along toward her new objectives.

Edna knelt down and, for a moment, looked around at the statues, wooden pictures, stained glass and other religious ornamentation. Such an array of symbols continued to affront her evangelical sensibilities. Though she had converted to Catholicism, it was difficult to eliminate the annoyance in her emotions at such "idolatrous" artifacts—a source of "distraction" and temptation so "successfully" removed from Christian churches after the Reformation.

There of course was the statue of the Virgin as large as life in such a prominent position. Actually, who else would one expect in a church named after her, Our Lady of the Mount. But the appearance of such a striking figure instinctively aroused those subterranean fears still festering in the swamp of unredemption within which her dissenting protestations had for so long gripped her psyche. Suppress them completely she could not; redeem them she would, bathed in the effulgent mercy of God.

Mary, a Virgin, had suddenly appeared immaculate, after an ancient history of animal slaughter and gory stone altars crowded with bloody pelts and entrails— great haunches of lamb and beef, heifers, rams, doves. It was all very primitive, very fleshy and very raunchy to the civilized pagans and their vaunted mental abstractions of election, predestination, reincarnation and self-justification.

No indeed. It was a keen embarrassment to a Gnostic spirituality and shimmering veils of elevated thoughts. It was a direct affront and a scandal to the Greeks and any others down even to her own day of new age imaginings. They for sure would vehemently exclude themselves from a tribal in-group wallowing in the blood, guts and trembling tissue of such flesh-filled oblations.

What was being learned and experienced from such an abattoir mentality? Surely something, someday, more explicitly spiritual would emerge in equal billing from these primitive lessons about humanness—not separated out but united in the flesh and sexuality as it had been in the original garden. And here it was—Mary, remembered in that statue up there so prominently mounted in liturgical history.

There she was a woman of flesh and blood to whom an angel appeared and hailed her with the opportunity of obedience in love. The world had suddenly had—not a summons away from the flesh and blood of oblation which "high" minded effetes might have wished—but a union of the most High with gynecology, obstetrics and a living birth. The whole ensuing story of that conception has continued to bother both "religious" reformers and apostates, and especially to enrage atheistic abortionists.

Against the liturgy and re-enactment of these events has continued to be pitted the whole satanic litany, the grinding iteration of titanic abstractions and the storm and stress of malevolent dissent. Faith was opposed to works. The words was arraigned against the sacrament. Inner devotion was set against enactment. The bible was thrown at church tradition. Even the very mention of Christianity was expunged from public observances in the vain attempt to separate church and state.

The God who had spoken a promise to Abraham continued to do so for another two thousand years in the blood, sweat and tears of a downtrodden conglomerate of tribes, slaughtering animals and birds and pouring out the first fruits of their vegetative labors. Then, in these last times, He spoke through the birth, death and resurrection of Son made flesh in a human womb. God continued to speak, she believed, in his Son now clothed in the bread and wine of re-enactment.

As of a moment, her attention refocused on a tiny prick of light from a lamp hanging near the left side altar—proof of his presence until the end of time and every beyond eternity. The light lodged in her attention like the great bear star herding his sons compelling her awareness of the Divine presence she as a Catholic knew was in that tabernacled tent. With that vector in her thoughts, all the religious "furniture" recalled the huge drama of Redemption.

The surface of things all around her bespoke of the Reality underneath. Even her posture, dress and gesture complemented the surrounding artifacts. They all conveyed meaning to her beyond the mere utility of words. Here for a few moments, she could withdraw from the verbal empiricism of the city and let down the anchor of her psyche in the secure reaches of a religious harbor.

What was it about all these accouterments that bothered here? Was it the beauty in the array of symbols or the distractions that could be aroused, holding her back from going directly to the Source? Could she indeed go directly to that unseen Source without being led there by the symbols?

Of course, the ultimate goal for humans is to set affect-on things above, not on things of the earth. No one can expect a continuing city here below—the world passes and the lust thereof. The local of spirituality is in the heart, sufficient that one hear the words of salvation and meditate on them.

If that were entirely so, why had she come here today? She had had considerable experience meditating with the tapistry of idolatry images. Then, why had she come if she had wanted simplicity, dignity and quiet? Could it be that subconsciously she only came to resent and mock the profusion of graven images?

She had come, she wanted to tell herself, to do something, to make an act of worship. She had not come only to get something. But the distraction of the disjunction in her thoughts was unsettling. This was not an auditorium. Neither meetings nor speeches, or even discussion occurred here. Actually, nothing else but an act of worship was expected.

Nothing in the atmosphere inside the church seemed to have been made to create a feeling of good-buddy familiarity. And yet, there was nothing cold or stiff about the place. Obviously, whatever it was that was expected did not depend eventually on having some ministering priest establish any sort of group dynamics contact with the congregation. Even the notion in her head seemed grotesque, irrelevant and embarrassing.

The only reason to come to such a place as this was to offer something to God, specifically, the sacrifice of praise. Worship builds into the very structure of the act itself the glorious antiphons of charity that must ring back and forth in heaven and all across the cosmos. In prayer, she on earth could begin to learn the script of heaven in a phraseology that could have very little to do with how she may be feeling at the moment.

For an instant she was troubled again—to accept the prayers of the antiphony or fall back on the supposedly extemporaneous vocalizations so favored by evangelicals. Why continue to deceive herself? Admittedly, those prayers she knew so well were really but stock phrases strung together and regurgitated on demand to suit the occasion. Was the old dissenting feeling of her Protestantism to tempt here again?

Why be bothered by the separation? Prayer is prayer to suit the occasion. The sponsored prayers of the liturgy would lead one into regions of consciousness. Left to one's own resources, such felicity might never have occurred to the imagination. Thus the individual, rather than mumbling fitfully, learns to move from solipsism into sustained mental praise and step from egocentricity into community by taking an appointed place among other selves.

Was not her trust of set forms in itself a temptation? Why, the very wish to escape from symbolism was surely evidence of its power. Who among us is a bare intellect, flaunting a desire to approach the most High like the seraphim? Shall the desire for reformation separate us from the Via Dolorosa of sense experience, refusing to settle down and land, extolling the Fountainhead of all shapes, colors, textures, sounds and smells?

Surely the eternal Father did not create a charade or a trap in making all this wonder, frugally symbolized in a paltry few religious artifacts in a church. All the descriptive sensations from the bible rush from his superabundant creation in freedom, love and exultation. Everything seen, heard, tasted, smelled or touched cries out in sensation, conveying meaning.

Awareness of inner church surroundings wavered. Attention shifted inward, became more self-reflective than judgmental. Her thoughts called up unresolved remembrances of an earlier life.

Even though forced into a child-marriage, she had been old enough to expect some non-sexual companionship and even friendly comportment. Instead she had been loaded with two pregnancies, she'd had to endure alone, under the insatiable lust of a much older individual given to porno compensation for the "hazards" of ministerial life.

Eventually she had managed forgiveness and learned to pray for that sexual predator and her father, also, who had been negligent in protecting her immediate and long-term interests. In time, the emptiness of life had led her to the superabundant resources of Jesus Christ.

Even being sustained by the sacraments, He had established for her benefit, there remained a longing. In considered discernment she had concluded that, now once her children were practically on their own, a continued dedication to a single life was still in her best interests.

*   *   *

All of a sudden, Edna felt the inner dynamics of her psyche change. The muscles in her shoulders softened and she could, once again, look at her hands in humble gratitude. Her mind had, for the moment, spent its wad of lingering Protestant resentment over things Roman—a deep seated tension that my yet return before eventual easement in light of the amazing grace of her sacramental rebirth in Christ.

Down on the nave floor, Edna was not surprised to see the older women kneeling and hear their muffled voices in rosary recitation. They were clustered in a somewhat disorderly fashion, up front on the left side of the church— praying before a statue of the Immaculate Heart of Mary.

Almost immediately, the slow refrain of lead-prayer and response in near-diatonic monotony got to her. In fretful mood, she was sorely tempted to belt out the "holy Marys" in a loud efficient voice that would easily carry from her height in the balcony to their ears.

Then inhibition struck! Who was she to soup up recitation, but an interloper passing by on the way to somewhere else. Disruptive behavior was out of line, nothing more than a brief irritant with no staying power to effect changes in the slow and measured vocalization of their prayers.

After all, religious as might be, they were but creatures of individual her-stories—not that much better, if any, than others suffering the personal limitations of hang-over entrapment imposed on democratic citizens by new age social planners bent on tax-levied vested-interest aggrandizement at the expense of otherwise fully-functioning subjects of the community.

What could she have accomplished but pester the worshippers who were praying together. So she ceased the initiative and followed sotto-voce as an exercise in overweening control which lasted for a decade of recitation. This recension quickly settled her down, all the way approaching a sort of near-fatalistic pout—almost as if she would pity herself over a self-imposed martyrdom for not having her own way, requiring everyone else to follow, conformed to her way of thinking and modality of behavior patterns or distribution of personal activity.

Then in philosophical counter-reaction, other thoughts prevailed, leading her to the concluding maxim: to be patient without the pout. She would take the air of the present moment without rancor over the happenings which might occur while events unfolded—holding herself in tense apprehension lest something go down that contradicted the scenario-in-her-mind.

Even though such mental behaviors might overlap there was always an inner layer of thoughts, emotions, impressions, sensations that differed significantly from the show of one's presence. While outer manifestations might be comparable to here, she remained deeply apprehensive, even suspicious of what some fellow could be thinking about her motivationally expressing. Though in proviso, it could and would eventually emerge to influence and radically change her own outer behavior.

In other words, the rug could be pulled out from under her feet. Basic psychological and psychic support could be suddenly yanked away, placing her in jeopardy and giving the lie to the old adage of possibly being two people in one flesh.

No one could expect complete uniformity in an alter ego. What might more realistically be anticipated was a considerable degree of overlap in personal viewpoint, philosophical compatibility and negotiating personality traits together with an understanding commitment to work cooperatively on whatever life throws one's way.

The effect had been to settle her down in a renewed sense of patience that was thwartingly devoid of the anxiety provoked by needing to get on with things, compulsive over tying up loose ends, fretful about the slow moving agenda of events—especially those proceedings scheduled by humans, even those rites and rituals of the liturgy conducted by alter-Christs.

11

For some time Edna had been kneel-sitting at the edge of the balcony in the old church of Our Lady of the Mount. Thoughts had wandered while her body remained in near-comatose state.

She came to, not with a start but gently as if roused by an unseen hand on her shoulder. She refocused her eyes and looked around slowly so as not to jeopardize her position by appearing startled had anybody at all been nearby.

However, there was only the low murmur of women's voices praying up front in the church. The sound was reassuring. Surely she could not have vacated from reality for long—not more than a few minutes if calculations based on the vocals of rosary recitation were correct.

Then suddenly from down below came the squeak of ancient iron hinges indicating that the church front door was being opened. Gingerly Edna pulled herself erect, poised to lean back on the edge of the seat, if necessary, to protect her privacy.

The figure of a young man stepped over the threshold, reached into the waterfront and blessed himself. Startled into temporarily forgetting her own presence, she recognized the fellow as the young speaker Father Thompson had had her observe surreptitiously.

To her consternation, instead of advancing further into the church, he stepped into the rear pew beneath her and knelt down. "Who does he think he is anyway?" she complained to herself in a near irritable growl.

Was he trying to be more publican than the gospel story had suggested? Surely the fellow could not be so proud of his humility as to have not advanced at least a few more pews forward.

Momentarily, Edna leaned back in the seat, more out of line of direct sight from below. She could not possibly afford to be seen, even if by chance her own excited thoughts might attract his attention through mental telepathy.

Then she caught hold of herself. So what if he did look up! No recognition was possible. He had not ever seen her before!

Yet she could not bring herself to hazard the possibility of a chance acquaintance. There was something about the young man she was unable, or unwilling to handle at this early date. Was it the resentment still clinging to her that now began to simmer again? How could anyone, especially this male creature, have had such similar thoughts as herself as were expressed in that speech to a young adult audience?

It was deeply troublesome to think anybody would consider that the two of them might have anything at all in common. And yet, she could not shake the rising presentiment that for better or worse they shared any least measure of a common trait that could only be managed in reciprocal mutuality.

If as Ann claimed he had judges-in-his-head she, surely, had scenarios-on-her-mind that gave every indication of keeping her alert. Perhaps it was a nail-biting anxiety lest things happen contrary to expectations of how events ought to exist according to some script-in-the-head "that seemed right" in light of her experience, her background and her, her, her…whatever!

And yet that disturbing something would certainly have to be dealt with, if ever an encounter were to occur. There was a difference, sometimes enormous, between internal behavior as one feels and external mannerisms—an expression of one's perception of what society's others think of you.

At the mere possibility of such an eventuality, her thoughts rose upwards. She directed a prayer forward to the tabernacle where Jesus Christ waited under a red lamp on a side altar in supplication for the strength of self-control at some future date.

Maybe He even had a hand in arranging the small miracle of this present coincidence. If so, what was the message that so far escaped discernment?

That good news might take some time in transmittal. In the meantime, she again let her thoughts eddy around the "holy Marys" being offered to the Virgin in supplication by the women praying the rosary.

Still holding her body back from the line of sight to the young man below, she breathed a sigh of relief from entrapment in a psychic-blind. Full relief would come when an entire rosary could be prayed with the intention of binding over to the Immaculate Heart of Mary her children and herself. Then and only then would one be cleansed of the awful burden of improvidence.

Come Gabriel, come! May the scales on the skin of consciousness fall away and be scraped clean—leaving my boundaries of soul intact, but able to absorb the imperatives and opportunities of the present moment without psychological recoil. Deal with me objectivity, free of subjectivity especially most of all the escape mechanisms of a pout, and the pull of an unrequited rage that simmers up and down the totem pole of my her-story!

*   *   *

After a few moments, the fellow down below got up from the pew and made his way to the front of the church. At the vigil candle rack beside the side-altar, he ignited a remembrance of whatever it was uppermost in his mind.

Then to her frightened awareness, she realized he would soon turn about and return, facing her presence in full visibility. Horrified, but as silently as possible she crouched down on the kneeler, almost in a laid down-position.

In what seemed like an eon of time she heard footsteps on the ancient wood floor. Eventually the light tread walked to the front door and swung outside again.

Gingerly, lest it be one of the women, she straightened her body, letting the strained muscles relax from the awkward stretching and realign themselves more comfortable in seated position.

The trend of her thoughts, rudely interrupted, was not so easily recaptured. In fact, she was a prey to anxiety and the impatience of wondering just how long to wait before attempting her own departure.

For a few moments she sat sideways, right arm gripping the balcony railing. But reverie was gone, replaced by the worrisome urgency to get away.

Then she heard a sound out front, surely resembling the rapid grind of an auto motor starting. In a moment she too got up and returned down the exit stairwell.

In trepidation she opened the outside door a trifle for an unobtrusive view of the surroundings. Gradually she felt comfortable in widening the gap. Nothing except her own car was in view.

*   *   *

Soon after escaping unobserved by the side entrance to the church balcony, Edna was on the road motoring eastward out of Port City. She had entered the interstate cutting across the district beyond the city and getting en route to the interior regions of the state.

In a few moments she would pass River City, crossing the high level bridge over the mighty river draining the interior of this coastal state. Then for hours the interstate would follow the south bank before turning northward and eastward again into the Inland Region an enormous fertile crescent of numerous villages dominated by North Town, Middle Town and South Town.

Edna had considered taking a newer toll road which actually was only about an hour shorter in driving time and much more heavily traveled. However, she was more familiar with the accommodations off the older interstate highway in existence for many years.

For Edna who did not like driving long distances at a stretch, the hours to be taken and the travelling would seem endlessly depressing. Of course, the magnificent scenery might be considered sufficient compensation, but not quite!

Others she was sure would make the trip in one driving. But for her, it was more than she could take. She would have to stop halfway for an overnight rest.

For the present, Edna had set the cruse control and settled into the inevitability of the long drive ahead. It was good to let her thoughts roam through the wealth of impression during the last few days enriched by the remembrances of past developments as a human being.

Eventually, she came to from reverie. She began to focus more on the stimuli aroused in perception of the passing phenomena. She had effortlessly it seemed, as she spun along with the tires revolving a threnody for her thoughts.

It was not that her musing had been direful. It was only the impression of the spinning rubber on the pavement that carried her along. But it did match the mood of impatience arising within as each new mileage sign flashed by. If there was anything which bugged her, it was those mileposts every few miles that kept up unwelcome anticipation of the great distance yet to be covered.

Not long, her attention was caught by a large poster off right hand of the roadway. The marker was an indication of a lookout for tourists further on ahead. As she came closer, the smaller letters revealed this to be the last spot for a panoramic view back westward out over the great river she had traveled alongside since leaving River City, the delta lands and other salt water nourished settlements.

She decided to take a break and ease the impatience eating into her sensibilities. Soon the pull-off appeared and its deceleration lane. She released the cruise control and let the vehicle throttle down off its own air resistance before turning into the exit. It was a long slow curve up into the tourist area on the south side of the interstate.

Edna pulled into the commercialized compound area. She checked the gauge panel and pulled up to the gas pump. While the attendant service the car, she used the toilet facilities to ease herself before the next leg of the journey.

On return, she moved the car over to the snack shop for a hot cup of tea to go. She parked again and absentmindedly started for the entrance. She walked toward the entry and without realizing it pushed on the wrong door marked "out". It would not budge.

Then all of a sudden she felt a powerful thrust on the door panel from the other side. It came open sharply, revealing a longhaired young man backing out with a heavy packsack, almost knocking her down in contact.

"Sorry," he apologized.

Then apparently realizing it was a woman he was backing into, he dropped the objects he was carrying in a seeming flutter. A book flop-eagled onto the ground, both covers open to see. It was a bible.

"I am sorry," she echoed automatically, "doubly so because of the word of God."

"God be praised," he mimicked in what sounded like a hollow voice. "It's okay." He stooped, picking up the book.

In a moment, Edna recognized the tone of voice which so many of her erstwhile co-religionists used to simulate as representing the graciousness of God. But it sounded so sanctimoniously self-righteous coming from an unexpected source—as if the fellow were making a special effort to ingratiate himself.

Despite the gritty taste in her mouth, a natural graciousness came to her rescue. She replied, without thought of possible implications and entanglement, in typical evangelical fashion.

"Be blessed, Brother."

"And the Lord be with you, Sister!"

For a second she paused, wondering at the young man. There was something about him that instinctively raised suspicion. It was not immediately possible to put a finger on the source of concern; nor was she going to wait around for an inevitable encounter to develop.

Why let his way of dressing bother her that much? After all, so many young gals and men in her own father's congregation were not any better attired. "It is not the clothes which make the person," she mused to herself.

Instead, Edna stepped through the in-doorway as he departed on the other side. She turned to the task at hand of getting some refreshment for the next leg of her journey.

*   *   *

On returning outdoors, she looked around cautiously. But the young fellow had disappeared, thankfully, probably having found someone to give him a ride on his way. She got back into the car and moved it to the other side of the parking spaces overlooking the vast panorama westward.

Edna got out and, in the cooler air of this mid-altitude, walked to a point along the parapet. Far to her right, as she stood facing the expanse of scenery, it was possible to make out the upper north shore mountains above the inlet harbor on the far side of Port City. Closer inland the highlands reached ever upward, stretching precipitously into the peaks of the coastal range.

Swinging the coin-operated binoculars again, she glanced out over the sweeping vista. The river laid itself out to the west, turning southwest in the distance this side of River City. At that point the meandering arms of its slowing water-escapement turned once more, leaving Delta City on its alluvial banks to the south.

And the city, oh the city! How wonderful the glitter seemed down there through the binoculars. And yet, perhaps as a result of cultish upbringing, awareness of the tri-cities was pulled back in reflection. For the life of her, Edna could not stop the words coming in a paraphrase of the Savior weeping over Jerusalem. "Woe unto great Babylon! If only you had listened to my words of consolation and strength."

See the towering buildings gleaming in glass, steel and concrete! Closer up, not only were blighted neighborhoods obviously repulsive, but also the minds of human beings. Oh, the minds of people constantly dazed, bombarded by blipped images and words, stumbling along, feverish and confused—to the sheer delight of new ager hang-outs and the mediated might of svengali allies soon to be contorted.

For the communications elite, those who are active users of language, the "knower of truths" and especially those with opinionated interests crowd around the structures which knowledge has built within the city proper or its affluent suburbs. The quest for power leads to ever deeper involvement within the confines where ever newer buildings are constantly being erected to the glory status of this individual or that institutional consortium.

Only the knowledge of technology could be tolerated in the city by the power structure whether they be in exploitative mass culture, degree driven education, roilery-shrouded politics, or the machinations of economic enterprise. Philosophical knowledge and wisdom—being non-cumulative and thus less amenable to being cornered on the market by the franchised privilege of toll positions—are driven off from the centrality of an information society, being vortexed through the warp holes in the universe of knowledge.

Suddenly, the remembrances of the city called her attention back to the trip ahead. She returned to the car, deciding to eat the sandwich and drink her tea in transit.

Out on the interstate, the long black roadway stretched ahead vacant and lonely. There were no cars in sight. It was just an open highway with traffic signs it seemed for the control of nothing at all—only a solitary woman making her way home in the early afternoon, eating "lunch".

Out here, in this hinterland scenery, she could ignore the cacophony of babel and set ears to the nondirective and non-power laden sounds that could be heard when listening to the deep speech rhythms about the fullness of time. Out here, far beyond the city limits and the outskirts of mass culture, the folk rhythms could come alive to be transmuted in mind into the high culture of knowledge as distinct from the power technology of the city center.

Edna was somewhat less than half the distance to the spot where she had already planned to spend the night. She expected to reach the temporary destination before nightfall. There, she could find a motel room, rest awhile, and continue the more arduous drive over the canyon road along the banks of the great river.

She was immediately struck by how rapidly the scenery had changed. That lookout, back there, was certainly the indicator mark of a rapid transition. The landscape had already lost most of its undulating characteristics. The rocky embankments, though not as craggy as mountain ranges, exuded a premonition that ruffled emotions and troubled her thoughts.

Could distraction be projected onto environment, using the world to screen those disparate formations and externalizations? Was she always to be subject in passage to the designing ravages and distortions as these enormous "hills" and danger threatening ridges? What sacrifice could possibly placate the gods of unpredictable weather or fogged-in collisions with unseen obstacles as she scurried along this narrowing gorge?

What was this feeling within if not but a source of energy emanating from an expression of need? Was she to be alienated from herself by drives projected on the crueler and now more relentlessly raw environment? The compulsive power seemed to depend on the voice within, that murmured, continuously surfacing gush of interactions from remembered daily events and interpersonal negotiations.

Upon whom would she find any support? Had not the choice already been made in religious conversion? Perhaps contrary to the born-again certainty of salvation, it would be her fate to continuously verify the validity of the experience, laying it out vicariously, testing its goodness of fit on her emotions and aspirations, clinging to the belief, hope and trust in the love of God.

Surely she never lost her proper place as a child of God and she had lived her mature life in an analog of that location. Now, her hopes were pinned elsewhere, a home that was beyond place and time and settlement. Regardless of whether she stayed or left any place at all, whether psychological or ground-fixed, she was now one of those remnant persons for whom the glory of the Lord Jesus would shine in eternal fulfillment. So why not become evident with what she could not now see, hear, taste or feel? Even Paul could not detail what such a revelation would be like in time to come.

Here she was speeding through a wilderness firmament, relentlessly rugged in an upheaval of fixed mountains ranges, uninhabitable and mysteriously isolated On her way to another part of the state, it was exhibited separately in imagination; the familiar was commonplace, endowed with the widest possible range of connotations. Was this journey back up into the interior but an apprehension of considerable symbolic dimension?

What kind of information was she to receive from such an environment of mountains and precipitous wilderness? It was an ever more forbidding, dangerous kind of world supposedly filled with evil beings as the ancestral spirits would have believed. Indeed, could anyone ever be sure what actually was lurking out there just behind the irregular edges, rough textures, curvilinear lines, and continuous gradations of shape and dark blue depths. Whatever other anthropomorphic premonitions could she have?

Could she really compare this land of the wilderness gods with the world of man-made environments? Urban domains seemed so safe, at least on the outside surfaces of regular lines and edges, sharp breaks and abrupt transitions, highly regular and smooth surfaces. And yet behind the façade and within the buildings, the heart of man could run even more riotously and savagely than any weather up on this sometimes forbidding topside of the world.

12

Once again Edna was alerted by a poster in the distance. On closer inspection she noticed that the sign up ahead warned of new highway patterns. It was the "Y" junction where one roadway turned north and the other eastwards towards the toll road through the worst of the mountains.

She had already made the decision to take the northern route instead of the pay-as-you-go bypass. Anyway the miles sped by with the cruise control set.

The car radio was turned on. However, on neither wave band was it possible to pick up much of anything, hemmed in as the antenna was so low down in the enormous walled ditch of a river canyon.

The classical music station of choice was silent. The only broadcasts available were a talk show and a western country music channel. Before she could sort out either programming, her attention was caught by a road sign alerting drivers to a northwest junction which she did not want.

In a few moments the indicated five miles had quickly passed by. She ignored a follow-up sign which hovered into view, stacked to the exit ramp. Instead attention was caught by a figure walking further along the roadway. The individual turned and jerked up his thumb for a ride.

Aghast, she thought she recognized one of the evil enforcers sanctioned by the cult. She did not slow down, but kept on, hoping desperately to avoid the inevitable. To her relief, the hitchhiker did not seem to match her fears. But he could have been!

Just as she was about to flash past he waved an arm. Then, as he came into sight in the rear-view mirror, he shot up two fingers in a devil's sign of enmity and indecency.

An abrupt turn in the road erased him from view just as a sharp blast of sound rocked her ears. The radio shot on with the shrill voice of a doomsday preacher. As suddenly, the words were cut off. Apparently she had passed a wave break in the solid rock mountains.

On it came again, the radio wave peeking through some craggy pass to the north of South Town where she had ministered so mightily in the vineyard.

Hyper-suspicious, the preacher sounded familiar. "Woe, woe! you sinners out there! The day of the Lord is coming nearer…!" The voice trailed off with the changing land configurations.

The incongruity of the message broke her tension over the sinister hitchhiker's affront. Her breast heaved. The air in the windpipe broke loose in what for her was deep relief.

The brief light mood was quickly dashed. The ghoulish doomsday voice poured out again, skipping through intermittent breaks in the mountain ranges.

"Woe on that Jezebel…wanton out of the south…flirting us over the years… jading our ears, grouped around foreign ministries…polluting our spirits…gone back over to the roman antichrist…woe on her family when the enforcer comes…"

Nearly too late, she recognized Reverend Jarrett. But his bitter diatribe was clipped off by a raucous dash of electronic static. Quickly she rolled the dialing knob back and forth—masochistically rewarded only with random noise.

Of a sudden a voice returned. It must have been on another broadcast station. Otherwise, the context was too radically altered. "…so, you have just arrived?"

"Yesterday, God be praised!"

The instant recognition of the female voice startled Edna. Its satanic unctuousness and pretentious malediction clawed into awareness.

"Thank you Bishop for this public appearance on our show. Commendable beginning for your great campaign!"

"Time is the essence," the female prelate announced. "The forces of antichrist are released, already at work. The great harlot has defected, gone over to Rome, grandmothered into devastation!"

Listening, Edna was not fooled. Deftly she held onto self-control and awareness of the present. She for one would not get sucked into an altered consciousness that lied about antichrist for monetary advantage.

"Tell us, for our listeners, who is the great harlot?"

"Her name's in the dead book, known to all true believers. She was among us clothed as a minister to lead us astray."

"You mean before you came?"

"Yes, indeed! For that was I sent!"

"Bishop Hillstone, can you be a little more specific?"

"Call me Gaia, whyn't you. Everybody does."

"Will do, Gay-a."

"Everybody knows her. The great whore who came up outta the south, sowing seeds of disquietude and subversion. Outcast she is, never to rise again!"

"Why the big fuss then?"

There was a pause. Could it be electronic noise? No, the static was absent.

There seemed to be a human gasp on the radio wavelength, like an anger-riven slash across a cheek-boned face.

"Gay-a, you allright?"

"Yeah, heah. I'm allright."

The voice ground out the words as if that feminist bishop were in pain. Or, was it the enmity of full hatred?

"Are you here to enforce doctrine?"

"No," it growled. "Help people divine things for themselves!"

"Is the end near?"

"For her, yes! For us, a little more time."

"How'll we know?"

"Seminars all over to let people know what and how to do…" as once again it trailed off.

Edna was frustrated, too mortally fascinated by wanton evil to think—fear engulfing her emotions, to climax in a paroxysm, cramping every muscle in her body, pinching every nerve into a psychic squeeze play.

Seldom had her psyche been so suddenly knifed open and the stuffing ripped out with one vicious grabful. Edna's attention lapsed, oozing towards wanting to let the car drift. Even to make a small flick of a foot on the accelerator, that would release the vehicle into a drift, was beyond her, momentarily.

Unconsciously automatically, her hand remained on the wheel, impulsed from some subterranean psychic well, directionally vectored despite the suicidal nature of mountain travel for the unwary. So, she would ride on the tip of bi-location, carefully clinging to the visible and practical business of negotiating her way over a treacherous highway.

Why was she so drawn to the enormous spaces, expecting something more in this gigantic world and seeing none? Only the wind moved the clouds in the atmosphere—nothing else even stirred! But the force of these tremendous shapes, granite castellating against the sky was thrill-rousing enough.

So huge was the scope of mountains and peaks, and jagged up-piled rocks that one could only comprehend it in an abstract way. Devoid of humans, the environment seemed to be infinite, remote and stripped of the pulse of life.

The specially treated road surface held the wheels in place as the car sped along, joyfully responsive to the feel of her arms. A few shrub conifers and some dwarfed but leafless trees clung to the almost vertical heights on either side. Off to the left across and high above the river wall, highlands rapidly stretched upward, snow tipped and craggy.

The landscape was a deserted wilderness. All it had going for itself was the grandeur of its stark spaces hoisted up there eons ago by some gigantic earth forces, primeval and precipitous. Unknown and disdainful they remained. One could only be tempted to wonder, with Paul, whether this part of creation too was groaning for salvation.

What unity of experience could one associate with places like these? Where could real beings live in this vast mountain wilderness with whom to organize intercommunication and any mutual influences. There was no dwelling together here, no living people with images and memories except as noted, quickly passing in transit. To what appeal could such places attest except that of escape or a recluse's desire for purgation?

Yet could such a wilderness possibly be devoid of life, the hidden presence of millions of tiny organisms that help to render down the rock clinging soil, air and water into a biosphere. No patch of ground anywhere up there in the granite hills would be vacant of life forms. But with whom would it be shared except for a few animals and, perhaps, with a few rock-climbing vacationers?

*   *   *

Once again, the same radio broadcast signal broke through and was picked up by the car's antenna. The program interviewer-announcer was the same. The guest was different.

At first, the talk-show words seemed disjointed. Then one of the male voices, apparently not the interviewer, settled in on an anecdote. This voice sounded familiar.

"People better get upset about it. If they don't, they'll end up like the farmer's frog in a kettle of water over the fire. Little by little the heat's being turned up. We're all being cooked now!"

To her surprise, Edna recognized the speaker as the Monsignor, her converting uncle from Mother's side of an Episcopalian family.

"Who's doing it?" the radio interviewer asked.

"The FCLU," uncle replied.

"Oh, the Federated Civil Liberties Union. They're always in the middle of one controversy or another."

"It has taken some time to get things going. Deliberately delayed, everything's planned to happen gradually. Then nobody will notice. They take one thing away, then another, and before long everything's gone without realizing it. One problem is that few Christians do anything. We're not supposed to get involved in politics—separation of church and state. What a joke they've made of that!"

Since the radio host did not seem to interrupt, the religious cleric continued. "In less than a few years everything will be gone—Christmas, Easter, even Federation Day! We'll have raised at least two generations of atheists with taxpayer's money, indoctrinated in naturalism, stateism, socialism and world government. First thing you know, the integrity of the UFNAS'll be gone. We better get involved, the way they've stole it from us in the courts. Christians do not have counter-balancing strategy that's legally viable. It takes money, time, effort. Liberty depends on vigilance, even more so today than when the republic was founded. Our freedom presupposes a Supreme Being as well as moral values throughout society. But tragically, morality has been laundered for virtual relationships."

"Who is doing us in?" asked the interviewer. "You seem to imply it's a deliberate attempt by liberals to make a minority vote stick?"

"It's never been denied," Monsignor interrupted. "In fact, they are pretty careful to avoid confrontation, just letting diversity slip away in the night! The real issue is how soon they can coalesce movements supporting the rise of some post-apocalyptic antichrist who will establish a New World order under satanic domination."

"I'm confused!" the radio host exclaimed. "Are you saying antichrist's already been here and the apocalypse's over?"

"Partly yes. The bible's full of imagery squandered away by individual interpretation. The commercial clergy and media-churchers have exploited its spiritual potential like Simon-magicians to financial advantage. The last century was turned over to the beast so that it could have its worst apocalyptic fling. But the devil's power is limited and it's pretty stupid at times. Even now, even though its adherents are still riding high on the Trojan horse of power and arrogance, they've fallen prey to their own virtual reality. Blinded by apparent success and self-massaging illusion their expectations of an antichrist to come is a mirage. In delusion they resemble people of old still hallucinating for a Redeemer who's already been visibly at work for over two thousand years in the hearts of those who have no reason to reject him."

"Then have you got any reasons," asked the interviewer, "why the defunct of new age humanism has taken so long to work itself out of mass population consciousness?"

"By itself," the monsignor began, "nothing will automatically be changed, let alone rectified—not even the public's backlash and recrimination that's sure to come over the vast insufferable and irreversible harm done to so many women by apocalyptic industries of sex porno, contraceptive nidation, 'fast-foodsy' abortive cannibalizing and euthanasia."

"If not, why not?" the radio programmer asked.

"No human-made undertaking, or legal enforcement has the moral power to move people's consciences—no state, business, socio-cultural enterprise, especially not even the commercial clergy of the reformation religious establishment."

"Well, if I've got things figured out," the other voice ventured in inquiry, "that leaves in your estimation only the Roman Church?"

"No," the monsignor admitted, "the fifth column has been all too effective, particularly there where Satan's smoke has replaced the incense."

"Is that why you've been transferred up here to the interior?"

"I would think so," the cleric replied.

"Will the Catholic bishop allow you to operate as an exorcist?"

"Yes, " came the reply with elliptical caution.

"I know you're reluctant to discuss details. But would an exorcist operate differently in a large metropolis than here where the population is more scattered?" Obviously the interviewer was digging in, refusing to be put off from pumping his radio guest in the interests of the "people's right-to-know".

"There can be a shift in situational specifics. In general satanic possession is more evident here in the state as it was in Jesus' time when the lame, the halt and the teeth-grinders were in full view everywhere in the population."

"Isn't that the case down there in the metropolitan area of Delta, River and Port cities?"

"Satanic possession takes many forms," Monsignor began to explain. "But over there antichrist commands much greater wealth. Those whom it infects can easily hide behind vast power enterprises, all the while controlling multitudes through hench-person machinations."

"That's nearly the same here," the radio jawperson began in investigative confrontational style. "You've got a Roman bishop being manipulated by public opinion created by two outspoken 'leaders'—the female cult bishop and the industrialist out to do his 'civic duty'. Both of them used to be in Port City."

"Yes, and both of them are still heavily funded by Barren Parenthood, the Sexual Information Foundation, Yoofnas government grants, the pharmaceutical holocaust, Porno International, etc., etc. They're all dead-set against abstinence and chastity, or else the lust industries would soon die out."

"Does that mean your ministry will change?" the interviewer asked, then hastened to anticipate whatever the reply might be. "I know, for example, that the bishop—also deposed from Port City and down-graded up here—relieved you as dioscean pro-life director and put you in a parish where you had something called perpetual adoration of a white host. What was that all about?"

"That holy bishop acceded to my request to mount a spiritually proactive ministry. People came from all over to worship the Blessed Sacrament every day, twenty-four hours. Every morning during the week there still is a mass of reparation for the widespread sin of lust that is tearing society apart by its devastating psychological and physical repercussions."

"It's easy to get hung up on theological nit-picking. Could you give our listeners a non-religious explanation of how a once-called capital 'sin' could affect people in everyday life?"

"Lust breaks down sexual morality by substituting rationalized illusions and delusions for reality-verified thinking. The forces of antichrist were quick to exploit the porno industry's wishful serendipity and synchronicity, and manufacture a virtual reality touted electronically and inescapably everywhere."

"Hasn't information saturation make the knowledge revolution available to everyone?"

"Yes, but unfortunately its implosion has enabled epidemic immorality to relapse into masochistic recidivism. For example, what used to be 'living together without married enslavement' has empowered every young stud to stable lady friends—enticed to move in and then be kicked out when more desirable female flesh comes along. In metropolitan Port City, near a million of these young fellows living off taxpayer benefits have never worked since leaving school. Among them and other morally crippled adults, the suicide rate has exponentiated. Every condo building and apartment block has been zone-enforced to add a rooftop elimination room. Every electronic access channel—whether audio, video or holograph—has been regulation-imposed to synchronize such continual schedules of liberalized religious Yoofnasism that no one can escape being tuned in at any time of day. You can be sure your tax dollars are at work, not for your benefit, but for the vested advantage of wastrel antichrist hench-persons."

"So what are the alternatives? Or, would revealing them compromise initiatives?"

"Not at all. The forces of evil have so pre-empted the ordinarily usual methods that their overweening confidence is high. For them, no opposition is possible or even worth considering now that they've got everybody reacting at least negatively, if not savagely. Few if any persons are left who are 'instinctively' proactive. But lest a remnant of the good still remaining give in to despair, the words of Job should inspire virtue, 'I know that you can do all things. No purchase of yours can be prevented'!"

"If that's so, where do you see people becoming proactive and the 'work of the Lord' going forward?"

"It's enough to be anti-lust. We all have addictive tendencies that can only be eradicated by someone who is entirely free of all such inclinations. In Port City, for example, Jesus Christ is publicly exposed perpetually in the heart of downtown above the little Church-on-the-Square."

The radio jawsmith stifled a guffaw. "You saying that tiny white piece of bread will turn society around!"

"Indeed yes, if that's His will. In the meantime under his Mother's guidance, we'll raise up a new breed of priests and deacons trained and dedicated to leading people out of the treacherous information universe of virtual reality."

"You're as triumphalistic as that Roman church of yours. Nobody's gonna…" But the angry retort of the radio promoter was abruptly trailed off in electrified static.

Edna tried adjusting the station know. Not even any other transmitter came in with clear consistency. Apparently she was in another electronic tunnel of interference and turned off the receiver.

*   *   *

Edna has listened intently to the radio and was bolstered by the words of her uncle. The presence of his voice brought tears in appreciation of his support in her trials and wise guidance in handling the repairs of her life. Hearing him again made her wonder whether it was now possible to face up to the problems she'd been dodging all the while in Port City.

Still, she was convinced that the course of action taken was correct. Privacy had been self-imposed, suppressed-in-mind below a level where thoughts might form and inadvertently be released on anybody's astonished ears. After all, it was Uncle who had made the recommendation to Father Thompson without reference to the garbage that had gradually been recycled into a productive lifestyle.

Up until reflection at Our Lady of the Mount, Edna had successfully vacated her mind of the unfortunate matter in subdued toleration. Prayer and supplication had been ever so much better than any masochistic entrapment setting her teeth on edge by generation-imposed retribution for her own marriage break-up and annulment for cause.

She was still committed to a course of action leading her to start over again with Father Thompson and associates, unburdened by the past, when in a week or two at most she could return to Port City. That move would be permanent, putting behind her the clouded situation she was about to face and resolve.

In the interior, her personal predicament had been used against her dangerously by unscrupulous cultists, damaging the otherwise successful religious mission she had been forced out of and was en route to final re-engagement. Worst of all was the little human being sandwiched in the middle through no fault of his own.

Edna had eradicated any false sense of guilt, least of all remorse over what others had been prone to label as complicity in the matter. The role she had played had been honorable in protecting a grandson from the ravages or doggerel inquisition, and the limited value of a short cut dictated by Trudy's need to find herself under Mother's and Uncle's benevolent protection.

In hindsight, worth unlimited but unattainable merit, other options might have been explored. But the past remained unnegotiable in terms of present informative values. Only a resolve to make amends was possible while patiently waiting for opportunities to break open when favorable conditions would surely return with professional employment at Leland House.

As always in these and other matters, the sustained blessings of Uncle had been humanly supportive. She was also encouraged by recent phone conversations with Trudy and her own mother. Reconciliation on reasonable terms was finitely ever so much more attractive than any protracted arrangements by contracts.

At that, Edna sighed wistfully. In the long term, projected into the future, she could not help giving a thought as to whether the empathy of an intimate consort—long denied to a traumatized child bride—would ever come her way. Were such a happening to occur in reality, and not just in the serendipity of synchronous thinking, then Lord willing she would be rewarded by the experiential discovery.

13

In the distance up ahead, Edna spied someone walking along a stretch of road which appeared to be just past the exit to the next small town somewhere beyond the interstate. It was an individual who had a thumb up, hitchhiking.

Then she recognized the interloper, if he could be called that, as the young scapegoat with whom she had inadvertently tangled at the entrance to the coffee shop. Indecisively she let the car slow down, not fully certain whether to stop or not.

It was not her usual pattern to dawdle or pick up strangers while travelling alone. Yet his big smile and expectation appeared open enough. The fellow's stance and appearance seemed non-threatening. Were her previous suspicions really that well founded? They could hardly be worthy of a fellow minister of the Lord, if that were the case.

Finally, Edna brought the car to a stop several feet short of his location and watched him approach before unlocking the passenger door.

"Thank you kindly, Sister."

He sounded appreciative and, as he got in, a faint southern accent seemed to escape his intonation. "It's a long walk where I'm going."

"Where's that?" she asked, getting the car rolling down the highway again.

"Up beyond the Inland Region."

Edna did not let on that that was also her destination. Instead, she asked. "Are you from the south?"

"Yeah. I guess you can tell my accent."

"There's a trace," she replied charitably.

"Anywhere you're turning off's okay with me. I thought that guy who just left me was going all the way. Sure not much traffic here out. Anyway, the Lord'll take care of me. He always has."

"Oh, I'm only going half your way," she offered, shuffling her words in the hope of throwing him off untoward attention.

"I could drive if you want me to," he offered pleasantly.

"Oh no! That's okay. I don't mind."

She knew she had spoken all too hastily, chagrined at letting a slight note of anxiety creep into her voice. She ought not to have done that, she thought ruefully to herself.

Edna did not push her response any further. Better to let him play a hand. She would stand her ground and not let him take away the lead.

She noticed that he was approximately in the same age range, but taller than herself—too much of a hulk were defensive action needed.

"This is sure big scenery up this way. We got mountains where I come from. But nothin' like this."

She did not reply, feeling the need for more control over the situation. Let the fellow squirm for awhile. If he could not handle that, then the reaction might reveal something about any hidden intentions.

"Hitchin'a ride's been tough all the way up here. At first it took awhile to get started. But I got rides up to near Sound City."

Again, he looked at her which she noticed from the corner of her eye. But she still felt it was too early to respond.

"My mistake was not turning off at Sacramento and coming up north. But you know a southern boy who's never seen the ocean! Anyway, I been days connecting with anything worth while. Maybe this's not the best time for travelling," he paused, then added. "They tell me the coast's been pretty mild this year."

'Yes, I guess so," she finally responded, making sure a small note of distance sounded in her voice.

"Wish I were stayin' down in Port City instead'a having to come up here. Pretty hot'n cold, I'd say!"

"Often is, I'd say," she replied, again somewhat noncommittally.

"I'm a week late. They wanted me up there on the fifteenth so as to start on time for the new season."

The tone in his voice sounded more relaxed, as if finally he was ready to let himself become as open as his appearance seemed to be.

"Yeah. I finished up in the seminary last summer. You might'a guessed form the bible I always carry."

"Lotta people do that," she noted almost as if in protest.

"I been pastoring around home every since. Now's my chance to get an appointment as assistant pastor."

"Oh."

"The former pastor was a woman. She apostated to Rome."

"What's the matter with that? I'm a Catholic myself," she spoke up in mock protest, hoping to drag him out, revealing ever more of himself.

"Oh, nothing at all," he spoke quickly.

Almost gleefully! She was sure of it, especially as he began thumbing through the bible as if to call back to mind some argument or other he was about to lay on her, now that he was beginning to take her as a victim to be pounced on for new doctrinal alignment.

"She just up and took off, leaving the assembly floundering, poor souls without a shepherd. No telling what damage she'd done to their faith in the months before her downfall. It was a good thing her assistant was well prepared to take over."

Certainly his version of the story apparently was not complete, not even accurate for that matter. But who was she to place herself further at disadvantage. Now she began to regret making the mistake of picking him up.

She would not let herself be revealed, not now until she could feel herself to be in a stronger position. No telling what kind of morals an attractive young fellow, just about her own age, like him might have—seminary or no seminary!

The laxity in discipline had been bad enough in her own day, not that long ago. The relativity in doctrine and morals would only have increased, allowing much looseness in thought.

It suddenly struck her as puzzling why someone about her age had only so recently submitted to seminary training. What was there about his past that still continued to trouble her own security of mind and soul?

Then, she "knew" it! She could feel the attack coming on as the fingers in the bible and the notes in his mind seemed to fall into place. But at his words, she knew he was holding off!

"You know it! Might's well be up front about it. I was a Catholic once myself. But too many problems were always bubblin' up all over the place."

Indeed? She thought to herself. Was this a ploy or revelation? There was still something about the fellow she was unable to put a finger on.

"In fact, to set the record straight, I was in a Catholic seminary for several years. But the discipline got too tough for me."

There she had it, she thought. But until the suspicion aroused about the word "discipline" was removed, her mind remained in warning mode. Further consideration was needed.

"Yeah. You know the doctrines they cram down your throat! There's no flexibility for thinking in such an approach."

So, despite his protests to the contrary, his apostasy was surely not about doctrine. Of that, she was certain. He had been too careful in his preparations, trying to convince her, to be taken at face value.

Maybe she would have to wait for discovery. But there was indeed something else behind his story, so far too precocious to be fully believable. She would stake her reputation on that!

A likely fable that was, having to cross a continent hitch hiking! She knew her former homeland all too well for that. If "missionary" he was, any congregation down there would have forwarded such a recruit with a bus ticket at least, if not plane fare.

So there was something up! She observed him surreptitiously out of the corner of an eye, as he continued thumbing his copy of the bible. It was well marked and annotated.

While still wary, she was beginning to feel somewhat more in control of the situation. How many Christian students she had formerly prepared to mark up their bibles in the same way! And then put them through their paces, so to speak, in preparation for fieldwork.

"Witnessing", they called it—witnessing to the verbatim evidence of specific bible passages, even if these might on occasion have to be taken out of context. She smiled inwardly at the thought of the subterfuges and textual liberties they had considered to be well taken in defense of the faith as admittedly defined by themselves.

The young man seemed to be looking for something, somewhat desperately it appeared to have the end justify the means. So why not take the offensive? So, she would let it be done. "You spend a lot of time reading that thing?"

The words were phrased with pointed deliberation, as she let a faint smile of mockery play around the corner of her mouth. She would let herself appear to be a supercilious infidel, albeit a Catholic one.

"Quite a lot. Much more'n most Catholics do."

"Well yeah. I can believe that," she agreed.

"They never know if they're saved or not."

"And you do," she retorted with provocative emphasis.

"Only as they are born again and believe on the Lord Jesus."

"We're all baptized and confirmed," she noted, cautiously leading him on.

"So was I. But that was only an ordinance laid on innocent children who can't think for themselves. Child baptism is just an exercise. Only adults can be baptized after being born again."

"Does the bible say that?"

"Yes!" he stated emphatically.

"Where?"

"Well'a, it supports that conclusion."

"How so," she asked so tentatively that he could take the bait and back off. "You think the end justifies the means?"

"Why? What'dze that mean?"

Edna did not reply, letting her appearance seem to imply indifference. After all, she had done more than enough to give him fair warning. If he persisted in stumbling along, so be it!

"Sister, have you been born again?"

"As I said, I been baptized and confirmed."

"Then you're on the way to damnation, caught in the same sinful negligence I was."

"How so?" she asked.

"The Roman Church long ago compromised itself off from true Christianity. Even Newman…"

"…who's that," she interrupted for an enticing emphasis, as if she did not already know.

"Cardinal Newman, a hundred and many more years ago, admitted quite clearly that Constantine in the Roman Empire transformed pagan festivals into Catholic feasts. Pagan temples were taken over still ornamented the same way with tree branches, incense, lamps and candles. Holidays and seasons, the use of calendars, processions, planting and harvest festivals were all taken over from the pagan Romans."

Edna did not verbally acknowledge his statement, continuing to listen in great disbelief to such trash from a supposedly educated man. Either he was not what he said he was, or else he had fallen like a dupe, totally convinced of such falsity.

"All those vestments, the tonsure I was supposed to have—thankfully it's grown back," he added patting the top of his head. "The marriage ring, bowing to the East, sprinkled water, statues, ornaments of all kinds were taken over. Even the temple prostitutes came over in church nunnery. They listened more often to the sibylline and Delphic oracles than the pure gospel of Jesus Christ."

"You mean the Reformation corrected all that?" she asked playfully.

He did not seem to catch on, but headed pell-mell into his own convictions. "The first reformation has been unfortunately as anti-christed as the Roman Church has done. The mainline denominations are shot through with neo-paganism, humanist psychology and even demonic witchcraft. They're all running after each other trying to catch the world by a tail." He paused. Edna cut in.

"You can't say much for the born-agains either, can you? Look at those television-preacher scandals which continue to go on behind the scenes until the journalists ferret them out."

"Only a few been picked on. Then the press blows it all out of proportion to what actually happened. Then, they can't let a dog alone, hanging on tooth'n nail, worrying the man to death forever!"

"You believe in forgiveness of sin," she asked slyly and cutely.

"Once and for ever, the Lord Jesus forgave all sins. John says, 'Those who believe the gospel, their sins will be forgiven'. Paul in Acts 13 says the same thing. So does Jesus in Matthew 28. In all, there's more'n a dozen or more proofs that believers are forgiven once and for all."

Well may he assert, she thought to herself. But assertion is not proof, even if an impressive array of quotes could be mustered. She well remembered the technique of pulling quotes out of context.

However, that was not all which bothered her. Here was a young man who could have been a "splitting image" of her erstwhile self not that long ago. After all, she had been a very successful Christian leader, badgering almost into hiding the very same Catholics he was now inveighing against.

Woe be it upon her own complicity! But she had trained many co-religionists, young and old, in what could only be called the scurrilous tactics of browbeaten "witnessing". Who else but she would know full well that few fundamentalists ever really find "true" doctrine in the bible. Reading it only helps them pick out short quotations which they think substantiate already preconceived views, even prejudices walled up in their own psyches.

"It's like the invention of purgatory," he continued. "It's nowhere ever mentioned, let alone sanctioned by the gospel. It's a gimmick cooked up by Rome for prying money outta relatives having masses said for their dead." He seemed to want to savor self-righteousness before continuing. "Salvation always comes from putting on the Lord Jesus. Accepting Christ as my personal savior, born again, makes me dead to sin. Salvation has already occurred; nothing can keep me from heaven, no good deeds, no works."

So familiar were the words and so individualistic was the trap of it all, even idiosyncratic! The individual was to be saved on his own say so, without regard to much of a church, a congregation or anyone else—a one-to-one relationship with no mediators, no sacraments, just the "man" and the Lord's word interpreted by himself alone. How much more locked-in could self-sufficiency become and in an area over which no one had any control at all except through the besought mercy of God.

No wonder she had often felt so marginal in her relationship to everything evangelical—as if even a modicum of personal space might be considered apostasy. Everything had centered around her profession. All their friends were members—even her husband's clients—all their social activities were staged in the shadow of one man-made institution.

That institution had been their idol, fashioned in their own image and likeness, not God's. Not to attend almost daily evening services in addition to numerous weekend assemblies, not to participate in bible studies and youth groups, not to dress and act like everyone else in the congregation immediately put one beyond the pale.

Edna almost sighed aloud in relief in her newfound emancipation from the moloch of such tyrannical power engulfing their very humanity in its bellied flames of conformity. Hopefully, her husband and children would soon find the same liberation.

Outwardly, she found her voice in dissembling.

"Is that what the Reformation meant?" she asked with a show of interest to keep him talking.

"Well yeah. We're a continuation of the Christian faith which Christ established."

"What about the millennial and apocalyptic hiatus before evangelicals ever found themselves?"

"After Christ's death, we had to go underground until the first Reformation. Then eventually, we surfaced and came to America in the great awakening. That made most Americans consciously religious. The mainline denominations which we got from Europe, glutted on membership, were seduced by modernism and all its works and pomps."

"It wasn't until the holiness churches took off from the Methodists that we were able to come back to the gospel again—we, the remnants! Now, the evangelicals are all that remains of true Christianity. All the rest have fallen into apostasy."

"Evangelicals, if that's what you are must have an ego problem," she protested, "if not a divine complex!"

"That is blasphemy, Sister!"

"How can you be so sure if it wasn't for the Catholics you wouldn't have any Christianity at all?" she asked, trying to expose his cultist, not evangelical affiliation.

"Catholics are damned!" he almost exploded. "They're dead in their sins. Their confession's proof'a that, keeping a hold over them for life."

"We're forgiven in confession."

"Never!" he expostulated vehemently. "That is sacrilege! Only God can forgive sins. Men are only play acting to keep a hold've power."

"Christ gave the keys to Peter who passed that power down to all other priests today. Sure, God forgives sins. But confessing it to a consecrated man helps us to learn some humility."

"Humility be damned!" he thundered. "It's ego damaging, destroying self-esteem. No wonder Catholics are such namby-pambies!"

"Well I don't know about that." Then, because of his vehemence, she probed. "Were you ever ordained as a priest?"

"Instead, I learned to believe in the Lord Jesus. He is my rock and salvation—not some foreign bishop or foreign pope!"

"You seem to be saying Christianity has only been rediscovered by Yoofnas charismatics in holiness churches?"

"There's today a veritable outpouring of the Holy Spirit. People in all walks of life are healing others, prophesying, revealing the gospel secrets and ministering to all peoples in these end times. The rapture will soon be here. Then we'll all be taken up into heavenly delight."

"Catholics too?"

"Never! Only the saints."

"If all the saints are taken up to heaven beforehand who'll be left for Christ to reign over?" she asked ever so slyly.

For a moment he was nonplussed, looking sideways at her as if to strike out, or at least retort. She took the initiative. "You mean the Catholic religion is the opium of the people?"

"Indeed! Along with socialistic humanism."

"Sometimes, wishing makes it so," she offered bluntly. "What about the Methodists, Episcopalians, and Lutherans?"

"They're misguided surely, But not evil like Rome—the most nefarious institution in the world. It's the embodiment of eschatological evil. It's the tool of powers the average person's only dimly aware. They've made a pact with Satan to come out with Antichrist and kill off the other believers in Christ. But we'll all be raptured up before that."

"You sound like a jihad longing to die in battle for the Great One. He'll be immediately translated into heaven with all of its beautiful houris."

"Not a bad idea!" he retorted.

Out of her eye, Edna noticed a strange look flit across his face, almost as if it were a wolfish leer. Desperately, she suppressed a startled awareness, refusing to let any evidence of fear disturb her face muscles. And lest he were to smell that distress, she held her emotions in check.

Again suspicion crowded in on her, wondering about the motives hidden behind his visage. What could have gone wrong with him? Had he left the Church out of anger and frustration? Was he looking for consoling pats on the back, or out for revenge, or—God protect her—some promiscuous venery?

Certainly he was not poorly educated, if indeed he had ever been a Catholic priest. Nor could he be unschooled in doctrinal history. But there was definitely something missing, some explanatory factor not in place. It bothered her. The suspicions she felt in his presence added to her uneasiness.

14

Edna's uneasiness continued to mount. She was beginning to worry that fear would show, thus placing her in double jeopardy. She should never have given in to sudden impulse and have picked up this warped "Christian" of a man. But then, hindsight…!

Suddenly, with relief, she noticed a signpost announcing entrance to the district in which the town was located, previously targeted for an over night stay. It was a welcome sight. Almost immediately the fear drained out of her emotions, replaced by a hope for "escape".

For several miles now, the skies had turned grey, mists coming close, seemingly almost level with the canyon top on the other side of the river she had been following northward. A few raindrops were beginning to fall, hinting at more, perhaps in tomorrow's part of the trip.

In any event, it seemed she had better sound an alert to the hitchhiker beside her. Soon she would be turning off and hopefully be rid of her now unwelcome passenger.

"I'm stopping just up ahead for the night. I got another long haul in the morning," she explained.

"Oh'a, so soon? I was just beginning to feel at home," he added with a strange note to his voice. "Maybe I better stay over. We can team up again tomorrow."

Such a presumption! That was more than she had bargained for. But she force-held her cool and replied slowly.

"I thought you're going to the Inland region?"

"Yeah, up around there."

His voice modulated to a pointed coldness. Presumably that was calculated to make her feel apologetic. But she held herself in and lied nonchalantly.

"Oh. I turn off northwest not far up the road."

"You said you're going to Inland City!" he shot back.

The brusque fierceness of voice made her turn and look directly at him. She caught the tail end of a frightful look that at once disappeared in a sneer of mock concern.

Had there been other people around, she would have abruptly stopped the car and ordered him out.

But she felt a lack of confidence in her own resolve. Better to make the best of a situation, not yet come to a head until the security of the village motel came into view.

"I'm sorry if you misunderstood."

She let a note of conviction backtrack into out inwardly budging an inch towards any weakness of apology.

"I did not," he retorted again as if in a sour pout.

So be it! Let him high horse if he wanted to. Priest or no priest, he was in a worse state than herself. He was the one who had backed away from the truth and the security of Jesus Christ.

Suddenly, for some reason or other, she felt prompted to make the sign of the cross. If the person next to her was who he said, that should be no problem. But come hell or high water, that is exactly what she did do.

The man became agitated. She was sure his pursed lips had let some peculiar sound escape, more like a hiss than a vocalization. As she turned the corner of her eye, his face was jerked away by some unknown force, hiding whatever expression may have been registered.

Anyway, for the now, she had to give her own attention to the turn-off, exiting onto a secondary road eastward. The snow had not been as carefully plowed from the surface.

Safety dictated more careful driving. The passenger priest would just have to fend for his own thoughts as he sat staring away out of the door window. Any problems were his own doing.

Soon some outskirt houses interspersed with one-story buildings bobbed up along the roadway out from the now lightly swirling rain descending everywhere. Eventually the neon lights of the motel blinked into view. She turned in, gratified at the sight of this rather large traveler's haven.

As soon as she stopped, the hitch hiking "cleric" grumbled something unintelligible. She did not reply but carefully removed the ignition key before getting out to register for the night's accommodation. Edna made her way inside followed closely behind by her unwelcome passenger.

Instead of going directly to the registration desk, she turned into the closest gift shop to browse, hoping to avoid any further contact with him. After a few moments, she glanced around the lobby. He seemed to have disappeared.

She made her way to the registration desk only to find at the last moment the troublesome hitchhiker right behind dogging her every step. Now it was too late to make a change in tactics. The clerk welcomed her in a loud voice and handed her a card to fill out.

With her body she protected the written information from any meddlesome viewer lurking behind. But she was not prepared for the clerk's give away after registration.

"There you are, Ms. Masterson. There's your key to room 19 on parking level. Here's a location map to find it easily."

Almost impatiently she grabbed the key and diagram, and turned sharply off, returning to her car. The man did not follow but, obviously, he had enough information she he become the nuisance she suspected he might. Edna moved the car and parked directly in front of her room.

Once inside, she hoped to relax before dinner. Still fully clothed she lay down on top of the bed covers wondering what to do about the evening meal. She was not up to another bout with that young fellow. He was too precocious for her tolerance.

Relaxation would not come. Her sense of security had been broken and her body would not respond. She was of course tense from driving. But that did not explain all of the uneasiness at some heaviness pressing down on her.

Suddenly there was an inexplicable rapping on the door. In a moment it came again, followed by the words muffled by the wooden panel. "Message from the front desk."

Without more careful precaution she got up, walked over and opened the door a crack allowed by the chain bolt. Her eyes met those of Ariel, the worrisome man from the church seminar.

She could see a liquor bottle in one hand and drinking glasses in the other. "Come on Edna. Let me treat you to a drink before dinner."

In consternation, she fell back intending to slam the door shut. But a heavy boot was plunged into the bottom of the spread, wedging a threatening intrusion. The weight on the opening stretched the latch chain to its limit.

"Edna let me in! We got a lot in common. Rod'n I can share with you."

"Go away! I don't drink."

"I won't until we have a glass. Rod did a good job seeing you get up here—no delay!"

"No!"

She tried to close the door. But it would not, jammed open the few inches allowed by the chain. "Leave me alone! I'm calling the front desk."

She moved back to the phone and dialed. "Operator, call the police! There's a man trying to get into my room. Come right away!"

Immediate action! But she was not prepared for the scream of rage and stream of filthy language that tumbled out ahead of the ominous words, flooding her ears.

"Masterson, I know who you are!" roared Ariel. "You whoring apostate! Rome'll not protect you. I'll get my hands on you sooner or later. I'll tear you down wherever you go—you and your diabolical family!"

Could she believe her ears! Her conversion or lost influence must have been a greater blow to cult ego than imagined. Who would engineer this type of retaliation—track her down with two enforcers. One, Ariel, so typically named was to disguise mole identity. She could only surmise about Father Thompson's deception!

"That monsoor"ve yours's had it! He'll die like the devils he casts out. You think you gotta chance against us? Never!"

"Begone Satan with all your works and pomps," she cried out loud enough, making the sign of the cross reverently.

The last of the beast's words trailed off in an eerie growl. The latch chain went limp and a stomping sounded in her ears. Quickly she slammed the door, shut and turned the deadbolt down.

Her ears rang, buffeted by unholy curses. Edna would not let her body collapse into a threatened trembling frenzy. It was all she could do to control the shivering and turn up the heat some more, before returning fully clothed to sit on the bed.

She held herself in, adamantly stiffening resolve and determination to trust in the Lord. He had brought her this far, strengthening her confidence every step of the way.

Surely, faith would accompany firmness in accomplishment. She reached into a bag to retrieve the bible. Reading the psalms had always been a particularly rewarding experience at times like these.

The heat built up in the room. Edna's body relaxed somewhat, while her psyche was comforted by the verses. Surely these lyrics spoke of the Holy Spirit everywhere in space and time. Nor could they be any less applicable in this moment of trial.

Now, what to do, as she stood up thinking for a moment. She would phone her uncle, for verification of this devil's recruitment to the church. Then, she would order dinner in her room, checking and double checking on whoever would actually arrive.

*   *   *

On the second morning of her stay at the motel, Edna was finally though somewhat reluctant to leave its apparent security. She had stayed over on the advice of Uncle, expecting surely that the two enforcers would have left ahead of her delayed starting time.

Reflecting on the matter at this later hour, she was not certain whether such a delay could be interpreted as an expediency or a weakness. In any event, the time had been useful in catching up on her own work and in the reassessment of her position.

She had had an early breakfast and was out on the interstate following the river northward. The abutting canyon wall cascaded upward and backed off into the upper distance in gigantic columns of rock hurled against the sky.

The early morning was clear, a blue sky covering what she could see of the dome of the firmament between the precipitous cliffs on each side. It would be sometime yet before the strengthening sun would be able to swing loose and shine down over the sharply channeled canyon of the river, gorging its way through the mountainous sentinels forcing tributaries into cascading torrents.

Eventually, the highway left the canyon gorge with its castellating craigs and fortification of the blond gods. So long ago had those ancient ones internalized the inhuman environment that righteousness stood up in them, jagged and cruel. Fit dwelling place for the long headed ones, tobogganing over the snow-covered peaks, specializing in fantastic victories to be rewarded in the halls of the slain.

The wheels of the car began to run faster as she descended lower in altitude and into the outskirts of the region of sunny spaces. In a single magical sweep she was about to enter the home country—the fertile crescent that had been her main abode during conversion, and the wish-sustained undoing of painful losses and separations. Would she eventually lapse as a passive victim of circumstances, throwing back the remembrances of an active decision to leave?

Anxiety compelled Edna to hasten along. It would have been so nice to savor this great outdoors more leisurely, particularly with someone capable of mutual intimate sharing. In subdued anticipation, her heart remembered the songbook of youth.

> I sing the mighty power of God
> That made the mountains rise;
> That spread the flowing seas abroad
> And built the lofty skies.
> I sing the wisdom that ordained
> The sun to rule the day;
> The moon shines full at his command
> And all the stars obey.
> I sing the goodness of the Lord
> That filled the earth with food…

Her mind shifted, distracted by changes in the aggressively overpowering environment. Rugged peaks and erect castellations of enormous rock were gradually being transformed as the journey continued. Somewhere back along this route she had passed a boundary that unobtrusively signaled more gradual slopes and dense forestation. This home of the ancient naikoons was rich with animals roaming together in mutual symbiosis.

Edna figured she was now radio-clear of the worst mountain range static. She toyed with the thought of reestablishing broadcast contact. Instead, she straightened up her shoulders, and pulled in the reins of her mind—heeding the self-induced admonitions erected over the hewed-down years. Self-recrimination was never her style. It smacked too much of suicidal inclinations.

She would double resolve, not in some wound up tension ready to spring, but erected in more substantially paved ways that put solid building blocks under her lifestyle. Calmly and surely, she started to work strengthening the positive schizoid of he bi-located awareness. Culpable, perhaps if necessary; victim, never!

*   *   *

Up ahead, beside the highway, a sign revealed she was getting close to the region near Inland city, the seat of the local bishop for the half million, or so, total Catholic population scattered around the crescent territory. A glance at the instrument panel warned that another gasoline fill-up was soon necessary to complete the many miles yet before Inland City and down around the upper end of the chain of Finger Lakes into North Town.

There she and, later her grandson had been living "in exile" since last year when the announcement of her conversion had been made to the evangelical congregation in Middle Town. She had actually moved a few days before that news was released—a precautionary foresight that had proved to be provident. It provided the necessary interlude of reorientation, and self-development in the rite of Christian initiation into the Catholic Church.

At the junction of the main highway and the trunk road at the western end of the exit into the direction bypassing Inland City, Edna stopped the car for servicing and a cup of hot tea-to-go. She also used the restroom facility because there was a substantial distance left before reaching home.

Having completed the tasks, Edna turned the car back onto the roadway swinging around Inland City and paralleling the flank of hills on the East Side of the finger-lake chain. The view was magnificent out over the City in the distance and the river-cum-lakescape stretching in meridian direction to the next connecting river-neck.

The sun now glistened across the vast expanse of towering hills, rolling eastward far up to the lofty mountains ringing the distant horizon. Just before the lakeshore at the end of the bypass around Inland City she took leave of the trunk road for the not-so-well maintained highway turning southeastward up and through the undulating countryside on the way to North Town.

Eventually, the road curved again, more in a southerly direction, and onto a low plateau overlooking North Town in the distance. Directly off to the sides of the speeding vehicle were shrub-studded slopes falling gently into the body of water that lay out beyond the landscape on her right. The lake was formed as an upside-down exclamation mark. The narrow upper neck was but a widening of the tributary stream feeding down into its bulging length.

Very much further off in the distance, jaggering the eastern horizon in a long arc of the circumference, were the Great mountains. Even from this remote approach, the lofty peaks tore at the hem of the sky. In the antediluvian past, some long extinct but erratic breed of seamstress had left their rough edges sawtoothing the sky in a fit of impatience.

Had she herself become that impatient, sweating over the disenfranchised feeling that had, fog-like, come up and settled into her psyche? Was she really that fatigued from the drive? Or had the backwash from an enforced early retirement as an evangelical minister caught up to her—overwhelmed the formerly positive nature of her psyche, plaguing her self-esteem with the peek-a-boo game of regressive hide and seek? Was her self-assurance not any more stronger than that?

*   *   *

Eventually Edna found herself half expectantly approaching the edge of a small settlement on the outskirts of North City. It was located on the northern bank of another tributary which fed into the upper finger-lake right at the point where the small river emptied into the larger body of water. The village lay on the side of the roadway just before she would have to cross the bridge and continue on beyond the outskirts of the town.

Edna turned off the access road and entered small community. It was little more than two rows of buildings lined up on each side of a main street going nowhere. The road dribbled out, dirt surfaced beyond the last house. A side street seemingly located almost as an afterthought, wound out into the open countryside.

One store stood at the corner, serving all residents, stocking only those goods needed by adherents to the local lifestyle. The other corner was dominated by an assembly meeting hall.

Behind the theocratic edifice stood the "rectory" for the liberated catholic pastor and his family with whom Edna had recently been acquainted. She pulled onto the "church" grounds and drove around to the front door of the pastor's residence.

For a moment, Edna had the feeling of being watched. Sure enough, just as she pulled to a stop, she noticed the front window curtain fall back into place.

She parked, got out of the car and stepped up to the front door. Almost as soon as she knocked, there was a muffled banging sound inside. But it was loud enough to be unmistakably heard.

Of more startling import came the cry of what sounded like the cry of a young boy. But the plea was abruptly chopped off, as if forcibly made mute, gagged on the words he might have wanted to yell out in fear for his life.

Fear seized her as a distinct impression fell heavily upon awareness. Somehow she "knew" that that cry was from a grandson, struggling to speak. Her grandchild! Could it be?

The sudden fright made her knock again—pounding more insistently and loudly. No more sounds came from inside. Nobody made any attempt to open the door. It was as if a coffin in a grave had already been filled in!

Aroused by the possibility of danger to the child, Edna was determined not to leave it at that. There was somebody in that house. She was sure of it and had more than enough right to be recognized.

She was about to pound again for admission when, to her abrupt surprise, the door was opened slightly, but only to its chained extent. Consternation struck her in the face. The hitchhiker glared out at her in a strangely violent way.

"Go away! No Roman Jezebel's welcome here."

What was he doing here? Where was the rector who had been, at least in appearance, recently friendly?

Again the sound of a scuffle, followed by another cry for help. That was indeed her grandson!

"Timmy, Come here!" she called out.

"I can't. He's holding me."

Once again, came the sound of a struggle, followed by a cry of pain this time from a man's voice as if from a suddenly savaged leg. That couldn't be any other than Pastor Boyd.

Then, two seemingly unrelated events occurred almost simultaneously. Timmy apparently broke loose from the pastor and started in kicking the hitchhiker who disappeared in anger from behind the cracked-open door.

Behind her, a police car suddenly came round the assembly hall and skidded to a halt beside her own. Surprisingly, one of the local constables got out of the vehicle.

The burly policewoman ran up the stairs almost pushing Edna aside in her haste. She banged on the door loudly and ordered the individuals inside to open up immediately

The scuffling stopped. The door was momentarily closed while the latch-chain was removed. As it was opened, Timmy ran out seeking grandmother's sheltering arms.

The constable let the boy pass and stepped through the doorway.

15

"Timothy, what happened?" Edna asked.

"They took me! Said you in trouble."

"Is that true?" demanded the female officer, in heavy voice, facing the house occupants.

"No, no, officer! Not at all," replied pastor Boyd trying to ameliorate the situation.

At that, the hitchhiker pushed Ariel aside and stepped forward in what looked like a threatening manner. Abruptly, pastor Boyd intervened to caution the hitchhiker with the command. "Rod, don't!"

"What's going on here?" the policewoman asked harshly.

The hitchhiker stood brazenly solid, arms ready for confrontation. The constable gripped her paddy-stick in a threatening way and ordered. "Back off!"

Then, instead of being confused by this interruption, the female constable demanded of the hitchhiker. "Who are you?"

"Rodney Jarrett, the new church administrator."

"Which church?"

"Reformed, of Middle Town."

"Whatta ya doing way up here in North Town!"

"Conferring with Pastor Boyd."

Edna cut in, disbelievingly. "On your first day in the area? And in a different denomination!"

"You got to start somewhere," he shrugged in a big-man sort of way.

Apparently feeling that something was missing from the discourse, the constable addressed the boy. "Timothy, what did they do to you? Is there something you're not telling grandma?"

Tim glanced at the hitchhiker. Edna could feel a tremor in the boy's body as he stood close beside, her arm on his shoulder.

"Young man! Did they do something to you?" the officer repeated.

The boy shook his head. Edna "knew" he was hiding something.

"Who called me?" the constable queried.

Pastor Boyd shrugged his shoulders. Rod, the hitchhiker, answered for both of them. "We didn't, officer. There must have been some mistake. The boy was hitchhiking up this way to meet his grandmother. At least, that's what he said. So, we gave him a lift. Pastor Boyd can verify that."

"Yes," muttered the pastor unconvincingly.

"Are you alright, Timothy?" the burly policewoman asked again.

The boy nodded his head. But that, to Edna, was not convincing enough. She would get to the bottom of this later on.

The female officer backed off from the door, and turned to Edna with a question. "Do you want to file charges?"

"Ma'am,' she replied. "I don't know what the problem is yet."

"Neither do I." The policewoman was obviously at a loss over what to do.

Edna commented. "I don't know what my grandson's being forced to do here. Pastor Boyd used to be my friend before that one came into town."

Edna tossed her head slightly in an indicative direction towards the hitchhiker who was standing behind Don Boyd. The pastor seemed like a diminutive youth in front of the taller man.

"Why would he come way up here the first day in town? Are you too long time friends?" While the constable addressed the question to Edna, she looked directly at the hitchhiker. But Edna responded.

"That is highly unlikely, to say the least, unless there's some premeditated collusion. It may be circumstantial, but why pick up my son out of hundreds of others?"

"Good question! Any responsible answers?"

Again, Edna interposed. "Well, I'm going to find out. When I do, I will get in touch with you."

This time, the pastor interjected himself. "We were going over some resources for an immediate ecumenical service to welcome the new leader."

"You want to come and see?" the hitchhiker added in an almost openly mocking way.

"No," replied the constable. "But I'd sure like to know what's going on."

"Well," Edna added. "I am going to find out. When I do, you'll be the first to know."

"Fine! Call me at the barracks."

Once again, Edna added her weight. "What they're proposing is so unlikely as to be impossible. These two denomination never worked together before!"

"You envious because you didn't get it done before you defected?" the hitchhiker shot back in a bitterly condescending tone of voice.

"Allright, that's enough!" commanded the constable. "Now, Pastor Boyd. Can you vouch for that man behind you?"

"Yes…" he replied with some uncertainty.

Edna, observing quietly, was certain the pastor was under some duress or other.

"Do you have an address and phone number?" the constable asked the hitchhiker.

"Yes. I'll write it out for you."

The hitchhiker flipped open a notebook, scribbled in some information before tearing out the sheet and handing it to the policewoman.

"Thank you! Now I'm off," as she turned her heavy frame. "You allright, son?"

"Yes'um."

In passing, she touched the boy's shoulder in a compassionate sort of way, as if to assure him that all adults were not out to get him.

"Thank you, officer. I'll be in touch."

Edna was grateful to the officer for such consideration. Never had there been a worse time when young people and especially children were so victimized by adult irresponsibility.

As the constable departed, Edna turned towards Pastor Boyd.

"Don, can't you tell me what all this is about?"

He shrugged his shoulders and twisted his eyes sideways as if to see whether the hitchhiker was still behind him. "We told you everything we know."

The words were pushed out of the side of his mouth in a snuffling sort of way. Edna could see he was uncomfortable, even cowed by some force which he was reluctant to consider visible.

"Edna," he continued to grasp at straws to retain her. "I could make some coffee if you'd like."

"Is Rebecca home?" she asked.

"No, but…" His obviously suppressed nonverbal plea was interrupted by what appeared to be a jab in the back of the ribs.

Edna made an attempt to collaborate with his suborned cower. "Well'a, thanks. I'll come back later."

"Y'er welcome. Maybe we can talk sometime?"

He seemed to reach out to her with a gesture of his head, as if he would draw her back into conversation. She waved him off and turned, taking Timmy's hand as they returned down the steps.

Edna wanted to escape before he could draw her into an encounter. She would "retreat" for now, hoping for a better moment later when she was more in control of the information needed for a decision.

*   *   *

As Edna and Timmy walked the short distance away from the infamous rectory, she was somewhat surprised to see the policewoman still sitting in her car. Apparently that worthy individual was writing up some notes for her report.

Edna was about to pass by. But the police officer motioned for her to approach the vehicle's open window.

"Timmy, will you go and sit in the car while I say a word to the police lady?"

"Yes'um."

She let go the boy's hand and approached the police vehicle on the driver's side. With her back to the rectory doorway, Edna leaned forward to bring her voice more at a level with the others.

"I was wondering about your daughters. Are they okay?"

Edna hesitated momentarily, reluctant to say anything that would acerbate the rumor mills. Probably there were already too many ears itching for the latest "juice" about her and her family.

"Yes," Edna answered reflectively. "Thanks for your concern. Tamar's doing internship at a counselor's camp in the Valley outside River City. It's her last assignment before teaching school. Trudy's on her way here to pick up Timothy."

"Blows my mind, how fast they grow up!" the constable exclaimed and then asked more directly. "You know anything about that new cult leader?"

"No, not really. Only that one was being sent from back east." Edna responded in an off-hand manner. She could not bring herself to anecdote the happenings back at the hotel, feeling uncertain how to handle the incident. Indeed, would any credence be placed in her version of the story, anyway?

That new preacher's got a look about him that brooks no good."

"He has that," Edna agreed.

"Kids're being victimized all over the place."

"Actually, there're few children left anymore," Edna observed. "Seldom, you see a pregnant woman, or else she's gossiped about. We must be coming to the end of the world."

"Maybe," the constable mused, apparently in agreement. "No where's safe! It's getting worse'n worse, adults working inward. Parents don't parent! Churches don't care! Teachers can't cope! Pushers hustle'n marketers ravage."

"The young need close, intimate relationships with adults. Adolescents are so fragile and vulnerable. Look in their eyes and you see the future. It hurts more'n more."

"Everybody's banging on the kids. If the prevalence've abortion's not getting' into their heads, weighing them down with dread, then violence is hittin' on'em everyday! There's hardly any safety. Go to school and see the brutality of kids on kids. It hurts too bad to go home. If adult violence don't get'em, the info-mag will!"

"Somebody's gotta offer them affirmation, hope and love. Adults've gotta take another look at themselves. At-risk kids need adult protection and friendship."

The heavy-set woman responded. "Your grandson looks like he's got a level head.. You must have hadda time pince-hitting for his mother."

"Trudy's had to make sacrifices," Edna replied, holding herself in check, not really wanting any further conversation on the matter.

Seeing the hesitation, the constable remarked. "I believe him about what happened. But what can I do when them two adults back each other up?"

"How did you find out something was wrong?"

"Oh, the usual anonymous call. We have to check them all out."

"I am glad you did," Edna replied, backing up the constable. "I just stopped by to see if the pastor's wife had anything for me. She's baby-sat for me, off'n on."

"Well, let me know if you ever have problems with that new preacher. He bears watchin'!"

"I will. There may be more to it before he lets go. Thank you, so much!"

Edna eased herself up while the police constable started her car and backed off, to leave the area. Edna glanced briefly up at the rectory, noticing Pastor Boyd standing behind a large glass window looking out.

The hitchhiker was not visible. But from the look on the Pastor's face, that ominous one could not be far behind. Whatever the import might be, Edna was in no position now to lend a hand.

But then, the heavy beat leaped out again with increased intensity. So compelling was the decibel urgency that it grabbed attention, brow beating awareness into dependency.

"You like that music, Terry?" she asked as gently as possible while maneuvering the car, getting underway.

"Yeah." Then he protested. "I not 'Timmy'! I'm big!"

"One of these days," she corrected and added. "You know what the words say?"

"Maybe."

"Does it help fill the time when I'm away?" Edna asked.

"Mis' Boyd won't let us," Tim replied, apparently not phased at the possible hint of dependency.

"What do you do then?"

"Play the 'net," the boy offered.

"Does that frighten you?"

"Yeah."

"Can I turn this down a little?" Edna asked. "It hurts my ears."

"Me too."

"Why do you listen?"

The boy shrugged his shoulders.

With the radio turned down, they rode some way without speaking. Still, Edna knew that the matter of Terry's kidnapping would have to be faced, if for no other reason than the boys' damaged feelings of security.

"Timmy," she started gently as possible. "Do you know why Pastor Boyd and that man took you from school?"

"Not school!"

"Where?"

"Where Mis' Boyd went."

"She went to our place!" Edna exclaimed in surprise, "with her girls? Wasn't Missus Boyd back from where we come from?"

"No."

"Then what happened?"

"I hadda play like kids."

Edna thought for a moment before continuing. "No, I mean with Mister and Missus Boyd?"

"Fightin' at our place."

"Is that where you were playing?"

"Yeah."

"Where were her girls?"

"Movie."

"Didn't you have anybody to hang out with?"

"No."

Again she was silent, not because of wanting something to say. A dozen responses could have leaped to her lips. But that would have led to extenuations all to confusing for a young mind, perhaps even her own!

Certainly, the questioning of a boy would never pull up enough enlightenment for decisioning, or anything else for that matter. Nevertheless, it might fill in some background information.

"When you were with Pastor Boyd and that man, did they say or do anything?"

"You need', me."

"After that in the car, or at the house?"

"Huh?"

"Man did they touch you?" She let the words come out as low as possible, devoid of any anxiety or apprehension.

"On your shoulder?" She asked in anxious anticipation.

"No."

Timmy was vaguely non-committal, as if the remembrance of the event were being squeezed into forgetfulness. He brushed his hand towards the lower torso and legs, then cringed inward.

Edna almost let her anger seethe up and escape in a growl of pain. But that would have let out the cat-scratching fury of her anger to inflict more wounds indiscriminately.

She was tempted to ride on, silently musing to herself, letting the bubbling anger percolate upward. But such recourse would be obvious to the boy and add to his already badly damaged sense of security.

Instead, she had to say something, not just in babbled-out words of vague import. But what, where, when? Any cautions would have to be couched in soothing sounds and have meaningful significance to a child not yet ready for the road to life development.

*   *   *

It was not long before they arrived home, at the small house into which she had moved on resigning from the evangelical ministry. She pulled up to the street curb and hesitated before entering the driveway.

Timothy had immediately leaped from the car, almost before she could stop the vehicle. He would have rushed off inside—in boyish care-free neglect—had she not asked him to pick up and carry one bag to the front steps before going to the rear entrance.

For herself, she sat hesitant, scarcely willing to turn off the motor and let the vehicle grow silent, indifferent and inert in the face of consequences to be faced, neglected and dealt with in respectable order. The house seemed so transitional, so provisional, so empty of the continuity of a lifestyle given up for another dimension of reality.

Could she go inside and face the wife of Don Boyd who had something to do with the abduction of her grandson? That house! Had it really been her rental? Would she have to go inside? Could she suffer through with it, return even briefly to an existence that seemed to be so makeshift and so uncertain of the future?

Edna made an effort to rouse herself and succeeded only to the extent of pulling the car forward up past the driveway and in shutting off the motor. The abrupt silence after so many hours of driving fell with the suddenness of snuffed energy. She sat still almost transfixed. Escape? Could she now? Was that at all possible?

She was enervated from the trip, and letdown from contending with the hitchhiker. Nevertheless, she could no longer sit in the car. It was time for action, for breaching lethargy of mind.

Edna forced herself to remove the key from the ignition, get out and hoist her second travelling bag from the back seat. It was heavier than the one already deposited on the front steps by Timothy.

After climbing the few steps to the veranda, she lowered the bag to the floor and stood steadying her purse against the porch stanchion, supporting the overhanging roof. In a moment, she found the key. Before she could place it in the lock, the door opened to reveal the expectant figure of her unforeseen guest..

16

"Edna. Thank the Great One! You're safe."

Such warmth in the greeting momentarily took Edna aback. Could Rebecca be that sincere, or was this but a prelude to a trap?

Here was the actual presence of Rebecca Boyd hoved to before her eyes in all of its bruegelean luridness, spiritually suffocated—a spooky, empty demeanor preventing her from scarcely ever making eye contact.

Here again Edna was struck by the woman's appearance in contrast to the beautiful voice of this female as singer. Past association flashed across her mind. Edna was moved in mind by the remembered intonation and quality of evocation that this plain looking creature could command as cantor for religious services.

Part of the unattractive impression given off by Rebecca came from a gimp-eye—one of which sometimes looked away, while the other seemed ever ready to trap any uncomfortable associate in unwitting surveillance. Her distorted, strangely lighted face alternately appeared to reek of stupefied despair, or else it was sprung tense by a skin-reddened rage triggered to erupt at the first puff of confrontation.

Edna decided it was wiser to be commiserate while waiting for more evidence to emerge, lest she be damned and dogged by a wrong turn right from the start. "Rebecca, I'm sorry to have been so late in coming. I stopped by the rectory. Don didn't say you were here."

"Oh, he's like that all the time. Can't change! He's got his nose into things everywhere."

"Don't be too hard on him, Becky. Ministering's not all that easy."

"My name was given, Rebecca," the woman shot back in sharp reprimand. "Our religious contacts're no reason to belittle me!"

"Oh, I'm sorry, slipping like that!"

"Slipping you are into that double talking Romanism you got. Bad association's sure to spoil useful habits. Even the evangelicals you come from are backsliding enough!"

"Where's everybody?" Edna asked trying to head off being trapped in a religious argument.

Rebecca was a strange mixture, at one moment friendly enough to be accommodating. At the next, she would suddenly pull back, snuffling out any interpersonal good will, any benign inclination that might lure her down into what she called the devil's trap.

Edna knew she had few other friends, that is if she could ever let herself be described as such outside their denominational contacts. At one time in the past, Rebecca had been a Roman Catholic; and a mixed marriage had been performed in the Church. Later, defection was apparently inevitable under her husband's dominance.

Right now there was something different about Rebecca. She seemed to be uptight, doubly so, as if she were watching herself, being overly careful not to reveal some dark and repulsive secret. Her eyes constantly shifted in that double-take vision peculiarly her own.

"Rebecca, you're not telling me something. What's the matter with you?"

"It's not me. It's Timothy!"

"Didn't he come in?" Edna asked.

"Just now, yes. But earlier I sent him out to play. Gone to hell! That boy's gone off. His mind's all scrambled. I don't want him near my daughters!"

The denunciation was so strong and threatening that Edna felt a startle of fear, and uncanny compunction nibbling at her ear.

"What's wrong?" Edna probed.

"Spends all his mind cooped up on those rock heavy tapes pounding in his ears. Spites me whenever, and bunges around with no good boys doing evil things to themselves."

"Where's he now?"

"Up in his room wired into them head sets, peckin' at hisself alla time."

Edna mused to herself. That was pretty agitated talk even for a pastor's wife. Out loud, she added. "Rebecca, what are you telling me?"

Again, the pastor's wife was hesitant, nearly to the point of letting her agitation get the better of her. But seeing that Edna was waiting persistently, and obviously would not be put off, Rebecca made a start. "Don wanted to pick up the girls. I wouldn't let him."

"So?" Edna wondered.

"They went to a matinee of the Shot Ball, stirred up by friends've theirs to twist a movie outta me. Our congregation would be scandalized."

"From what I hear that movie'll only do them good. You can't keep them under your thumb all the time."

"It's a waste of their minds when they could be out campaigning for God's work," Rebecca charged.

"All work, and no play gigs the devil's view!"

"That's them backsliddin' Romans again gaggling on the devil's talk!"

Edna, however, refused to be put off. "Perhaps," she offered in a melliferous sort of way, "there is something more to this affair than what's come out yet. Rebecca, are you still keeping something back from me? What is it?"

"Well, uh…"

"I already know that Don was here with the man who tried to rape me back in the motel."

"Oh hoh…" Rebecca snuffled the cry in her mouth, letting it echo out in a sob. Her eyes were lowered. She turned her head sideways so as to avoid anyone observing the shame burning into her face, and moaned. "They wanted my girls!"

She groaned out again nearly under breath. Then turning, facing back towards Edna, she lifted her bilocated eyes and resolutely added to her response.

"I wouldn't let them."

"So," Edna began, "that's when they kidnapped Timmy. Better a boy than the girls!"

"Oh hoh…" Rebecca barely voiced the sound.

Again, that disconsolate moan as if she were a barren of the earth, despoiled of everything she had ever owned. Rebecca's shoulders trembled. She jerked her head back into a sideways position.

"Rebecca, Rebecca, Rebecca."

Edna softly crooned out the name, trying to cleanse the sorrow with the words. She stepped closer and raised a hang to lay it on the sobbing shoulder.

"Rebecca, you've been triple devastated—as a woman, a parent, a zealous church goer. If I understand what you're telling me, you've been hollowed out while trying to keep up face as a pastor's wife."

"Hoh, hoome…"

The sound trailed off in indescribable sorrow.

"Have Don and that Jarrett fellow known each other long?"

"They'a…they've been on a some trips together, back east."

"Now, they've been brought back here?"

"Yes."

"Either one with NAIDS?"

The shock of the question sent Rebecca into another spasm—moans concatenating with the rhythmic heaving of her breast.

"Come Rebecca. We've got to get on with it."

Then, in response to a sudden insight, Edna added.

"You and the girls could stay here tonight."

Like a touch of magic, the invitation seemed to draw Rebecca's attention upward and outward to some possibility of restoration. She responded with all the relief of a deeply troubled child who has suddenly been offered a turn at redemption.

"Could we?"

"Yes," Edna repeated.

"I'd ever be so grateful. I can't show my face at the Rectory anymore."

"How long is Jarrett going to stay there?" Edna probed.

"I don't know. But it's an easy drive to Middle Town for them to get together anytime."

"How did he get the Evangelicals to appoint him, anyway?"

"Maybe," Rebecca started, "because of a trip back east over a year ago he was secretive about. Anyway it explains why Don and that female bishop had to travel so closely together."

Abruptly, the telephone rang. Edna would have ignored the call, but the sound came with particular insistence. She took a step over and reached for the receiver. "Hello…hello…hello…"

No answer came. Edna hung up the phone, worried.

"It's been doing that," Rebecca explained.

"Somebody's keeping tabs on us," Edna concluded.

Edna refused to let the fear eat into her and thought for a moment about proposing a meal.

"Rebecca, is there enough food in the house for a meal?"

"I think so. I'll get it ready."

"Oh no! You're the guest."

"We'll do it together then."

"Okay," Edna agreed.

Scarcely had she turned, anticipating the tasks at hand, than the phone rang again. Again, she reached over to the instrument.

"Hello. Oh, you want Rebecca. Just a minute."

Edna muffed the transmitter against her clothing, and directed her attention to Rebecca in a low voice.

"It's Don."

"Oh no! I can't," Rebecca balked.

"Well, I could tell him you just left," Edna offered.

"Oh'a, all right."

She reluctantly pushed out the words and took the hand-held instrument.

"Yes? You'll what!" Rebecca nearly screamed.

The words came out in terror as if she had suddenly been accosted by a sidewinder out on one of those desert patches in the nearby countryside. Rebecca continued arguing, beside herself in fear and worry. "No. I've been invited to stay overnight at Edna's. No, no it's not! No, you cannot! The girls are staying here too. No Don. Don't come by! Why not? Because you are not!"

Shaking with emotion, Rebecca hung up the receiver. As it clattered back on the cut-off hook, she shook herself free.

"He is taking Jarrett to Middle Town. They want to pick up the girls," Rebecca reported. "When he shows up, Edna, don't let them. They'd want to picture the girls...undressed!"

"He'd abuse you too?" Edna asked with sudden apprehension.

Rebecca hung her head, nodding ever so slightly.

"How soon you expect him?" Edna asked anxiously.

"Any minute, he said."

Edna reached for her purse and found the calling card she was looking for. Quickly she dialed the phone number of the policewoman who had come to her assistance earlier.

After some routing, Edna was connected. "Hello, officer? Yes, it's me again. We're gonna have trouble again with those ones we had earlier...Fine! Thank you."

Edna hung up the phone. "She's coming right over. Sure hope she can make it in time!"

"Thank the Lord! I am so afraid."

"Rebecca. Did you phone the police earlier this afternoon after they kidnapped Timmy?"

She nodded her head slowly, reluctantly confirming the suspicion that had been troubling Edna.

As a result, Edna expressed appreciation. "If it hadn't been for that policewoman, who's coming over now, I don't know what I'da done."

"Edna. Don't say that. I don't know what I'd do without you."

The words were scarcely out than the front door bell rang with long and loud demands. At a distance, from the top of the upstairs stair well, she heard Timothy call.

"I get it!"

Edna abruptly turned and raced for the bottom of the upstairs landing. She caught Timmy just as he was about to jump over the last few remaining steps.

"Timmy!" she shushed urgently. "It's those two men who kidnapped you this afternoon!"

"Oh!"

Timmy backed off, up a stair or two, while Edna hastened to bolt the double security chain in place before turning on the porch light. She took a deeper breath than usual and settled down her composure.

She would have waited longer except that the promise of the police constable seemed reliable enough. Again she motioned Timothy back up the stairs and then opened the door a crack. From outside it was banged open to the limit possible allowed by the security chain.

Suddenly, she was face-to-face with Pastor Boyd. Behind him stood the larger framed and taller hitchhiker.

"I come to get the girls!" he ordered.

"They're not here."

"Where are they? Where's Rebecca?"

"She can't come. She's sick!" Edna lied politely, but with conviction. Better to be adamant now and take a strong position right from the start.

"Open that door!"

"No!"

"I have my rights! Jarrett, break in that lock!"

"Sure! It'd be a pleasure to get at that Jezebel. Then, Rome won't wanna see much'a her anymore!"

Edna tried to slam the door shut. But the counterpressure was too strong. She found Timmy down beside her trying to do the same thing. But their combined push was not enough.

Abruptly came the first heavy blow of a battering-ram shoulder directed squarely at the door's edge where it could have it's worst effect just below the chain latch. The whole casing of the door scarcely stopped shuddering when the second blow rammed again.

Any third ram-blow on the door would surely break the chain loose. But before it came, the deep voiced roar of the police constable echoed into her ears.

"Don't you try that again!"

What wonderful relief!

"You may be big and mighty in the religious community," repeated the heavy voice. "But you can't go break down citizens' doors!"

The sound of the burly policewoman's heavy boots came up the outside stairs, then paused.

"Now, what did she tell you?" the constable demanded.

Edna could see Pastor Boyd shrug his shoulder and shake his head.

"Come again," the policewoman repeated. "Or else I'll book you both for forced entry."

"Ah'a…She said to go away."

"So! Why are you still here?"

Edna could see the constable handling her rugged nightstick in a threatening way.

"Okay. Get on with you!" the policewoman ordered.

Edna watched the two men skirt past the constable. Only then did she loosen the latch chain and open the door.

"You want to come in," Edna invited, "and have something to drink?"

"I could for a minute, while I get notes for my report."

"Hello young man, again. You protecting Mommy?"

"Hello," Timmy replied, nodding his head.

The policewoman smiled at the boy. But Edna shushed her grandson back upstairs.

"Come in officer. Please sit down. I'll get you a cup of tea."

"If I may, I'll just come into the kitchen while you make it."

"Sure. Come along."

As Edna held the door, half way turned between Rebecca and the constable, she noticed them look hard at each other for a somewhat longer period of time than usual. A conviction seized Edna that they had had some prior acquaintance. It was soon verified.

"Rebecca, are you alright?" the constable asked.

"Sure Connie. I'm holding up."

Edna paused, almost too amazed to speak. Then as Rebecca began setting up the fixings and serving quick tea, Edna asked in conversational support. "You know each other?"

"Yeah," the constable replied. "I don't know how much you know about her."

"Well'a…" Edna hesitated, "we been friends awhile."

"I just told her," Rebecca filled in quietly.

"Well, then," continued the policewoman. "I been trying to get her to lodge an abusive husband complaint."

"That'sa lot for church-faithful wife!" Edna exclaimed.

"You're telling me!" Connie agreed. "But the police can't do a thing until she does."

"What about the social agency?" Edna asked. "That'd be easier'n going to the police."

"Maybe so. I can't do it for her!" Connie protested.

"Why not report the evidence you have?" Edna advised.

"We've done that. They can't act until she's ready to testify."

"I thought they changed the law?" Edna asked.

"They did," Connie replied in Rebecca's continued silence. "The only cure's divorce. He won't go for psychiatric help."

"Yes, but we go no-fault laws," Edna informed.

"I know," Connie agreed. "You tell her that!"

The two women joined Rebecca in silence for a moment as they continued to sip tea. Then Rebecca opened her mouth. "Edna, you know I got no work skills outside keepin' house'n singing. I was married off young in the church."

"What about your parents? Couldn't they help?"

"They wouldn't take me back after defecting like I had to. Now I can't go on living even around here anymore!"

"Welfare could help you while you get some work training."

"Not around here. Edna, you know the gossiping'd go round everywhere."

"Ya gotta start somewhere!" Connie the policewoman interjected.

Rebecca sighed in resignation.

Yet before anyone could pick up the conversation again, the front door bell rang. "I wonder," Edna mused and then offered tentatively. "Let me see." This time, on reaching the front doorway, she noticed that Timothy had not leaped down the steps. Instead, the boy stood at the top expectantly.

Edna cautiously did not remove the safety chain fastener. But as she unlatched the door, the precaution was unnecessary. It was the monsignor.

"Just a minute, Father," Edna called.

On hearing identification, Tim leaped down the stairs from behind and called out loudly, stirring Edna's ears.

"Uncle!"

For a moment, the two embraced. Edna let out a sigh of relief. At last, another part of her tattered family was together for a sharing.

"Father," she interjected. "How much I'm grateful for your follow-up back there at the motel. I couldn't have made it without your support!"

"May God be praised at your relief! He's got you tagged for great things, Edna."

"Maybe," she demurred. "Anyway, right now, would you mind joining us in the kitchen?"

"No better place for a get together. I heard you got home after that terrible ordeal at the motel."

"My, my! How the 'news' does travel!"

"Wanna too," Timmy proposed.

"No," Edna replied gently, but firmly. "Let us get our conversation done. Then, you can come."

Monsignor gave his nephew another hug and kiss before sening the boy back upstairs. Timothy seemed to accept the turn-around gracefully.

Uncle followed Edna into the kitchen and greeted the other two women with big, "Hellos!" Their response was courteous but brief, apparently, in the sudden presence of what they perceived to be a rival denominational.

Lest the icy fingers of interruption harden into a conversational impasse, Edna offered enthusiastically, "Father, I really enjoyed hearing your interview on the radio, at least before being cut off by mountain static."

"I'm afraid they turned it into a kind of swain song at the end. Anyway, that's not why I'm here," he announced, looking first at the constable and then directly at Rebecca, gently asking. "You having trouble?"

Edna demurred out of deference to Rebecca. But it was the policewoman who started to fill in for the reluctant pastor's wife.

"Rebecca and Don are having problems."

"That's hardly unusual between husband and wife," he replied, courteously smiling at Edna. In acknowledging remembrances, she smiled and nodded.

Connie went on to explain. "These problems are pretty serious. Now they triple compounded by abuse. I been there often enough to know what's going on. But Rebecca won't lodge a complaint."

"You said there were more problems?" Monsignor asked.

"He started banging on the girls."

The priest gasped, now in focused attention. "He couldn't! That will damage them for life."

"He's done it," Rebecca moaned in scarcely suppressed dismay.

Edna added. "Now, he's joined up with that hitch hiker who tried to proposition me in the motel."

"Damned to hell they'll be!" exclaimed the priest hastily.

"No use cursing," cautioned Rebecca. "God'll take of it."

"God helps those who try to help themselves," Connie objected.

"What's that hitch hiker doing here?" Monsignor asked.

"That's the butt of the matter. He's the new evangelical associate in Middle Town. He's taken Edna's assistant place as a faith-counselor, so called!"

17

In the shock wave of momentary silence over this now common intelligence, and before small group awareness could erupt in any more discussion, the female policewoman got up from her seat in a move to depart.

"I've gotta report in," she explained, then glanced at her watch and added. "It's almost time for that movie to be over. I'll pick up your girls and bring them over."

"You're an angel," Rebecca smiled. "They'd be safe!"

"Maybe this time. But whatta you gonna do in future?"

"I dunno," the abused wife replied. "I'm kinda wondering what'll happen to us."

"Well, anyway—see you later!" Connie promised. "I can find my way out."

As the policewoman departed, on her own, Edna turned attention to the bestraught woman. "Maybe we can help you."

"There surely would be employment in Port City," Monsignor added assuringly. "That could be a start on a new life. Abused wives and children have the right of protection. I could recommend you to a very effective Catholic center in the City."

"I couldn't do that," Rebecca interrupted vehemently, "—not down there where the great Satan's got everybody in grip!" Then more thoughtfully, she added, "Pastor Boyd would call that damnation."

"He's long lost any marriage rights by abusing you and pornoing his own daughters," Edna disputed. "If it comes to a divorce, that may have to be."

"Isn't that the end justifying the means?" Rebecca countered with a certain bitterness.

"Divorce is a legal thing, not sacramental morality," Edna continued, apparently attempting to protect her uncle from any over-immediate repercussive entanglement."

"You mean every civil, or non-Catholic marriage is only a legal contract to be broken whenever?" Rebecca asked.

"Not at all. But all too many are; perhaps the majority of legal certificates are obtained as a Band-Aid in lieu of sacramental integrity. A non-Catholic minister does not guarantee validity. Look at it this way—how many such broken marriages ever feel the necessity of annulment? "Indeed," Edna continued, "to what other jurisdiction could the married couple possibly turn! Despite the words, 'by the authority vested in me', the state is merely the state if it does not acknowledge and let the ultimate authority of God pass through."

"If that's true, it's not surprising the divorce rate's so high. There's really nothing except whim and sex to keep couples together."

"Pretty slim motivation," Edna agreed, "in the face of the male porno-addictive imagination doubly aroused by intercourse. As a result, the female's slightest need for reflection and discernment is confronted by the male as a rejection-experience of major thwarting proportions."

Edna's voice had risen to a near-heated level as the memories of her own tragedy and life entrapment came flooding back.

In contrast Rebecca's comment, "I'd need to get an annulment," seemed like a polar meekness.

Edna returned from her momentary inner psychic detour with the interjection. "Why?"

"I was force-married as a Catholic and later beaten over the head to join Mr. Boyd's religion!"

"You have many ground to get out of a martyrdom that's turned you into an animal!"

Edna was about to get incensed all over again. Fortunately, the monsignor was able to catch her eye and, in beckoning, ameliorate further aggravation.

Since Rebecca seemed unwilling to continue the dialog, realization tipped the scales. Edna turned to Uncle with a conversational change of topic.

"You know," she began, "It seems sometimes all we do is put out brush fires, perpetually ignited by agents of the higher ups to keep us busy and distracted."

"That's exactly the point," Monsignor agreed. "That's so we all won't get together and throw off the overlords."

"Why doesn't a 'Moses' ever come anymore?"

"Spiritually we do have one whose providence is ever present. His grace is sufficient to the tasks at hand. He uses the overlords for our exercise in maturation. As a result we gain entry to an eternal home while they exclude themselves to perpetual anguish."

"Sounds like the old story over'n over again."

"It is," he agreed. "The bigger picture is the Lord's, and such organizational structure is possible. Ours is the daily struggle to save ourselves and others from dependency upon the addictions scattered around by the overlords to keep us tempted into servitude."

"We never going to be able to get at them directly?"

"No plebiscite will ever get them. They are beyond the poll, hiding behind influence. People think they can have an effect by the campaigns mounted. But change ebbs and flows as an illusion fostered by the wealthy and powerful. Even politicians are at their behest."

"That's pretty fatalistic and hard on the ears of anybody living in a democracy." Edna concluded.

"Especially in a democracy, " the monsignor echoed, "where the movers and shakers are so well hidden behind the deal-makers and politicians. The elected ones strut before the cameras and spout off on the media."

The monsignor paused, momentarily, and then picked up his thought again. "The fall-out and aftermath from the reign of antichrist may be with us yet for some while, if the time is not shortened by God's will and design. These ill effects are still everywhere evident in near universal extermination of human life by legal cannibalism promoted by radical feminists and licentious homos—no phobia intended! Only gradually will the death-camp cohorts of euthanasia, abortion, contraception be won over by prayer, sacrifice, and reparative worship. There's a lot of behavioral crud left in the sinfulness of divorce, fornication and perverse homosexuals. Eventually, however, moral virtue, spiritually validated truth and non-virtualized knowledge will prevail. We have the promises of Our Lady."

"Can't conditions be made evident by investigative journalism?" she asked.

"Not when the reporters are infected with the same hype of liberal contagion, moral laundering and verbal dysentery—all symptomatic of the aftermath left by the apocalyptic epidemic of inflamed imagination, logorrhea and sadistic cruelty still rampant throughout the world."

"Will it never stop?" Edna wondered.

"Little by little common ground will be reinvigorated by Judeo-Christian applications as restoration seeks the power of God in prayer, discernment and consensus building. Already the democratic process has been counterstrategized to reduce spiritual benefits and set the clock back. Look at the effect of the Cardinal-Bishop down there in Port City. Over the years his policies and developmental initiatives have established the legal standard for defining the beginning of human life at conception in a female womb. Also, his work on socio-economic parity passed into positive legislative action. Thirdly, the 'liberated'—so called Yoofnas Catholic Church is really no longer viable to all intents and purposes. So, you can't throw up your hands in despair."

"That Cardinal," Edna began, "has profited from the apostolic zeal of the holy bishop transferred from Port City to Inland City, and by whom you had me confirmed in the Catholic faith."

"Yes," Uncle agreed, "he's suffered much trying to re-invigorate parish life and take advantage of post-apocalyptic opportunities now in this era of gospel good news. Our bishop is living a continual martyrdom stymied by a sizeable clerical dissident group in this are who are compromised by the strings of psychological dependency. All too many clericals lack the guts to set up personal boundaries and cut the cords binding them to special interests. They've been infected by the religious socialism of Yoofnas Catholicism."

"Isn't that the case most everywhere else?"

"It's compounded in this region by the liberated Catholic Church that has been actively promoted by a female bishop with financial support of an industrialist. Both have an avowed record of anti-Roman destruction."

"That's the same couple, among others, who instigated Yoofnas Catholicism down on the coast?"

"Yes, but their evil forces were thwarted by our bishop's efforts down there. Now, all over again, he's had to contend with their savagery throughout this inland region."

"What trump did he have then?"

"Only God's, guiding the events of the time. Back before then, there was a lay hermit who lived in a makeshift hut in the woods behind the Church-on-the-Mount. He was a fierce defender of Church rights—fire'n thunder zealots like the prophets of old. Anyway he was murdered by vigilantes 'working independently', at least that's what the media called it! Nothing was ever proved, linking the killing to the city's overlords. Anyway, the bishop labeled it a martyrdom and organized the funeral as a pilgrimage from that Church-on-the-Mount to the Church-on-the-Square downtown. That little edifice had always been there; but the bishop instituted perpetual adoration and the liturgical recitation of the hourly ritual which exists to this day. As a result, in order to bring about such spiritual benefits, he and I were transferred up to his region where Yoofnas Catholicism is more deeply entrenched and satanic possession more prevalent."

For a moment Edna was silent until a thought broke out in observation. "You admire that hermit, don't you Uncle! Has he been a role model?"

"Both he and our bishop have so been, to a great extent." Then he paused, seeming to wrestle with something inward of great intensity. The impulse came out, deeply serious. "Yes, I'd like to be like them. Someday, Lord willing, Catholic and evangelical populations will have become liberated from abortifacent-addiction and profiteering on cannibalistic 'mercy' killing. Once more we may see women with children and families populating the parishes again."

"That will be a time of great rejoicing!" Edna enthused.

"In only a couple instances has our good Bishop been able to rejuvenate a parish life that responds to the marked differential in socio-religious dynamics. In the long run, overall, church delivery systems can no longer count on the resources once available from the dedicated but now dwindling religious orders. Support has become dependent upon volunteers and a partially remunerated lay apostolate."

"Does that mean that Catholics for the first time in their lives have got to tithe more?"

"Definitely, but the implications entail a more advances attention to individual motivation than has ever been mounted previously."

"What does that mean?" Edna wondered.

"The twin delivery systems of the Church—religious services and info-educational with a catechetical component—have to be systems-analyzed for efficiency and productivity."

"That sounds pretty managerial and even mechanical!"

"It is, if an example is not set by the priests in sacramental primacy—supported by an ordained and disciplined deaconate. Ministerial overload could be lessened by delegating delivery system tactics within the overall parochial spiritual, liturgical and catechetical framework. Sacrificial commitment is kindled by volitional fervor. Discernment is nourished when hearts are set on fire."

"Looks like the motivational round-robin of a proverbial 'chicken'egg'!" Edna observed.

"Goal setting is a problem because the process breeds the greedy-gimmies unless referenced by altruistic values and validated spiritually."

"That kind of aspiration is often nonverbal. Words are difficult to articulate, let alone communicate for catechetical and instructional purposes."

"Augustine in discourse, maintained that the psalms are cries of joy—indicating that aspiration of the heart are being brought to birth in words. In everyday affairs such high hopes are realized in perpetual adoration and the diurnal recitation of the divine office by the liturgy of the hours."

"People are more familiar with the hymnal than ever they'll be with the ministerial prayers of the Church," Edna concluded.

"Admittedly, hymns can serve accompaniment, but song-books in many instances are but a distant reflection of scriptural texts."

"Does that matter?" Edna asked, posing a dubious tone.

"It does, if it is necessary to build a spiritual foundation where motivation gushes from the rock of truth in a Roman Catholic Church. Instead, tragically, when your gimmie-goals quisle out, the liberated Yoofnas version will seduce whatever wishes you want to project into imaginative serendipity."

"You suggesting that a replica of the little Church-on-the-Square of Port City be established in this Diocese of the Interior?"

"Yes, a duplicate—together with the Liturgy of the Hours cantored daily in the spiritual voice of a Rebecca Boyd..." Uncle paused briefly, apparently to let the implications sink into another's awareness. "But attendance would be sparse in this thinly populated region unless that liturgy were satellite broadcast. Unfortunately, that initiative has also been violently opposed by the area's feminist bishop and her industrialist ally."

"You know, Father," Edna began as if having mused over the topic, "your comments bring up the matter of rescuing Rebecca from a fate worse than the imagination."

"How's that?"

"In a few days Trudy's coming to take Timmy back to New England where she's getting established near Mother's family. Tamar's to be employed in Father Thompson's mixed generational school. I'll be in Port City with a position at Leland House."

The monsignor immediately leaped to the conclusion. "Sounds like you could use that house, still in my name, near Port City. It's now empty and big enough for you and Rebecca if she wants to relocate with her two girls."

At that point, Rebecca blurted out in protest. "I got no work skills to live on my own."

Uncle rejoindered. "I've heard the cantor for the liturgy at the Church-on-the-Square is about to leave for another position. Your voice is admirably suited for spiritual purposes. I'll recommend your appointment."

"Father, I'm a lapsed Catholic baggaged by guilt, and remorse—compounded by marital entrapment."

"Sacramental forgiveness is only a penitential rite away. You can be released from legal servitude by the staff of the Battered Women's Center in Port City. Up here in this region you'll only be pilloried forever. Your daughters will get swamped in a flood of suggestive advances."

"No, no, no," moaned Rebecca. "I can't…"

"You need some time," Edna commiserated. "I'll be here for a few days yet. Even afterwards, when you're ready, I'll come and help out."

*   *   *

That was the end of their conversation. Abruptly, interruption came in the form of a commotion at the front door. Rebecca, surprisingly instead of Edna, got up and moved towards accommodation. Timothy appeared, bouncing down the stairs.

The door opened as the girls let themselves in accompanied by Connie, the female constable.

"Praise the Lord," Rebecca exclaimed at the joy of reunion with her children.

The youngest informed her mother in all serious excitement, "Connie brought us in a police car!"

"Connie," Rebecca offered, "thanks again for your kindness! The Lord will bless you."

"Well, I could use a little special help," the policewoman acknowledged. "In the meantime, I hope you can get relocated along with these good folks."

Connie nodded her head towards Edna and her uncle, before taking her leave in good-byes.

Section 3

Downsized Togetherness

18

Two months of moping-denial had not left Bill Scolan in much, if any better mood than previously suffered. He had long endured the critical dissatisfaction of transitional development.

This morning, nevertheless, he was up early expecting to catch his thoughts without interruption as he sat in a corner of the dining room at Leland House finishing breakfast. Later in the morning he was scheduled to interview some female priestess turned Catholic from a Protestant cult.

She had been recommended by Father Thompson. Bill had been told that the visitor was a friend of Mary Bulinsky. Worse still, he had learned that the woman had already been hired as a counselor without consulting him. That gossip had been hard to countenance.

If true, why had she done such a thing, particularly Mary, the daughter of his surrogate mother back in early childhood? Like Ann, both of them—at least ten years senior to Bill—had then ganged together with other adolescents to remain judges-in-the-head for all too long in his still youthful adult mind.

As the senior administrative associate at Leland House, Mary was also the one who had done much to rescue himself from the oblivion of addictive guilt and suicidal depression. Now, it seemed that she was at it again, doing her level best to help another "lost soul" to find a way out of the fate deserved by their own religious doings.

For an uncharitable moment he wondered about that young female preacher whom he had not yet met. Surely she had to be experienced and old enough to escape immature entrapment?

Yet, his conjecture speculated. How did she fit into Mary's predilection for walking a fine line between actually healthy inter-personal support and the enabling of victims for the kick of it?

Shaking off an involuntary shiver over a lack of psychological immunity from envious thoughts, Bill pushed aside the empty food plate and raised a half-finished second cup of coffee to his lips. He had scarcely taken a sip, struggling to swallow in fright, when the possibility of impending disaster fell upon his unprotected ears.

He had seated himself for breakfast in an improvised nook of the Leland House dining room. No one else apparently had found this hidden corner which, so far, had suited his need for privacy just fine.

The unobtrusive recess had been left unused next to the cafeteria exit. The temporary construction screened him from view but not the sounds coming from the tables beyond on the dining room floor.

Bill was not particularly trying to hide. However, this out-of-the-way location had offered him protection from stray observation and gave him surreptitious privacy from many other hungry persons who would surely want to press acquaintance were he otherwise available.

He had just heard two people slide food trays onto the table adjacent to the other side of the temporary partition. They pulled up chairs to sit in the corner right around the edge of the screen protecting him from view. His muscles tightened at the real possibility of unforeseen discoverance.

Then abruptly his body froze with trepidation over the near certain eventuality of catastrophic recognition. The voice of one of them was so unmistakable familiar that confrontation was beyond any ability his strength of courage might bear,

To his utter dismay, inner reproach raised its backhanded presence from the subconscious. Surely he ought to have been able to have learned by now how to deal with past guilt now threatening to erupt. But fortitude was not to be found this morning in the lucky cards of serendipity.

Once, if triggered by personal exposure, the bitter remorse of psychic devastation would cling to him with oppressive weight despite the sacramental forgiveness he had received. Even so, he had been informed the residual scruples remained a hangover temptation to be resisted according to the priest to whom he had gone for absolution from the parental legacy of heretical Yoofnas Catholicism.

Then descent into personal damnation deepened as more words came from behind the improvised screen to flood eavesdropping ears. His body was fixed-in-chair, stunned immobile by an inner compunction that had not yet completely atrophied.

A youthful, but unfamiliar voice asked, "What's this fellow Scolan like that I'm apparently to be working with?"

"You must have formed some impressions," Mary's voice came back at Bill's itching ears. "Didn't you observe a lecture of his once for Father Thompson?"

So, Bill thought to himself, that was the way things were stacking up against him! Just what else was needed—another judge coming out of his head, and a younger woman at that!

"Yes," the female newcomer admitted. "But you know how artificial a situation like that can be."

"I suppose so," Mary agreed. "Anyway, he's okay. We been colleagues for years now."

"I've heard he's got a terrible reputation, almost worse that my estranged husband. I can't imagine you working together."

"Oh, you know," Mary replied, "there's a redemptive quality in everybody."

Big deal—Bill mumbled soto voice! Was that all she could say in his favor? What a letdown expectation from the carry-over daughter of his surrogate mother.

Abruptly Mary filled in the brief silence. "You have an interview with Bill Scolan. Then Father Thompson has arranged a luncheon reception for you at the new adult school."

"Oh!" exclaimed the female preacher in what sounded like a disappointed reaction. "I've known that priest for awhile, and his regard for Bill Scolan."

"Will it be a problem, then?"

"Not necessarily. But I've already been endangered by one of Thompson's proteges. He turned out to be a mole."

Bill's ears picked up on that one, but apparently not Mary's. Anyway, she expressed no curiosity.

The young woman renewed her probe. "What can you tell me about that young fellow? Who is he, anyway! Has he a nice manner?"

"He's had a pretty sordid past," Mary cautioned.

"Who hasn't! Anyway, gimmie the details?"

At that point, Mary seemed to demur briefly before adding in near-conversational shift. "You remember, Terry's been no saint either."

Had he missed something, Bill wondered. Where were the details about his dastardly life? Had they passed a note, or something, between them—surreptitiously concealed, aware of his presence behind the screen? That couldn't be, surely!

"I can hardly remember. I was so small then," came the reply seemingly deflected from original intent "How's your children?"

"Quite the adolescents, stretching into young adulthood as fledgling workers at the Youth Center."

"So're mine—scarcely a year apart in age, but not any much younger than yours."

"You were so young when they were born. I was too, but not that much," Mary ruminated slowly.

The other female voice changed, bitterness filtering through the words. "What else can you expect when you been marriage-raped, over'n over by the older colleagues of a father who forced you into a wedding at scarcely twelve years old!"

"That was a terrible time!" Mary agreed. "Do I remember you had both pregnancies by age thirteen?"

"Yes, but successful only by the grace of God!" replied the young woman.

Seemingly, the words stretched themselves out, of their own accord, until attention snapped back. "You haven't said anything at all about Bill Scolan!"

Mary reacted slowly to the challenge. "Well, he's our head consultant. He does psychological research for a book he's been writing."

"I don't mean that!" exclaimed the young woman in near exasperation.

"Well, he lives alone in a top floor apartment here at Leland House. He's had an on-again, off-again relationship with a female understudy in our counseling program."

"Is it off-again?"

"Yes'n so far, it's been platonic—at least, far's I know."

"Why do you say it that way?"

"With his past, I'm surprised at the recovery," Mary replied matter-of-factly before adding in livened tone. "Anyway, I'm sure it's been my mother's prayers from beyond the grave."

"I'm sorry! Has it been recent?"

"Oh no! Some years now, just after I came back from that furlough down your way."

"That was long ago." The female minister sounded forlorn. "My pregnancies were at twelve and thirteen."

"So you said!" came the more matronly response.

"I was a child bride," the other repeated, "bargained away by father to an older associate whose imagination was tampant."

"How could you have become a minister so early in life?" came the question in full inquisitive swing.

"Mother rescued me. She helped care for my children and put me through school. She had money and influence back east among the Brahmins where father trained before returning, taking her to a southern ministry."

"As I remember, you were an only child?"

Replying in the affirmative the female preacher paused, possibly looking at the woman carefully and forcing suspicious thoughts under control.

Before the searching mind of her senior could pry any further, the young convert brought matters to a head. "I converted because of mother. Her high church ways had always seemed more Catholic than the Church itself. You can be sure her Episcopal convictions had embarrassed father more than once in his circuit-riding ways. In fact, the enmity of my former husband's cult still simmers at near eruption at any Roman sell-out defection."

"Are you...?" Mary tried to ask.

"Yes," came the hasty interruption. "That enforced connubial has been annulled. My girls were raised in the east with mother's relatives. It'd be nice to get a little family togetherness before they're finally out on their own. But now that Trudy's taken Timmy back with her to New England, I wonder?"

"I'm not counting my chickens. Young ones these days have got a mind of their own!" she reacted. "Anyway, let's see how things work out here with the Cardinal and Father Thompson. Hopefully, we'll make it down here permanent, sooner'n expected."

"Since leaving here, your bishop up there in the interior has continued controversial?"

"He's tried to be diplomatic with others, but completely in tune with Uncle's way of posturing. They've been up against a hotbed of cults, almost mobish in tracking down anybody they brand as dissenters."

"Are you in danger?" Mary asked.

"So far, my defection as they call it has not attracted too much attention. And Uncle—they've not yet figured out yet as an outspoken monsignor."

"You're fortunate to have someone like that."

"Uncle took over for Mother, his sister, and tried to make up for what Father was unable to correct." Behind the words the message came out, at least to Bill's ears, as a compelling mixture of apprehension and regret.

Abruptly, it seemed, the young woman changed the topic—returning to what surprisingly was a worry. "What about that woman he's had an off-again relation with?"

"My, oh my!" Mary exclaimed. "It's Ann Patterson. You've met her, I'm sure."

"She's so old!"

Mary's laugh tingled Bill's ears. "She's my age, perhaps more than less. Does that make a difference?"

"If he's gonna have children!"

"Why's that?"

"What woman could ever be safe with the imagination he's got? Probably no other way."

"For what?" Mary asked with an odd intonation of voice.

"Oh, you know," came the non-compliant answer.

"Is that what saved you from your husband?"

Perhaps the young woman nodded her head, or even shook it. Anyway, the two women seemed to have reached a plateau in their relationship and remained silent for a few moments.

Then Bill heard Mary suggest departure. "Bill'll be waiting. After that I'll take you over to Pastor Thompson. Between times, I got a stack of paper-work. Don't forget the lecture series Father expects."

"That'll have to wait a week or two. So…maybe later in the day we can compare notes after follow-up with your Bill Scolan."

"He's not my Bill Scolan," Mary protested.

"Nor anybody else's, even his own, far's I can figure out!"

*   *   *

Hastily, Bill glanced around and realized the jeopardy of his situation. Reluctantly he returned awareness to himself.

The chance of not being discovered would not hold that much longer, especially if the two women were to exit by the same open doorway next to him.

Rather than push luck any further, he eased himself up from the table gingerly and moved his body ever so carefully out the nearby escape route.

It would have been much more satisfying to continue attending to the hearing-presence of the young preacher. Surreptitious curiosity had yet to be sated. Neither Mary nor Ann appeared to hold as much promise as that newly acquainted female seemed to have.

How could it be any more than passing interest that she and Mary were previously associated? But then what did he know of Mary and her whereabouts during the many years spanning his own childhood and reassociation ages later after Terry's contributions to electronic systems analysis?

At the moment however it was not Mary who was uppermost in mind. Even after departure, his senses were preoccupied with the intonation of the other female voice reflecting in his ears.

There was something about that young preacher which hung in awareness, compelling attention on her beyond deliberate control. Yet who had ever heard of attraction at a surreptitious initial hearing still uninformed by first sight?

Despite himself, interest remained sustained even though tempted towards chauvinistic suspicion. Who'd ever heard of femininity being that compatible with the status of an ordained minister in a Christian church?

Yet how uncharitable could he be, if for nothing else! How could such a though have turned that dastardly in nudging consciousness?

In momentary retrospect had his own conversion been no big deal, more like a coming home again? Was it but a non-event of transferred loyalty, facilitated by Ann's mediation and Mary's ever present nurturing?

The fleeting remembrance soon passed. As Bill was en route from inadvertent eavesdropping, a strange sensation troubled awareness until inquisitiveness provoked attention towards how to frame answers—the question being how to handle future behavior towards a newly appointed associate whom he had only now been allowed to interview after-the-fact.

Though curiosity mounted and drove him towards the only option in which he felt the matter could be handled, he did not turn back. Bill hastened down the hallway in the direction of the administrative center of Leland House.

Still without a glance behind to see who might be following, he entered the counseling suite and crossed over to his office. Once seated he would wait until Mary had time to return from accompanying the young female convert.

In the meantime, his mind floated into reverie triggered by the pretense of organizing thought patterns. He was reluctant to become confrontational; but Mary had long been for him one of the judges in his head like half-sister Julie.

At the remembrance of those days imagination began to spin with a sensual delight that electrified the lower organs. The sensation ambushed him. It was similar to those experienced whenever Julie as a juvenile had made him, a child, look at pictures of naked girls and boys in her sex ed textbooks from school.

Even more vividly the feelings of guilt and shame had surfaced—only to be driven back by her giggling permissiveness. Many times in the years following had he given in to her precocious female needs.

Regardless of whatever sexual liabilities there may have been, these clandestine visits were the come-on of any day probably just because they were forbidden. There, apparently, any female child could have been the bait—strange to some, but succulently desirable to the artless duplicity of a growing male child.

Even the postman, "she" said, must not know what they were doing—which, to Billy as a boy, seemed a strange way to put it. More importantly, it appeared that one should never think straight—not at all like the predictable way adults did, or seemed to.

In a moment he was abruptly shocked back into present moment awareness. An acute sensation of heartburn and indigestion brought him into actuality. For a moment his breath was caught on a near-hiccup.

The impression was real enough although the cause seemed to be produced by a distress in mind rather than from bodily condition. For a second he ground his teeth together, hoping for relief. It did not come.

He tried to swallow. But that did not stop the bile churning up secretions whose bitter taste revolted upward to sicken his mouth and tongue, injected with a copper-brown apprehension. An obstinate body was well on its way towards a vomiting and haunting awareness of shuddering dread and throbbing head.

The fury of a Judas seemed to have entered him as the fantasy of a smiling, no leering priestess hove into mind's eye. The illusion resembled that of the voluptuous young woman in mini-skirt who, not that long ago in memory of the days before conversion to Catholicism he had witnessed at the schismatic service in a Yoofnas Catholic Church.

Sparked by envy and suppressed hatred, hindsight clearly revealed the lustful glances of that heretical minister-ess. Sitting ex cathedra across the altar space behind, her worthless clerical associate would surely have had a direct view of the shapely female legs topped by a suggestively abbreviated skirt.

Bill remembered having been tempted to call out in spite, "Hey, how's your little female priestess? Is she gonna give us another 'sermon' about psychological Christianity and religious socialism?"

But that would have tipped his hand, doomed him in the eyes of all the congregation as addicted to the envy and hatred of women, especially young ones, aping the priest—tooling themselves up for the sooner take-over of sacerdotal ordination!

As the conceited thoughts would further down into the worm of his ego, they revolved and repeated themselves with intolerable insistence. They ground around in a little hole like the screw of an oil well in mud. Yet before injection could puncture the crust of insanity, a reflex trophism sprung up in the psyche.

It was all too easy to court a ritualistic suicide and fall upon the sword of one's own conceit. The devil's spell, tecking away in the imagination, had to be broken. No longer could he let such images shuttle back and forth, cavorting before the impulsive squalls of pride.

Looking back on himself, Bill had to admit that these thoughts were pretty devastating both for any unassessed continuity in his previously developed style of life as well as for the omission of any consideration in altered patterns of existence.

There was no trustworthy support system on which he could count. Only the Catholic Church was a reliable guide to the grace of God needed on a continuing basis by his impoverished soul. Virtue, self-control and character integration could only be achieved through voluntary action, freely chosen habits of moral behavior as well as steadily pursued and reverential self-actualization.

How could they call themselves free—those who were dependent, disintegrating under way of the "spirit of the world", or the new age others of the era, or even those codependents such as peers, friends, families—all who had acted out of necessity, not chosen, barely understood and difficult if not impossible to resist.

For anybody, each individual had been thrown into history at birth, along a trajectory not of one's own self-making. So what else was new! What was the big deal? Join the human race! Everybody else does. No one could ever be wholly free of all restraints.

19

Bill quickly returned to his office lest he be unnerved by discovery. Were he thrown off poise, an unsteady manner might reveal more than he was willing to take a chance on.

He was determined not to dwell upon his own guilty feelings. After all, they had intruded on his space sought out for privacy. Instead he would suffer through the initial disease and settle down into at least the appearance of having something to do.

The moment would soon come when it was necessary to interview a young woman for the newly dictated position as associate and catechetical counselor at Leland House. He was expected to welcome the new recruit, a convert from a religious cult, and facilitate her entry to the staff.

It seemed fairly safe to gamble on the predictability of Mary's behavior. She would take some time, he was certain, in parading the young female priestess around, showing off this most recent acquisition to her staff.

He felt quite confident in this estimate of the coming sequence of events. Based on previous observations, Mary had grown quite comfortable in her well-earned accomplishments.

Nevertheless resentment had mounted in him not only because her outside interference might upset the developments he'd been able to effect through torturously practical applications. Irritation also resulted from the manner it had been initiated by Mary and carried into finalization by Ann.

The fact that Ann had been involved at all was humiliating until a certain realization dawned. While it might not quite have been another matter with Ann, the conviction was growing in him that any interest in their personal compatibility had cooled.

Indeed, he was almost certain that his release from any semblance of commitment had been finalized. There might even be some net compensation for the apparent bypass. Could the last strings of dependency on any judge in his head have been severed?

Yet the fear of rivalry remained. The newcomer would at once have all the opportunities he and Ann had worked so hard to open up. It didn't seem that a converted cult priestess would be able to handle responsibility without some initial professional apprenticeship.

Nevertheless his patience could be long suffering even though Mary's precipitous audacity was aggravating. Obviously he was not powerless to react. But then how could he take out frustration on her, thus despoiling the memory of his surrogate mother.

Instead he mumbled to himself a prayer to her for intercession before God. "You got me into this dependency. Pray to the Lord for my strength to endure this imposition. Help me work it out with your daughter and preserve the Lord's work at Leland House."

He was convinced that is was only through surrogate mother's spiritual influence that he'd had enough courage to have a Yoofnas church baptism and confirmation regularized in a Roman congregation by Father Thompson. However, he had to admit that conversations with Mary and Ann, especially, had been instrumental over the years since he'd taken up a career at Leland House.

He thought for a moment. Maybe he'd better make another pilgrimage visit to the old church of Our Lady on the Mount. Private reflection had seemed to come to him better there than at the more publicly frequented little Church-on-the-Square.

Bill felt confident enough in this assessment to relish the feeling of inner release. He took a deep breath, realigning back muscles, straightened his head and shoved back shoulder blades as far as the stretch would allow.

The brief adjustment in posture seemed to have cleared his thoughts and released all the ropes clinging to his need for co-dependency that had impeded psychic movement. He turned slightly, sitting at an angle in the swivel chair behind his desk.

Subconsciously awareness had shifted as if some activity, shadowed through the opaque glass wall of his office, indicated the presence of an intruder. But attention relaxed as the reflection passed from view.

Still, the evanescent event did bring to mind an impression carried over from surreptitious eavesdropping. An experiential sensation was taking shape in the epiphanized fantasy of a woman he'd never met but whose partial personality had been revealed in listening to a non-consenting conversationalist.

It didn't seem to matter yet who she might really be. That possibility was immaterial serendipitously, to the presence appearing in mind's eye under the influence of an excited imagination.

Compared to his own inner development as a personality, she could be the apex in the evolutionary emergence of a new psyche for himself. Marvelously eloquent she was—coming to him resplendent of all he might ever hope to be able to realize.

Though the features of her face had not yet formed into an image and the shapely voluptuousness of her body remained indistinct, he had already apprehended the essence of her personality. That intuitive illumination appeared as a revelation emerging from the aura of himself.

Consciousness was aglow with the transcendence of a personage reincarnated from what he could have become had the child inside been allowed to peterpan its way out of the aspirations held out to him by a surrogate mother.

Once again, a shadow moved over the opaque glass partition of his office. As the reflection of somebody passed by in the hallway, Bill's eyes abruptly came to, recognizing the nothingness of their staring. The illusionary fabric fell away, crashing down while the curtain protecting expectations shriveled up.

He was back in the real world of a human development that had been fashioned by more willful hang-ups—aided in regression by less than courageous parents, a compliant Julie, and the baleful eyes of two other judges in his head.

His mind retreated even further in regurgitating events long cloaked in memory. Drooping shoulders stiffened as an attempt was made to compensate for the marginal benefits eked out over the years in paying attention to the remaining four talking heads lingering in awareness from childhood.

Bill had no difficulty remembering the currents and eddies in the flow of happenings that had once been constrained by the banks of existence. Nevertheless problems would obtrude without warrant or invitation when it came to a question of differentiating the beneficial from the detrimental movements of imagination. It was all too easy to let desire fixate on the lacy kerchiefs of enticement rather than temper inducements to achieve a higher good.

Reincarnated expectations should have been cautioned by the checkered experiences of those days now gone. But eagerness had not been chastened. The transformation remained a quasi-reconfiguration like the balloons of virtual understanding which had so often been lofted on thermals of hot air rather than rising with the leaven of born again experiences.

Even the presence of Mary and Ann, of particular benefit to him, had already faded in comparison to the new hope aroused just now by a single surreptitious hearing. Indeed he'd better, for real, soon meet this female priestess or else imagination would have her fantasized into unbelievable dimensions—images that would seriously inhibit any reasonable expectations of an actual woman.

He'd suffered enough in the past from the less desirable hang-ups of female over-idealization which only mocked-up differential women that just had to be treated either with contempt or seduced in an ever-increasing need for dominance.

*   *   *

To get imagination off the fast track plunging into porno-imagery, Bill had been re-reading the resume of the female newcomer. Though complete, indicating adequate preparation for the role of consultant, the professional vita told him nothing about the young woman as a person herself.

Anybody could have read her-story and have learned little about the real human being soon to be coming before him for a "placement interview." It was surely another matter whether she could stand up to any of the expectations calling for a fully functioning individual personality.

The tactics he would want to employ in the interview may otherwise be considered unorthodox. But he had already been the enabler in all too many so-called helping interviews that had bombed out over the years of experience in a developing professional career.

He did not have long to wait, if indeed the knocking on the door was the woman in question. If so, she was prompt—in fact early by a full five minutes.

"Come in!" he called, refusing to get up for the greeting.

The door opened and a figure appeared. As she stepped across the threshold, the full joy of a female body in youth was revealed.

The open radiance of a humanly beautiful countenance beamed on him. He felt compelled to get up from the seat and face her on a level of equality in glad adulation.

"So, you're Dr. Scolan!" she exclaimed boldly.

"Yes, why?"

"I had a completely different impression from what I'd heard!"

He made no reply, entirely absorbed in the presence of this remarkable young woman even though the preoccupation threatened to place him at a disadvantage.

"I'm Edna Masterson," she greeted in an attempt to break his male trance.

He could find no voice. In consternation he was held inchoate, deeply impressed if not disturbed. No words came. He stared open-eyed like the child he was with a surrogate mother whom he had adored beyond any possibly comprehension.

She held out her hand. But he remained immobile in silence, staring uncontrollably.

She stepped back and protested. "Dr. Scolan, you're staring me out! I thought this was to be an interview. But you're overloaded with a much too familiar interest!"

At that, he hesitated, caught himself and motioned her to a seat. Only then were his vocal chords released as he cleared his throat and sought to ease the embarrassed encounter with a quip.

"You know," he began, "once before in my life a woman said something the same at me. Only she thought I was lusting after her."

"Were you?" she demanded, firmly keeping control of the situation.

"No, I wasn't!" he retorted, instantly coming to his senses at the cool affirmation of another human's personal integrity. "Please forgive my rude behavior. I'm not a sex harasser at all!"

"Nobody would've believed it," she replied, boldly establishing her self-worth with a directness that left him near aghast.

He had not expected such a dimensional shift right up front in a professional introduction. Confusion surged into awareness, threatening to rob attention of driving towards a semblance of managerial skill in the situation.

He had to do something, anything at all to shift the focus from himself and allow him the opportunity to regain equilibrium. He just couldn't let her keep the upper hand and enslave him with rapture of her body and a remarkable personality.

Fortunately or unfortunately she must have perceived his dilemma. She asked, "So what am I gonna be expected to do here?"

He was certain her tone of voice resonated in affront, however polite the question might otherwise appear. Still it allowed him to offset an uncharacteristic lack of control.

He was able to mumble a few words in near half-sentences. "We're swamped with patrons…You'n Ann're associates…"

"You dumping your case-load on me?"

The demand tore into him and provoked a sudden flash of temper. He was thunderstruck! Seldom had it ever been in him to exhibit such raw emotion in context. Vaunted sophistication was ever ready to mask, virtually, that kind of revelatory behavior.

In looking at her directly, he recovered himself. "Not at all. There's plenty to do if you can stand up to it!"

The words were out before realizing the challenge. But the possibility of being taken to task for misinterpretation steadied him. He was resolve not to back down.

"So, what are you going to do?" she demanded again.

Her continued direct approach cooled him. Bill looked at the woman, letting his stare penetrate. He was ready and determined to appraise her ability objectively no matter how seriously he'd allowed imagination to compromise him already.

"What I have always been doing," he replied evenly, "counseling, research, writing."

"Are you writing a book?"

This time her voice seemed to have softened—as if she had made some preliminary judgment about him and was willing to consider an accommodation.

That shift in attention led him to consider a possibility. "I've been listening again to some taped interviews I did awhile ago when getting ready for doctoral research. It never paid off then…"

"Oh," she interrupted. "I thought you had the degree."

"No," he replied, letting the ellipsis in explanation widen into full silence.

His mind was made up; the hiatus would be tolerated for a complete moment. That would allow the memory of this thwarting experience to benefit both of them.

Though deeply attracted to this beautiful woman, he would not have that allurement take advantage of him! Still, he had to figure out some way of enforcing self-detachment.

No completely satisfactory solution seemed available. Only slowly did a temporary put-off seep into mind. "Maybe you'd like to hear some of the interviews I've recorded? Your insights would give me new hypotheses to consider. At least it could be a way of facilitating your getting to know me."

Admittedly he made a venture, sticking his neck out. So why not go all the way? Unfortunately though, the self-deprecation sounded less calmly than blurted out. "Whether it ever helps me to get to know you better is another question!"

The woman looked at him with what seemed a newfound interest. In point of fact though, he was sure it did something to enhance the allure so sought after by females in protecting the mystery of their secrecy.

Nevertheless she revealed no clues as to verification of the interpersonal hypothesis. Instead—deliberately and calculatingly, he thought—she exclaimed. "You scientists are so detached in your way of thinking—almost like you couldn't care less which way the facts lead out, poker-facing any possibly outcomes!"

All at once, Bill laughed. Equilibrium was restored at the prospect of maturity in a female of such engaging presence. Little did she know, however, at what price such apparent objectivity was often obtained.

"Seldom ever," she continued, "in my life have I ever been able to stand outside myself and look in to observe what was going on—no semblance of detachment whatsoever!"

"Well, I can't say it's an easy thing to do," he replied cautiously. "Sometimes it's more apparent than real, succumbing to the enticement of virtual thinking."

Once again there seemed to be a new twist in the way she regarded him, and responded. "Such a willingness to be honest with yourself and your ideas! All the people I've ever deal with have an agenda—some more opinionated than others. But to my sheer aversion, they've all known for sure what's wrong with me and how to fix it! Funny how nothing other than my own way of thinking ever works out!"

Bill was amazed to have heard himself characterized—nearly labeled with two traits that to himself seemed least typical, "honest" and "detached"! Just wait'll she heard more about his past from anybody with less charitable inclinations!

In any event, he was not about to let her apparent words of appreciation foment intelligence with the sauce of conceit. Instead he was inner-prompted to make an attempt at character rectification.

The words which emerged struck him as sincere, even though a trifle surprised at himself in adding. "Little do you know at what cost such virtues are accomplished. More often than not, the wolf of paranoia's been huffing me down!"

She stared at him so intently Bill was thrown on the defensive. Could you believe it! Here they were becoming masochistic—indulging, even, in the lukewarm fluidity of disparaging self-addiction.

Really, could she think some accusation of cowardice was being laid on the threshold of her entity?

Instead, she smiled calmly. "I may look like a bimbo—but…I've paid my dues to the lord of carnage!"

Bill was instantly won over, not by her words—which remained like a sphinx. Rather, the leverage come from the resigned conviction in her voice. The intonation resonated with that long-suffering determination to survive which he too had so long struggled to maintain.

"That's not something easily achieved," he offered. "We been trying to support people in accomplishment by our counseling program."

"That's what attracted me. Your orientation to proactive personality and the positive value of virtuous aspiration is so different from new age warm-overs of psycho-sexual motivational determinism."

"You do think—for a woman!" Bill exclaimed, instantly expressing male admiration for a sought-after female quality. "Hang on; I'ah…" he abruptly tried to back track. "I didn't mean. I ah…"

"I know," she filled the gap with a comedown. "You're like every other male. Chauvinism's just a built-in hang-up you can't surmount."

The words stung into him, leaving an impression-in-mouth that inhibited response. What could he say that would not be taken as self-serving?

Caution returned with sudden force. No use waving a red flag in front of a bull! Better to wait for some opportunity to extrapolate results that were not in confrontable overload.

As a turn-around, he changed the subject. "I'm surprised you heard about our program. We been so busy doing things, there's been no time so far to publicize it."

"Oh, I've known Mary'n Ann for years. They've been kinda like mentors, or seniors. However, without Mother, I don't think I'd ever've made it outta the behavioral ghetto."

"Sounds like my own voyage of self-discovery," he replied. "Only, I had a surrogate mother and seven judges-in-the head."

"How peculiar!" she exclaimed. "Whatever that means I'm sure it must have had something to do with the quality of your contribution to counseling."

Bill felt the intoxication of what seemed like sincere appreciation. But lest he be tempted to gulp down more wine of flattery, he suggested. "Why don't we get on with the listening. Your originality of thinking can be put to good use."

20

Bill got up from the swivel chair in which he had been sitting since Edna Masterson arrived. Admittedly, it had served as a protected location in the encounter that had been the occasion of some unsettling moments.

Now that he had recovered most of his accustomed equilibrium, he walked over to the electronic equipment by means of which some research interviews could be listened to.

"I hope," he stated, "you can hear okay from here. If not, some adjustments can be made."

"I'll let you know," Edna replied.

"There's pads and pens there on the corner of my desk," he called over his shoulder as he sat down beside the playback mechanism.

"Thanks, I'll make out okay."

Before turning on the sound projection of the old audio recorder, a carry-over from the days of doctoral research at the university, Bill paused with pen in hand resting on the note pad beside him. As usual when listening to interview tapes he wanted to recall the mind-set conducive to productive reflection.

The fundamental philosophical orientation of the respondents was still particularly relevant to present conditions in society. Each of the individual's interviewed had gone on to become important figures in the socio-political environment regardless of whether he, personally, agreed with them or not.

More regrettable, however, was the fact that despite the years intervening since the faculty had rejected his thesis topic, no appeal for reinstatement had been successful. The rejection, to an extent, had been softened by the loyal encouragement of Mary and Ann in continuing support of the counseling services for clients of Leland House.

When the refunding proposal for client services he and Ann had been working on was completed, he had found time in the evenings to resume efforts on a revised approach to publication. Instead of re-visiting thesis completion he had developed the materials for an alternate method of communication, a book developed on his own terms.

On the basis of initial listening sessions, it had been possible to identify certain themes. Preliminary reflection had suggested the juxtaposition of those tapes which seemed to fit together. Such was the re-organized hearing sequence he now planned to follow in anticipating a better compositional pay-off.

At the switch of a button, the sound of someone recognizable from the past came over the speaker, quite clearly.

Bill heard himself introducing the topic of the interview. "You have been described to me, by people in the know, as a 'king-maker'—a business leader to whom others turn for endorsement and support in their campaigns for election to public affairs."

"You flatter me," the other voice began. "Any power I may have is limited to what people think of me."

"You were instrumental in the protracted negotiations which led this territory into the Yoofnas Federation of North American States."

"True enough! But what has that got to do with what you want from me?"

"Well, I'm studying motivation. Many in the intelligentsia are saying that motivation is more intrinsic that what it has been in the past. Some maintain that the values critical to unlocking its power are of a higher spiritual order?"

"It sounds like to me like you been talking to one-worlders?"

"Yes, in some cases," Bill admitted.

"Well, to all that, I would apply one word, 'bullshit'!"

"That is refreshing! But I've been told that universalism was the driving force behind the original common market. And that world order was the objective of the Federation?"

"On a media level, yes. That is superficial info-dissemination for the masses, especially those still hooked on new-agerism."

"Aren't those important factors?" Bill wondered.

"For propaganda purposes, to satiate that great egalitarian shibboleth, 'the people's right to know'. But it's not got much to do with what I'd call the whore-house character of practical politics."

"What's that?" Bill asked.

"You see, the info-net and info-mag make up the near perfect analog for keeping people in line by holding them amused in pseudo-involvement and mock-seriously occupied to such an extent that any individual drive for real-world activity becomes dormant. In a generation or two, occupation is atrophied. Nobility is all in the head, aided and abetted by the electronic convenience of having everything available within reach of a sitting chair—a soft one at that! All the accoutrements of earning a living, seeking entertainment, and indulging the 'creative' use of leisure time are nerded right into a sedentary existence before electronic screens banked at hand for easy access from ergonomic chairs. Prefabricated food is delivered from convenience locations by immigrants carefully selected with scientific precision. Eventually hominoids will be put to use expertly cloned for type of fit. This virtual existence is devoid of all interpersonal relations whatsoever, and to such a point that individuals cringe from any outside contacts. Even sexual satisfaction is readily accommodated by holographic prosthesis that can jack off a body whether lesbian or gay."

There was a silence on the tape. The speaker had only paused momentarily, as Bill remembered it, before continuing. "It was a stroke of their evil genius that the originators of virtual reality preserved the consortium nature of the supporting electronic system. Any user now has the feeling of personal control which only kingmakers had in the past. The democracy has been almost completely de-democratized in an atmosphere saturated with inclusive pluralism."

Then Bill's own voice broke in again. "What about the external suppliers and minority bodies who do the legwork, pandering all the errands still necessary to keep the king-majority supplied with the accouterments that equip even a modest lifestyle?

"They have every chance to work themselves up in status and participate on an equal basis. As I have said, immigration keeps a constant supply of these people until they too are seduced into a virtual lifestyle. This keeps the population at a steady-state while allowing a regular harvest of fetuses for medical research and feed the cannibalistic rituals of faddy diets."

"I suppose those mercy killings are done for the so-called greatest common good?" Bill asked.

"I hope your question doesn't indicate the naivete it implies?"

Bill shrugged. "I'm only trying to get at the implications."

"Let me back up my say-so. Fundamentally, there are two models of the way socio-political power operates. In the Judeo-Christian ethos, power is infused directly by God into the people. They in turn loan a limited power to a government which supports their efforts at a common good."

"So what else is new?" Bill downplayed. "That characterizes democracy."

"Only one of them," the speaker corrected, " and even that one—the so-called 'American experiment'—has been subverted as the cherished achievement of the Yoofnas intelligentsia. The Federation is European, imposed by two-faced liberals. In this model, God's power is usurped directly by the state. The state puts itself between God and the people, becoming all things at all times for all purposes. Not only in effect, but in all tragic consequences, the liberals have created a civic idol, scorned in the words of the bible:

They have mouths but cannot speak;
They have eyes but cannot see;
They have ears but cannot hear;
Their makers come to be like them,
And so do all who trust in them."

The speaker did not long pause. He continued with scarce an interruption. "My quote may be but a paraphrase of what the psalm actually says; but it shows how fat the wasteful regression of the aftermath of a new age has been allowed to subjugate the people."

"So that's why social unrest and revolutionary agitation seem impossible to eliminate?" Bill asked with an obvious note of depression in voice.

"In point of fact, though, a more accurate perception of 'idol' fostered by reformation anti-logic would recognize the malignant genius of apocalyptic alchemy. Instead of remaining mute, new age idols were quickened by Machiavellian liberal humanists to proclaim anti-virtue in the wildest incantations of propagandistic glee. Their espionage and subversion have been working out all too well because a proactive world view requires a level of courage and conviction seldom seen in the face of 'wise' negatives to the contrary so prevalent in everyday life. The anti-Christ in its five hundred-year reign has been allowed to incarnate in hordes of intellectuals and people of influence who Trojan horse Judeo-Christian democracy with comfort behavior and the virtual gimmies. For most people god is dead and morality's been laundered out of existence. With inclusive pluralism, no behavior can be intrinsically evil. Even if it were ever again disassociated from simulated and holographic activity, democratically 'kinged' individuals can do whatever they want 'at home', or readily suicide themselves out of the way. As a practical expediency, abortion and 'mercy killing' make room for others in the population controlled by state policy; younger and healthier people from all over the world want to come here and get in on the 'good life'."

"Sounds hunky-dory, as they say, and motivation seems built right into a shakedown lifestyle!" Bill's voice sounded scornful.

Bill pressed the pause-button, remembering that the man had looked pained as if attacked on the skin in an uncomfortable place. Could some burr have blown in from the real world and lodged itself under his shirt, irritating the flesh?

When he released the temporary hold, the speaker went on. "Unfortunately there's been a growing group of fanatics in the population warring against what they consider the subversive remnant of a roman religion. They thought their 'good' friends in the Yoofnas liberated Catholic Church had them under control. But like all weirdos they failed to recognize the power of divine providence which created them and the universe, and whose providence is constantly manifest in history."

"Who are they?"

"The new agers, harmonic convergers, reincarnated universalists or whatever else they call themselves. Their propaganda would have you believe that human beings are rapidly evolving into higher realms of consciousness. But the reality of the matter, despite however much they want to delude themselves, is the same as ever has been, are now and ever will be probably until the people take back their power, hopefully peacefully in the ballot box."

"That is certainly is calling a spade-a-spade!"

"I'm not a particularly religious person. But when I see Christian concepts and symbols, its because I don't have anything else to describe reality. People are prone to evil, individually and collectively—spontaneous as in crimes of passion, and organized as in the planned killings of crime world infrastructure."

"Inevitably?" Bill probed.

"Not always. Sometimes people have aspirations to a higher spirituality but this has got to be spelled out in behavioral standards like the golden rule. It's got to be institutionalized as in the welfare system, fair employment and human right programs. On the political level it's incorporated into checks and balances."

"Do I take it you were against the movements for a constitutional convention before the matter of wider North American federation was brought up?"

"Yes, I was. And by the way, I was against your federal university."

"Well, ah…" Bill hesitated.

"Yes, I know! You only study there! But you'll more than likely be a leader some day and you can't listen to only one side of a story. You've got to learn to read between the lines. I'm not sure university students today are getting that."

"From what I've seen, you may be right."

"Spoken like a true academic, 'you may be right'!" the speaker exclaimed ironically. "Anyway new agers have their own hidden agenda."

"Yeah?" Bill wondered.

"Oh, I could down the litany of their covert goals. Of their overt 'aspirations', you've probably heard enough."

"Are you a john-birch conservative?"

"John Birch Society! I haven't heard that used in a long time. No. But I am a middle-road liberal."

"What do you mean whore-house politics?"

"That's an unfortunate phrase which I hope you won't use to label me in your research. What I mean is that in the affairs of everyday life, the responsible use of resources is absolutely essential."

"You mean money?"

"Money, property, intelligence, influence peddlers."

"Sounds like it comes down to money."

"It helps. But it has to be responsible and intelligent use. Not like carpetbaggers."

"Carpetbaggers?"

"Those who take advantage of others weaknesses. It includes the academics, media hypers, and information entrepreneurs. Anybody coercing others for profit."

"Are you socialistic?" Bill prompted.

"No. Private property and the natural law are still good grounding for human development."

"Natural law?"

"The rights of the human entity to be protected from all the hype artists, especially the intelligentsia."

"You mean advocacy?"

"Yes, in the sense of information consumer reports."

"That's not a new idea."

"Well, it's not much expanded, even though hyped over the info-net. Maybe its time'll come, if validation ever hits the info-mag."

"Anything else?" Bill heard himself ask.

"There is—the most important advance of all. But we don't have time to fully explore it here."

"Could you mention it briefly? Then we can come back on it on another occasion."

"Well, it's the prospect of an individual financial resource account based on a country's productivity. Like the conditions symbolized in biblical parables of vines and fig trees. There's more than enough wealth to go around to everyone."

"Sounds socialistic to me."

"Not to a hard-headed business man who makes more when more people have got it. It's an adaptation of the old keynesian theory. However this more recent approach is less doctrinaire in order to prompt smart entrepreneurs to get on top of things. The project could be financed out of the common treasury. Through reverse taxation, individuals could stockpile monetary resources to a limit possibly equal to ten years average earnings. Protected in such a family support enterprise, and free of inheritance penalty, each person could have more time to benefit from lifestyle maturity and enhance the socio-cultural climate."

"It's an interesting prospect," Bill concluded. "I'd like to explore it in another interview. In the meantime you have been very helpful in my research."

"You sound like an intelligent and thoughtful fellow. Have you ever considered going into law and politics?"

"Some," Bill admitted, "but not conclusively."

"Look me up again if you ever reconsider, or need help."

"Thank you. I will!"

*   *   *

As Bill snapped off the playback machine, he turned sideways in the chair to face the woman who had been listening and asked. "At the risk of violating a feedback principle, can I see if you have any comments?"

"He's got some interesting ideas. But they're all too new for any reaction from me," she replied.

Bill felt rebuffed. Edna appeared to have yawned herself into compliance. If that were true was she any different from other bimbos female-ing attraction into seductive connivance?

But then she seemed to return into awareness. "By the way, what feedback principle you having problems with?"

"After hearing new ideas, the mind needs some time to recover its acumen."

"That's me," she admitted.

"Well, maybe we could try one more tape before taking a break until tomorrow."

"Okay," she agreed.

"The guy in this next tape was a kind of guru in the university institute my half-sister Julie used to frequent."

With this brief note, hardly less than an adequate explanation, Bill turned back in his chair and started the tape rolling on the machine.

His own voice articulated the introduction. "As you know, sir, I am trying to develop an approach to the use of motivation in everyday life."

"Well, I'm not sure that philosophy can offer direct prescriptions. Philosophers are more useful in providing the understanding for assessing various options."

"That's what I meant," Bill had emphasized, "to gain a perspective on motivational phenomena."

"Philosophical study can help to do that—to set up guides to motivational variants."

"That," agreed Bill, "could help my independent study."

"Well, then. Motivation is bound up in the nature of the human person. It is part of the explanatory system which points out differences and similarities between the human and the rest of the environmental cosmos. During past ages, the questions asked have centered on a largely unchanging human entity. The perspectives elucidated were sociocultural pictures about the personalities of men and women. There are so many of these that they fill large sections of the libraries of the world. One can go there and begin a reading program that could be considered analogous to a world-wide trip of exploration, savoring the manifestation of human behavior under a multitude of circumstances.

"Today, however, as a result of evolutionary knowledge, the human entity is continuously and constantly under development, development that extends upward into the future. No longer statistically prone to evil after original sin, as in the Judeo-Christian tradition, men and women have escaped into the freedom of their own consciousness. They are constantly being redeemed—if ever again we can meaningfully use that term—by their own evolving awareness of the transcendent light that is the essence of their own good.

"They are becoming involved in their own powerful energy forces, bringing out their own healing processes, and creating their own environments by mind discipline, thought meditation and projective visualization. This is a unique amalgam of many previous religious tenets and philosophical positions. The result is a tailor-made and customized self that emerges from one's openness to the cosmic consciousness. It is not a church as in the institutional sense; nor is it Christ-centered as a carry-over from the historical past.

"It is a person consciousness that is completely individual, achieving an inner glow. As the outward manifestations of this inner light are perceived by others, there results a convergence of commonly felt light experiences. As more and more people focus together on a commonly desirable end, the import becomes tremendous, making way over obstacles, achieving an ever greater common good until eventually the whole world becomes the paradise men and women have dreamed about for eons, all the way up the evolutionary chain!"

"You don't hear that from most people today," Bill objected.

"That's because the media can't be very far ahead of most of the people. The concept of the information society, unfortunately, still has to be used as a metaphor for things to come. In the west, we still have to use language that is taken from Christianity. That's what people have relied on for too long to achieve but a limited and provisional freedom. Even the mysticism's of the east can only temporarily be relied upon for the transitional concepts and images that will lead more and more people to their own self-betterment through individual effort."

"You keep coming back to 'individual effort,'" Bill commented. "That's no different from the Christian way."

"No. You're right! But in the Christian ethos no individual could ever guarantee results. In fact, your prayers went up to some great big melting pot in the sky and by happenstance or divine providence, as it was called, some events would occur that, depending upon circumstances, one could interpret as an answer to prayer. That was like carrying water jars to Aquarius in the hope of getting some heavier water back, laden with some longed-for nectar.

"In the new age of philosophy, the pay-off for individual effort is more immediate and direct. One's efforts use the cosmic indwelling forces to achieve results. These results may not be completely guaranteed either, but the incidence of success is heightened. Instead of the random occurrence of happenings dropping from the sky, the individual can control events significantly beyond the operation of chance."

"Does this mean that god is dead?" Bill queried.

"Not at all. But it makes operational the prescription of the historical Jesus, 'Be still and know that you also are Gods'. God is within the individual. The experiences which flow from that revelation are tremendous. If indeed we are Gods, then everyone, each single individual expresses truth, goodness and beauty. The bottom line for the collective is that consensus, which emerges from the convergence of more and more individuals in harmonic cooperation, shines the light within to the outside creating a new reality and a new world order."

"How does this approach benefit the political and economic order?"

"In the past, and still today, political and industrial leaders have studied people's needs, or more accurately their hang-ups, in order to build these projections into political figures and products. Image building exploited such anthropomorphic projections to motivate people to action, to vote or to purchase products. Even educators used essentially the same techniques under the guise of experiential and mediated learning for individual differences.

"People were exploited, hooked on the bait of their own worst desires and fears. Now, individual people have control in their own hands. As they evolved into higher consciousness, aspirations took hold of them, facilitating their rapid ascent on the evolutionary spiral and into galactic events called forth by the power of creativity. They cannot but determine the nature of the figureheads resembling the leaders of the past. I use the word 'figurehead' because such entities have no power or energy but what converges on them by harmonic transference."

"Well, you have certainly provided me with the synthesis I need to complete my project. I'll work hard to fashion it to do honor to your brilliant philosophy."

"Let us say we'll do it together. Your consciousness will continue to draw light from the convergence of our two minds."

*   *   *

Bill stopped the machine, recalling vividly efforts to hide the mockery of his thoughts behind the words of flattery. He turned to Edna.

But she pre-empted any question on his part. "Once again Dr. Scolan, I don't have an immediate reaction. I will say, though, that voice sounds familiar even if I can't pinpoint where. Anyhow, let me think about these ideas until tomorrow."

"Okay, fair enough," he agreed, letting her depart in equanimity.

21

A few days had passed when, later one Friday afternoon after the workweek was finished, and Bill set out for the church auditorium where Edna was scheduled to address the parishioners. Father Thompson had asked him to introduce her to the audience assembled for a workshop.

Meanwhile in the interim since listening to the first of those research interviews, Bill had kept to himself—not necessarily avoiding Edna. He had thought it well to give her some space that might be needed in getting settled into her own unique, and probably unique way.

Edna's presentation had been placed last in the panel. She was already in attendance having decided as a newcomer to the locality it would be advantageous to have heard the two previous contributions.

Since the overall topic being considered was familiar, Bill had delayed arrival until just before Edna was ready to go on stage. Having estimated her ability and strength of character, he was not embarrassed at what to anyone else might seem like neglect.

Having pulled into the parking lot, Bill secured the car near the entrance and made his way inside the church hall. There he found Edna already talking to and glad-handing various individuals.

He was not surprised at such gregarious behavior, though he would not have anticipated it. But then he could be wrong in having surmised she was ordinarily a private person.

"Hello Edna," he greeted her. "I was sent to introduce your speech. But I see you're getting acquainted already."

"So Father told me. I just been having fun getting to know these beautiful people."

Before glancing at his watch, Bill noticed the near-by faces light up with a smile. He prompted her. "Well, Edna, Father Thompson said to start on time. It's near that now."

Edna put a stop to her greetings and turned to accompany Bill forward. There, he motioned her to a seat and then paused briefly to review notes.

The workshop audience seemed to be reluctant to let go loose dialog-level argumentation, vociferously chewing away on the sinewy remarks of the previous speaker. But reassemble they did, due to some "gentle" prodding on the part of the carefully selected ushers working the crowd.

Bill had to admit to himself that Father Thompson's cautionary preplanning had been done for good reason. But for him, what was the big deal? He had faced more than one dilatory audience in the past.

Be that as it may, Edna however had only herself as a resource under God's guidance, of course! Her own testimonial would have to become the shield of her resolve and the shadow of protection under the wings of the almighty Father in heaven.

In his introduction Bill briefly build upon some positive aspects of the previous speaker whose notes he had already reviewed before leading into Edna's introduction to the group. Then Edna rose and confidently walked over to the podium.

*   *   *

Bill found soon that his faith and trust in this attractive young woman's ability was not misplaced. Skillfully, even though note cards were placed on the lectern before her, she immediately got into personal experience as message verification.

"Evangelicals are seldom aligned with denominational membership in the traditional sense of 'old-line' churches. There is no 'holy' city like Rome, Geneva, and Amsterdam—no single founding 'father' like Luther, Calvin. They exhibit that simplicity, earnestness and indeed purity of heart, which the gospel expects. They feel more at home recalling the company of the apostles and ancient fathers than in the traditions and structures of church as institution.

"The original deposit of faith as given by Jesus is strong. Jesus was born of a virgin. He did not have a human biological father. At the Annunciation, something gynecological occurred under the power of the Holy Spirit. God had a son in the everyday world of human affairs who grew up to become the Jesus of the gospels. The 'verbal inspiration' and the 'inerrancy' of the bible message is trustworthy, important and God's word. If a story tells of a rod turning into a snake, or a of a withered hand suddenly becoming whole, then that is an absolutely true account of what happened in the real world.

"Evangelical spirituality stands or falls on private readings of the bible. To this day, bible events remain in my imagination as they were depicted to me as a child in little magnetized figures moved around on a storyboard. The bible speaks for itself. It doesn't have to wait around while biblical scholars make up their minds about its messages.

"We believed in Christ's atoning work for our salvation who in himself bore our sings in his own body on the tree. We preached being washed in the blood of the Lamb. That to many will sound like the salvationist, hillbilly religion which attracts huge numbers of converts. Some of you older persons will remember Billy Graham or Billy Sunday and their essential message, 'Ye must be born again', which sounded like the crowd arousing sermons of Peter and Paul just after Christ died.

"The Second Coming of Jesus is also near, we believed. In fact, the current emphasis on it could be considered an evangelical specialty. Their expectation of Jesus' imminent return is based on Jesus' own alarming words about watching for the event in the 'bridegroom cometh' and how suddenly the Son of Man will appear in his glory with the holy angels.

"Publicly, the evangelical may be reluctant to be considered too overtly associated with 'hell and damnation' sermonizing. However, in the conviction of his own mind, the individual all too often finds himself investing the words of Christ with something like their face value, no matter how crushing that may sound or how revolting to all human instincts.

"Religious drama must somehow include all the horrors—real evil and real free will and real perdition—as well as the comforting stories about the lilies of the field. Otherwise the thick darkness of the passion of our Lord is not such a thick shroud after all. If the gospel says nothing more than that we should all try to be amiable—sort of social simpletons as the new agers want us to become— then there is a great deal of smoke and dust in the bible that ought long since to have cleared away so that we could have left the 'gentle' story that only the moderns wanted to hear.

"You have already heard about the 'task-force' strategy of many evangelicals in witnessing to others. Closely allied to witnessing or 'personal work' we all since childhood were expected to do, is the missionary activity of carrying the gospel to every corner of the world. To come up here to the Pacific Northwest from the deep south was, for me, the great religious work of my life. We just had to make contact for the good of the person contacted. Have you ever sat alongside of an evangelical on say an airplane and felt how very much he or she wanted to start a conversation so as to hopefully lead you to conversion?

"But again, you have only to read the words of Jesus, Peter and Paul about witnessing. 'Be ready always to give an answer to every man that asketh you a reason of the hope that is in you.' You should remember, literally, the gospels spur us on to try to memorize scripture to use immediately whenever anyone seemed, on the flimsy-est of contexts, to be looking at us with the question, 'What must I do to be saved?' Some of you," she added with a wry smile, "are gonna say they never saw an evangelical who was too shy to initiate any contact. If you only knew the agony of shyness I used to go through as a teenager in trying to meet my self-imposed quota of contacts to be made!

"Anyway, for the evangelical, the New Testament is explicit, even strident in its assumption that the human race is divided into the saved and the unsaved. That literalness burdens our conscience. As a teenager, I've sat—writhing, perspiring, unhappy—wondering how to open up a conversation and witness to a person sitting next to me on a bus. The agony is almost indescribable. The sheer anxiety suffered is something like gasping out one" lungs before being pressed to death.

"The matter of finding the will of God for our lives was something very much more than an idle curiosity. Seeking was an imperative, laid on by constant prayer that God would reveal his plan for you personally. Sooner or later, by means of circumstances, scripture and inner conviction, God would make it clear.

"Evangelicals are always intensely watchful over themselves, even scrupulous about the quality of their Christian behavior. Non-evangelical Christians are never ever so hagridden with a personal sense of responsibility to remain clean in a world shot through with 'dirty' addictive behavior. All this is expected of us without any of the spiritual help that you as Catholics have so easily in reach— the sacraments. The sacraments are the most astounding help given by the lord Jesus and so readily available.

"Without such sacramental help, we had to get support and strength from out special in-group feeling. It was 'we' versus 'they', not 'us' all together as children looking for sustenance from a common father. This sense of separation was acute over such matters as alcohol, dancing, card playing, gambling, lipstick, and other baubles of the satanic one. As you can see, the evangelical has an extremely tender conscience. If the bible says no cursing, then the discussion is over—no cursing, not even foul words of any sort!

"To toy with God's word is a sin or to make light of any holy proscriptions. We can't pretend to be blameless, but we are never saucy about sexual matters. That may sound terribly puritanical in this day and age. But there is only one legitimate outlet for sexual activity—monogamous, heterosexual marriage with no biological hanky panky, except possibly natural family planning. In this regard they do not see it as fortunate that their most powerful ally and advocates are Catholics. Their minds are clouded because the Bishop of Rome is to many of them the antichrist.

"The center of an individual evangelical's spirituality is 'quiet time' or personal daily devotions, growing out of silent bible readings. The whole purpose is to 'get a blessing', however magical that may at times sound— especially when more or less futile attempts are made to wring spiritual counsel out of a long list of names—those heredity strings for which, for example, First Chronicles is famous or infamous as you might put it, or the hair-raising tales of butchery in Judges.

"Evangelical prayer is extempore. We learned that at a very early age to pray aloud. Usually we started with 'Our dear heavenly Father, we just want to praise and thank thee'. That was a safe start. Such openings as 'Almighty God', or 'Eternal God' were suspect, used by Catholics and liberal Protestants. To approach him that way, we thought they had not really met Jesus intimately, born-again. At the end of the prayer if someone said thanksgiving with just 'Amen', he gave everything away. He was not one of us! A true evangelical asks it all in the name of 'Our Lord Jesus Christ', or 'in Jesus' name, Amen', usually followed by a second 'big Amen' for added emphasis.

"Fellowship and testimonials are characteristic activities of the evangelical. Fellowship in Jesus is the bond actually uniting them to other Christians—not race, family, money, class, or taste. They have made something of a specialty out of fellowship. They talk to each other about the Lord. They meet in-groups to bring themselves together for informal bible study. Usually without a teacher, they pray and share—speaking openly about their inner burdens and about what God is teaching them.

"In testimony, one individual stands out and says something about his present experience with the Lord. He might talk about some victory in personal life— overcoming temptation and the sin, or a decision which God has helped him to make. This is the normal thing to do, not silent prayer bent over a pew. The embarrassing and tongue-tied behavior of other Christians is difficult to understand. They consider it to be quibbling and indecisive. They'll face right up and say, 'Let the redeemed of the Lord say so!'—not pussyfooting around hiding your face in your hands.

"With all that now, you are probably wondering why I would ever leave the Evangelical movement. If home bas was that good, why seek elsewhere, least of all in the Roman Church? If there is this much Christian earnestness, zeal and fidelity among the evangelicals, where else would a person turn? You may well ask such questions, because conversions from the evangelical group to Catholicism are not that frequent.

"However, once you start the process of becoming a Catholic you begin to realize all these activities—albeit good in themselves—are largely mad-made and man-driven attempts to influence God on our behalf. They can never be taken as substitutes for Jesus' freely given sources of grace—those sacraments which I understand Catholics all too often take for granted. Nor do they always recognize the very great privilege they have in priests, those marvelous alter-Christ's who consecrate anew everyday the sacred species of our lord Jesus Christ. If priests did nothing else than that, their contribution to the welfare of the human race is sublimely divine.

"Parenthetically let me recognize, here and now, the glorious vision of Father Thompson in establishing a seminary specialization in the deaconate. It has been the most consistently neglected ordination in the Catholic clergy, largely because its role was expropriated to advantage by all too many restless ministerial vocations dissatisfied with the so-called 'unglorious' drudgery of the priesthood. Instead of living the sacraments in people's lives, many Catholic ministers have craved the presumed visibility of the talking head more humbly performed by deacons. The resulting logorrhea has so inflamed the sacerdotal passions that in following their noses has led to many other unfortunate abuses whether moral, social or liturgical."

For a moment Edna paused and looked out over the audience in sweeping surveillance. Then abruptly attention returned to fructify a refocused mind.

"Anyway, for me, it was because of a holy bishop who taught me about Jesus' sacraments in the only Church founded by Himself—not by humans on personal bible readings. Like the bishop of Smyrna in the Apocalypse, he and his congregation were sorely tried by my coreligionists. In fact, as a minister, I had a very active hand in what really was a calculated persecution.

"As you get the picture from my 'apologetic' just now, we were really concerned about the Roman 'antichrist' at work in our community. It fell to my lot to hold a series of debates with that bishop on the local television station owned by an apostate Catholic. He and some of his associates set out to 'school' me in duplicity which set me thinking, reconsidering my position despite the enormous obstacles that appeared erected before me.

"The first debate went smoothly enough. The consensus of viewers was that I had come out on top. However, my own appreciation of the matter was much more reserved. I had kept the bishop on the defensive only because of the underhanded tactics I had been led to employ. Actually, we were scored to have come out about even.

"From then on, during the last two debates, I knew that the matter had started downhill for me. The bishop had the upper hand. He led me, but never appeared to do so. His charity of understanding, conviction of mind and holy subtlety never took advantage. He even helped to explain the Evangelical position to better advantage, and showed how generous it could become with the fullness of historical tradition.

"That holy bishop convinced a few others—not that many, perhaps because of the overpredominance of Evangelicals in that area—but some influential persons like the fallen away Catholic who came home again. For me, it was a New World vision, an upheaval in the ground of previously limited experience, almost revolutionary in the challenges it forced me to accept.

"Since then, under guidance of the Holy Spirit, I have been successful in helping Evangelicals to an altered dimension of their own spirituality. They, at least a few of them, have been led to perceive the influence of the Holy Spirit in the Catholic Church and to the broadening and deepening of their own more primitively expressed doctrines.

"On the other hand, Catholics seem to have been helped to appreciate their doctrines more expressly. Their attention has been caught by the Evangelical's fervor and dedication to the gospel message. Awareness has been deepened and expanded to more earnestly stand on the tenets of belief, not just chicken-out, as it is so easy to do in the addictive affairs of everyday life. They have been led into the apologetics 'business'. For the first time in their lives, many of them have had to struggle and learn to apprehend their own beliefs more thoroughly.

"In this regard, I can't help but remember the words of Jesus, 'Would that they were either hot or cold, not lukewarm'. My prayer is that Catholics and Evangelicals can appreciate each other the more. They could bring salvation and God's love to one another in greater measure. Together, they constitute a remnant of Christians still dedicated to a fullness of doctrine and virtue in their personal lives. So much of denominational Protestantism has gone over to the enemy in the slackness of morality and in the secularization of doctrine.

"Walking hand in hand, Catholics and Evangelicals could bring in a new Christendom. Marching together, towards the New Jerusalem, the world might see the joyfulness of our love in Jesus Christ for one another. That would be a great blessing in a world out there struggling desperately to recover from an era of antichrist where barbarism and terrorist violence were less controlled. A year ago at this time, some months before I was formally accepted into the Church, it struck me then as now how ordinary people live quite extraordinary lives. In every Catholic Church every morning, many noble individuals attend the sacrifice of the mass. How very remarkable is that event—a sacred happening of Jesus perpetually occurring, continuously sun-up throughout the world twenty-four hours of every day until the end of time!

"Whether Catholic, Evangelical, or other, so many peoples lives everyday infused with the grace of God. The Spirit moves wherever she will throughout the length and breadth of the world, especially wherever any human being resides. Can we not learn to love one another, in the saving grace of Jesus, and help each other to a better appreciation of the God-filled present moment?"

Edna paused briefly and, before closing her remarks, announced in compelling voice. "This is my prayer for us all and will be, God willing, all the days of my life. Thank you for this opportunity of sharing some little testimony with you."

*   *   *

The audience remained in awkward silence when she finished speaking. For a moment Edna stood her guard—almost imperceptibly rocking on the balls of her feet.

Several people looked one to another, nodding their heads, before a soft conversational buzz drifted upward. Then not as slowly the ground swell accelerated, rising voluminously until quite "unexpectedly" a general applause broke out—rollicking back and forth across group consciousness.

A wave of rising bodies crescended up from the assembly as person-on-person stood up in a round of loud clapping. Edna smiled and waved before turning and walking back to her seat in the front row.

Bill replaced her at the podium, clapping his hands and smiling broadly at the audience, then down to Edna and back again. He waited, momentarily, for the appreciation to slacken.

Then, he held up a hand for attention. The audience sat down while he voiced the general esteem. "Isn't she a jewel! It is so good to have our privilege recognized—reminding us of our nobility before God. You'll all get a chance to talk to her personally. But, right now please, let's take a moment for prayer. She needs God's inspiration as we all do. Let us pray that she will prosper with her family in this area. May she serve the people of God with her great gifts as a personal consultant."

Bill blessed himself and enunciated a short extemporaneous petition. "Oh Lord God, you are glorious beyond all mountains of human understanding. The beauty of your creation is ever abundant in blessings and high above all evil. You are the source of all divine grace and the river of all goodness. 'You have given everything its place in the world; and no one can make it otherwise'. You are the holy and eternal oil with which we are anointed, able to surmount the enemies onslaughts. Blessed are you who cause the inhabitants of heaven to rejoice and satisfy those who are on earth. O Christ, full of grace, make the assembly rejoice of all those who worship you."

Edna followed Bill's words in silent gratitude, while at the same time noticing how attentively prayerful the audience was.

<h1 style="text-align:center">22</h1>

Bill did not again immediately push himself onto the young female associate, other than brief encounters for business purposes. Nevertheless the attractiveness of her presence had become a constant preoccupation, a longing for something almost unfamiliar in past-life recall.

Unfortunately, the sensations aroused were larded with a recrudescence of remorse that approached overload. Even though he'd fought against the guilt that had blinded conscience ever since the previously near-lifelong affair with Julie, scruples remained.

On the one hand, there was enough work just keeping the counseling enterprise afloat. On the other, fortunately, other memories distracted him as the images shifted in the phantasmagoria of imagination. But as will all recall, he would surely have to expect disadvantages along with any chance benefits.

Only recently had he learned that the innocence of childhood—symbolized in memory by surrogate mother—had been lost. He had been deprived when in puberty the latent effects of original sin kicked in to darken consciousness.

Groping in the daemonics of a stealth-fog, psyche became grounded and shunted while the fallen angel of death hovered over his inner pool of emotions. Of the possible mentors once available, what little corrective action had been offered was not enough to effect positive results.

Even as adolescent rebellion had surmounted prudence, however admittedly latent—and the inner moonscape of consciousness waned—ignorance had corrupted self-knowledge and denied itself access to age-old wisdom. In the overweening light of virtual attention, so common among the information elite, all things had had to be re-investigated in general usurpation with "mysteries" quasi-scientifically packaged anew.

Long fallow, even polluted nearly beyond recognition as a human entity, he had allowed himself to be psychologically and spiritually handicapped. Inner daemonics became infected by invisible spirits who mocked him from behind blinkers woven out of the mischievous ideas of posturing intellectuals.

To his credit, he had sought absolution from the punishment due to a miscarriage of lifestyle with its many incidents of rebellion. The thorn had been pricked out, making it possible to cooperate with proactive grace.

Duplicity triggered, the tight-wire of deception had been loosened from its trap-set—sprung by divine pardon. Released by forgiveness, a firm resolution to sin no more—at least as far as he could affirm—had been to his advantage. Despite the temporal impediments which lingered, he had been acquitted of eternal punishment.

Over time, greater perspective had unfolded, receptive to divine pollination. Eventually the seed-bearing potency of his psyche had been incited into productivity. In turn, hope was strengthened by sacramental encouragement.

Nourished by the flesh of Jesus Christ his soul had been enlivened to countenance the insights of intuitive perception. Bill even caught a glimmer of discernment about the passivity and the immediate communicative moment of a glorified soul.

That near-instantaneous transplacement of a psychic traveler was far beyond the so-called rapidity of light waves. Voyages on the waves of the spirit could instantly project themselves through infinite realms. On the other hand, physical transport took so long to go hardly anywhere at all!

To think of how often he had miffed chances and despised possibilities in rebellion against inhabiting such a noble spirit. Instead of a shakedown that style of life was available to anyone receptive enough to put up with finite cleansings—making it feasible for humans to be released from the hang-overs of a temporal existence.

Upon occasion, he was nearly stuffed with regret at the time wasted. How sick had he become, pandering after the condiments of deception with which evil ones had flavored their pronouncements and sheep-skinned a humanistic manifesto! He all but caved in to depression, wallowing in the misery of what could have been.

Yet, why had he been spared and by whom? Why had he not succumbed? Why was he able to go on living while so many others continued to be defeated, if in fact any resistance were mustered at all?

Surely it could not be all that bad to admit dependency on someone else—not anyone at all, because such as those had bombed out all too often. It would take an A-one, an Entity accepted in filial obedience from whom all power flowed. Otherwise, as he had frequently experienced, vitality dissipated into the me-me-meing of connivance.

To his now present mortification, he had resented being budged by that reality which penetrated the thick clouds of the subconscious tumbling over'n-over under the centripetal rotor of fate. Through no power of his own, an awareness of other dimensions had blossomed.

Even in that long last minute before the cock crowed, he had heard a whistle calling. Who was he to have plugged his ears, or let his tail stiffen in enmity at the ages of covenant conditioning?

Had the dog of his dreams returned? Or, was the wish-fulfilling mechanism of illusion back at work in him, longing for the fix pandered by those judges-in-his-head?

Perhaps the spirit of Mary's mother was yet to return and puncture any remaining delusionary expectations? Maybe it was just his own sense of responsibility that, like retribution, had caught up to him?

*   *   *

Suddenly, realization shifted. He glanced at his watch. Mary would surely by now have returned to her office.

Bill got up from reverie, walked out of the counseling suite and made his way down the hallway. He rounded a corner and paused, taking a deep breath.

Of course he was not afraid to enter Mary Bulinsky's office. But he was uncertain whether the phraseology at his command was adequate for the inquiry troubling him.

Nodding to the secretary in passing, he rapped lightly on the opaque glass panel. At the sound of, "Come in!", he turned the handle and entered.

Closing the door resolutely behind him, Bill voiced the impromptu request. "Mary, I need a few moments of your thoughts."

"On what?" she smiled, waving him to a chair.

"Well,a…I think I don't think I understand the basic difference between women and men on sex."

"Wow! What brought this on?" she voiced in sudden surprise.

He could not reveal the surreptitious encounter of some days ago, when overhearing Edna and Mary together over breakfast. But he did comment. But he did comment. "I've got to work with that female protégé of yours and Father Thompson's. If eventually she stays awhile, we'd kinda be peers, leaving me sort've disadvantaged, maybe even handicapped compared to what you'n I, and Ann have gone through."

Bill smiled weakly, hoping it would draw her out without costing him too much.

But abruptly, she cut to a probe. "Your nose outta joint because of the way she was hired?"

"Well, no'a…" Bill reacted abashed. "That's not it at all!"

Sensing her blunder, Mary shifted back into a more appropriate response even though tinged with irony. "Whose sex differences you want—yours and hers or men and women generally?"

"Why, generally, of course!" he exclaimed, yet wondering at the irritation trifled by her implication. Not only that, but the knowing smile which flickered across her countenance bothered him.

"Bill Scolan, you are a child of this world!"

"You've said that before. But I never know what that's supposed to mean? You still putting me down like you judges-in-my-head used to?"

"Not at all—just a friendly give'n'take!" she disagreed with a tinge of disdain. "Come on now! What is it you want 'mama' to do for you?"

Bill glanced at her and, before reasonable thought could emerge, he heard himself charge. "Don't off-dump remorse if you feel that guilty not consulting me before hiring Edna!"

Then noticing her pained expression, he pulled back on the rebuff and added in a more conciliatory tone. "Don't get me wrong! She's an okay professional. I know, together, we can advance Leland House objectives in a significant way."

"I'm sorry, Bill. Let's not quarrel over trifles. Your request's just so much different from what we've ever discussed before!"

"Well, maybe we could try it another way—what is your take on the different characteristics of women and men?"

"Any response I could make would only open up a can of worms that may be insufferable."

"Why don't you try me?"

"My heart goes out to women who have been long-suffering. Women are naturally sexual because creature-endowed sexuality fulfills them in the procreation of other human beings. In other words, they can take it or leave it, savoring the after-effects like one does when hunger is abated. Men of course can take it but, unfortunately all too easily, have difficulty leaving it."

"What does that mean?" Bill wondered.

"Male sexual activity all too readily inflames the imagination and slips into second phase porno titillation. Male fantasy manufactures all sorts of extended positions, maneuvers and syncopated excitement which craves a prosthetic sex that is practically insatiable."

"So you assume women are pressured into a profusion of unnatural behavior by their inherent co-dependency in intimate matters?"

"The seventeenth century mathematician, Blaise Pascal, reiterated the matter in Genesis biblical metaphor when he stated, 'the urge of the woman is for the craving of the man'. Naturally inclined towards a helping relationship, the woman very easily becomes prey to predatory and addictive male inclinations. She's soon lapsed into an enabling role, turning tricks so as to entice male attention and supportive consideration. Females have a hard time with male silence—intolerable because of a her-story unfortunately being coerced by, and fending off the kinky, porno-addictive extension of natural sex that makes unwarranted demands. Thus women are forced to prostitute themselves into a whorehouse full of perverted antics and placate the unplacable—regardless of whether that whore-relation is a supposed legal marriage. Otherwise they live under a psychological tension that, if not addressed, soon degenerates into physical torture, rape, savage abuse and bodily damage. Some males, given to suppressing aggressiveness, wander into heterosexual exploration and profligation. Others, like peter pans, lace the suppression with disguised narcissism and cruise the villa-lined avenues for kindred homosexuals."

"You seem kinda pessimistic about wives and husbands if they can ever be fully functioning together?"

"Well," she began, "without matrimonial grace, whether explicit or otherwise, it is indeed a question if it is possible to handle sexuality without inflaming the male's trophisms and instinctive craving for the addictive extensions of copulation. Males easily fall prey to a feverish imagination. They manufacture all sorts of porno and kinky prosthetics that force females to employ abortifacents, backhand abortion, or looped and condomed intercourse. Females become desperate in trying to artificially compensate for sex on demand as a hedge against rape."

Bill asked for clarification. "You implying that males are forever doomed to be victims of imagination?"

"What a question!" she shot back at him. "Are you a john-of-the-crosser? If not, that is near endless in anxiety. Certainly it's a plaintive cry from the wilderness of male-female relations. That moody sob has reverberated in human hearts ever since Adam and Eve discovered their nakedness after the bliss of uninhibited cohabitation. Both men and women suffer deeply the profound sexual rift in human nature caused by sin estrangement. Nor is it necessarily enough only to receive the sacraments of reconciliation and reconstruction on a regular basis. Both sources of supernatural grace have to be accompanied by mutual discernment and proactive problem solving in the presence of third-part consultation. Sibling interpersonal relations as well as that of fathers and daughters, mothers and sons have been encumbered by the explosive potential of incest latency. Too often the inner gimmies of caved-in protectionism are not expurgated in mutual negotiation and reciprocal relaxation. Spouses remain impaired by uneasy truces which paper over and camouflage the stark crevice of isolation aroused by disobedience to the commands, God-given for human spiritual health."

Bill protested. "Yeah, but such meanderings don't clue me into anything specific that will solve the problem of sexual suspicion and rivalry."

"Well, Terry and I…"

"Thank the lord," Bill interrupted. "I thought you'd never get round to a case in point, giving meaning to mutual intimacy."

"You want something," Mary recommenced with a smirk, "to tit-me-for-tat with, don't you!"

"That means what?"

"Oh, forget it!" she spouted testily before evening out. "Anyway, Terry and I nearly broke up, or at least I threatened to do so when he took up developing a virtual phantasmagoria of female and male holograms. Those electronic simulations turned out to be more popular bawdy house prosthetics than the real bodies of male and female prostitutes."

"Yeah, I've heard of such a thing," Bill added without emphasis, hoping she would not recall his own despicable involvement.

Mary shrugged. "The ways of the world are the ways of the world. But the by-product turned out to be Terry's and my salvation—talk about God's ability to bring good out of evil! In the process, Terry was able to work through and divest his imagination of the worse of those male instincts which manufacture the kinky demands most men impose on, and enslave women in sexual depravity."

"How did that make a difference in your marital relations?"

"Terry was willing to accept a patience with himself and myself that was strengthened by sacramental reconciliation and reparation. We opened up to each other and explored mutual ways of recuperation. The major inducement to recovery came when Father Thompson got the Cardinal's permission to hear our mutual confession together. Without that reciprocal discernment I don't think we'd'a made it."

"That's novel!" Bill opined. "What happened deep down inside at the psychic depth of soul, or could you tell?"

"We established a basis in trust. Without that mutual self-confidence, I'm certain sacramental reception would have remained as shallow and spiritually unproductive as it had been previously. We're now convinced that the rift in our human sexuality comes as close to being closed as I guess we'll ever become since original sin."

Bill sighed, but would have repudiated any suggestion of envy were it hinted. Touched by the experience, he responded. "If only husbands and wives were available like that! I may be career inclined; but I don't want to be singled in lifestyle."

Mary smiled but refrained from inference conjecture. Nor did she demean the shared report by the customary reply—God willing, all things are possible!

Instead, she concluded. "Since sacramentally, marrieds are two in one flesh, we reasoned it ought to be available. Fortunately, in God's grace, the Cardinal agreed.

"For once only!" Bill added for his own summary satisfaction. "I'm sure that exception would not be allowed more than once in a conjugal lifetime."

*   *   *

Next day, all of a sudden—whether from the echoes in mind, aroused by scarcely tolerable memories, or due to his own feelings of melancholy—it seemed like the world as he had grown to know it was about to shrivel up.

Deep sensations shot through his skin and into the quick of his nervous system. So acutely felt were these apprehensions—as if deeply suppressed reproach had overloaded the scenarios being re-manufactured by the imagination!

He had been reading some reports when abruptly a sneeze disturbed attention. He looked up and mused to himself. By now the rising temperature of the morning atmosphere should have triggered even an ancient air circulating system. It had not.

Still he felt snively and got up to look about. He stepped over to an outside window overlooking this angle on the city. Again he shivered involuntarily like any one of his clients suffering psychological withdrawal symptoms.

He experienced a strange mixture of sensations as if he had been thrown an affront-to-dignity, from an unexpected distance, in a standoff space little used or frequented by attention. He was puzzled by the attack, it that it was, after these long years of adult sufferance.

The sense of retreat—from something or other that wouldn't come to focus in mind—deepened into a foreboding as if all the clothing around his body had burst open from some powerful explosion inside. Jacket, pants and underwear felt so fragile that on the least exertion the threads would disintegrate and fall from his body in long strips of decayed cloth.

He was shocked. Sure, he had compulsive memories the same as anybody else. But what was this massive stripping, this overload of withdrawal symptoms that could send the normal functioning of a body into shock—so close to the convulsive upheavals of particularly strained relationships?

The poignancy of displacement was upon him. The conference with Mary had left him with a feeling of disease. Frustration had continued to mount with little success in putting a name on the dissatisfaction.

He had hoped to find a way of severing the final cords of dependency, hanging over him from the last of those judges in his head. The influence of the others had dissipated, except for Ann-remnant.

However, she had never really shown that much interest in him; nor exhibited clues that could be taken seriously. Admittedly it was possibly a problem of his own making—a reluctance to rupture the ultimate anchor of singlehood in his existence without counting on a replacement.

Certainly they'd talked enough about things to have established some intimacy. But whether that attraction was the kind of first love he'd fostered in idealism was a question, or the foundation of a bonding that was expected to follow sexual relations in arranged affairs.

He was uncertain about commitment to another woman. Would it offer either of them the best chance to work through the unresolved issues of a previous lifestyle? Could they reveal to each other the needs cloaked in shame, or share the remorse of wasted personal opportunities?

Perhaps the problem was more his own, in the sense of not really knowing his inner self. Would he hostage himself out to another female by reeling with the punches and avoiding the uncertainty of mutual freedom—surviving until rescue, or possibly escape by banishment from the garden of mnemosyne—forgetting all else, staking out recovery?

But maybe, just maybe he had not listened carefully enough to the underlying message of Mary's comments? Perhaps after all it was up to him to divest himself of all psychological crutches in life despite whatever masquerade in which the guise was hidden!

23

This particular morning, Bill felt like a rat in a laboratory maze upon inadvertently finding the electrode-trip wired for pleasurable addiction…or, better still like he'd suddenly been released from work schedule to escape on an unexpected holiday.

Almost immediately his mind lightened, sensing the inspiration of a peacock spreading its fan. For a change, he experienced the leavening and balloon-effect of casting off, remaindering the last of a now unnecessary overload of ballasted precaution.

He hastened through bathroom ablutions knowing full well that the elation was not a serendipitous high. It was the direct result of an impending encounter, the interpersonal prediction of many a season—an entirely different event than anybody would ever have believed possible.

The issues anticipated had for the moment coalesced into this one magnificent sensation, a complete rapture of mutual exchanges fantasized out of nothing at all! Were he never to meet another person, the potential expected was more than rich enough in possible extension to last a lifetime.

As he completed toilet comportment his thoughts settled into the more measured sequences of daytime deliberation. Though astute in the appraisal of other individuals, Edna struck him as being more extroverted than Ann or Mary.

Certainly her range of interests could be expected to expand with the environment—enticed by curiosity and ranged in discovering people, place and things which could be represented in a compelling manner. Already mementos of behavior would flick through awareness.

Accurate in observation and denotation, her presence for him in any situation resonated with connotation. Obviously a part of that stance was a desire to be accepted and secure enough with others to engender personal liberation.

Sometimes disparaged himself at being stonefaced, Bill could really appreciate her semblance of scorn at habitual solemnity and the inner detachment of spirit which relieved herself of being taken too seriously. Having suffered times of orgiastic nightmare, she apparently had overcome her own witch's sabbat with initiative and self-determination.

But trouble with doubt had been an unfortunate hang-up of his own psyche. If stonefaced he might have been on occasion it was because of the fear of that power which an intimate could have over personal satisfaction. In fact, it could have been this negative reaction to even a semblance of dependency that had contributed to the alienation of many others.

*   *   *

Once having arrived at the counseling suite, he found that Edna was already there, visible through the open door to her adjacent office. Ann had apparently not yet come in. So he felt comfortable enough in making polite advances at Edna's threshold.

"Are you always an early bird?" he asked.

"When my mornings are not too complicated. Tamar's decided on her own apartment; and my house guests have found a location on their own."

"Already, you've had guests?" Bill noted in surprise.

"It's too long a story for now. In short, though, I've been responsible for the protective custody of a pastor's wife along with her daughters."

"Are they on the lam?"

"Not the police. But cults have been terrorizing Christian congregations in the Interior for years. Rebecca's nearly had it, saving her daughters from porno abduction by their father, a sect minister."

"That bad!" Bill exclaimed, and offered. "What can I do?"

"Nothing immediately. Perhaps in time, some review of their predicament might be needed. Then, maybe your offer'll be accepted."

"Sounds okay to me," he replied agreeably. "Well, soon's you're available we can get back to those tapes."

"In a little bit," she parried. "Maybe we can get finished by noon time?"

"Okay."

*   *   *

An hour passed quickly enough, although Bill wondered whether Edna was really that interested in having herself backgrounded in this way—listening to his audiotaped interviews.

When Edna did arrive, nothing in her manner appeared that would indicate an imposition. In fact, he felt the sunny side of the impending interlude as an opportunity which could emerge for realization.

"You know," he ventured, "it's better I tell you nothing beforehand about these interviews. Afterwards, comments can more accurately reveal reactions."

"You think I'll cut the cloth to fit," she countered with a twinkle in eye.

"No, of that I'm certain!" he stated emphatically.

"Looks like we'll get along okay!" she agreed.

Bill shrugged, stepped over to the playback machine and sat down before turning on the mechanism.

"Professor," came a voice from the past. "You seem to indicate that our psychological understanding has been in evolution for some period of time?"

"Well, yes. I suppose you could begin anywhere over the last two centuries. But skinnerian behaviorism is a convenient point because it pushes to a logical dead end the over reliance on the observation of external behavior."

"Isn't that the reality for all psychological inference?"

"I suppose so, but in a common sense sort of way. Reward and punishment, stimulus and response, pain and gain, all too closely underlie rote animalistic and even instinctive behavior. The human being becomes an adaptive control organism resembling the homunculus mannequins of alchemy."

*   *   *

"Bill, stop!" came the near-shout of Edna's voice behind him. Bill abruptly pressed the pause-button.

An apology followed. "Sorry, I meant Dr. Scolan. I know that voice."

"First off," Bill countered, "let's get on a first name basis. We can't go on formally, while working in the same unit."

"Okay, Bill, thanks for breaking the ice. I'm not that proper, really! But you know…"

"Why'd you know who that speaker is on the tape?"

"Don't you know who that is?"

"Edna, let's don't play games. All I know, he was suggested to me as a useful subject to interview."

"He's really an industrialist masquerading as a professor. You must have interviewed him before the Yoofnas liberated Catholics eventually recruited him for their cult. His philanthropy has been a mainstay, supporting evil causes like porno production and vigilante attacks on Uncle and our saintly bishop in the Interior."

"Whatta ya know!" Bill exclaimed. "I'll bet the story behind this interview has something to do with Rebecca. Still, why not finish listening to this and one more tape before we huddle on the matter?"

"Sounds alright," she agreed.

*   *   *

Bill released the playback mechanism and heard himself continue with a prompt to the "professor". "That bad, eh?"

"Yeah! There was no place for the mind, or spirit for that matter. So there was a humanist reaction that essentially stressed the inferences which could be derived from external behavior as explanatory positions for a study of mental activity. Intentionally as the predecessor of behavior was anchored in the mind and could be revealed by introspection and recall. Like the soaring of flushed-out prophet birds and the grumbling of disturbed animals, intentions emerge and condition awareness."

"That's graphic! You got a way with words."

A non-verbal sound from the "professor" could have been condescending. Nevertheless, Bill's question continued. "I thought the humanists considered us creatures as the measure of all things?"

"That a moral idea better considered in a comparative religion class," the "professor" pompous-ized again.

"Can you separate the two?"

"Not really! Comparative religion's been a great help to us in the Institute."

"I thought it'd only confuse the matter?" Bill asked, questioning.

"That's a naïve question for an academic to ask. Even a student should know better than that!"

"Well…I'm trying to set the parameters of my topic."

"That's better. From that point of view one should consider the side tracks taken by a naïve psychology and a naïve physics."

"I thought they were departures on the road towards cognitive psychology?" Bill wondered.

"In a way, yes, like the neobehaviorists and the perceptionists who worked their way through the reinforcers and extrinsic-rewards people need in everyday life. But these are culturally determined and concensually felt to be necessary so people can get satisfaction and pleasing results."

"These are not needed?"

"Oh. Yes in primitive levels of development. But in the hierarchy leading towards mental activity, information processing takes on greater significance."

"Great enough to eschew behavioral activity at all?"

"Yes. At first we had to use words taken from external behavior to describe mental activity. Those models were behavioral analogs and got us started along the road of cognitive psychology. Then, as computing and neural network software and machines became more powerful, we could transmute the essential elements in metaphoric expression for software design and development."

"Metaphoric expressions?" Bill noted.

"Yes. Instead of using expressions that go back to what people do, like a realia referent, we use expressions that make mental sense."

"Such as?"

"Well, At first they have to be mathematical because we have been limited to electronic digital machinery. Now, with light wave technology, we can factor in extra sensory phenomena that stem directly from mental activity devoid of, and unhampered by traditional notions of an experiential base."

"Wow! That blows the mind!" Bill exclaimed.

"It oughtn't," the professor smiled wryly. "Because it comes directly from the mind exclusive of old fashioned sensual mediatories."

"There is direct infusion then?"

"Well now, that depends," as the professor seemed to be squirming around in his thoughts. "Here again, you seem to want a religious explanation?"

"Well, my other two majors are philosophy and comparative religion."

"Oh well. That explains your bias. But speaking is a more carefully psychological manner, we have to take the mind as the source of perceptual manipulation. Then we can expand our understanding of its own cognitive behavior."

"Sorry to bring it up again. But is it the 'measure of all things' which I asked previously," Bill probed.

"Yes. If you so naively insist! But then only as concessions to your other two majors."

"But sir! I really ask it seriously. I don't understand whether motivational psychology has any place at all in a more cognitive, mentalistic approach?"

"Well, it does. More directly and more individually than we've ever understood before."

"How so?" Bill abruptly queried.

"The source of motivation is the mind, the mind which is responsible for self-development and self-actualization. The individual mind becomes the center around, and through which all external activity revolves and spirals. Like the reverse or reciprocal effect of an incandescent light bulb radiating through the universe, the individual can no longer be referred to as a one-directional flashlight or a guidance-seeking diogenes emerging from the emotional and experiential bases of reality. But a mind seeking, probing, stirring over the depths, creating paths of influence and achievement previously unknown in human history."

"That is a very fitting ending to your contribution. Your explanation has been particularly enlightening. Thank you for such valuable help in my research study."

*   *   *

"Any comments you want to make yet, Edna?"

"No..." she hesitated momentarily. "Painful memories are not that easily absolved."

"Okay then, let's roll another tape."

As he released the sound mechanism with one hand, Bill turned his head to observe Edna off to the side, partially behind him. He could see that she recognized the voice of the taped female respondent.

Bill again reached for a pause.

Edna's voice hardened not that prettily, as an explanation gushed out in a vociferous charge that gasped. "That's the female bishop who's terrorized everything Roman. She's a witch pretending clerical orders in that heretical catholic church. It's in cahoots with extra-religious sects who subverted Rebecca's husband."

Her eyes rolled, and hands trembled.

Troubled over the implications, Bill offered. "I can stop right now."

"That wouldn't be professional. I can hold out for awhile."

*   *   *

Bill released the button. As the audiotape started to play, he heard himself repeat the introduction.

"Dr. Vernal, Julie and I have listened to your lectures with interest in the comparative religion classes. Now, I was wondering if we could explore the trends taking place in human motivational research?"

"Well yes. There is a greater emphasis on intrinsic motivation today as you know. In fact, we are moving away very rapidly into a new world about to take place. We have a much greater awareness of ourselves. We can create anything that happens to us, any reality we want. This new approach to what we believe goes on in the psyche as world peace is created in ourselves."

It sounded like the female prophetess had paused for emphasis before going on. "A comparative religious approach has helped people to focus on themselves, on what to do in bringing out their own healing powers. As they say—'be still and know that you are god!' Each person can go into her body and explore it. The results powerfully release creative forces, almost unlimited realization for convergence on what needs to be done—'I have found god in myself and I love her dearly'!"

"Does this movement," Bill's voice prompted, "if one can call it that, have historical roots? Or, is it a recent advance?"

"As with most other things there have been various manifestations. They have failed because people then were looking for a movement with all of the usual hierarchical infrastructure of officers, leaders, etc. But it is rather a new consciousness in the individual who, focusing and visualizing in common with so many others, can bring about vast changes. Not only can, but does bring about vast change."

"Are these changes in the social world, political events, or the natural environment?"

"In all, and at all times making changes especially in the social and political realm. In the natural realm, it is only once in awhile when the planets are aligned that they can be cleansed of bad vibrations like the erratic thumping of an unbalanced balance wheel. Then, we have human and natural forces cooperating in a very powerful force for good."

"What is the 'good'? Or, should I say the belief system of this new awareness?"

"It's not a belief system in the traditional sense with its emphasis on denial to earn an afterlife reward. Instead of a 'green stamps' approach, there is a more positive openness and actively present participation in the universal emanations and cosmic intelligence's that strum the harp of reality to make such beautiful music as the human ear has not heard until now."

"Sound like the old primitive anthropomorphics?"

"Oh, Mr. Scolan! That's so naïve!" she scolded.

"Well then, if the traditional belief system and churches have been replaced, then the concept of 'sin' has evolved?" he ventured as a tempting throw-off to the affront.

"Why yes! You put it beautifully! We do not replace the churches. They'll just fall into disuse as more'n more people come to consciousness. 'Sin' has evolved into a higher mental life. The greatest failure is to not open oneself and become one with universal intelligence."

"You mean like...?" he hesitated, drawing her out.

"Yeah, 'God" was but a blip on the evolutionary spiral, a primitively naïve Christian forerunner in tuning to the great cosmic emanations."

"Are you saying that God is not dead?"

"The 'god is dead' people were also forerunners. We become God. All of us cooperating together in consciousness manifest that supreme force and make it applicable to the needs of living people today."

"Through transcendental meditation?" he asked, tongue in cheek.

"Yes, and other methods. We intensify our methods to strengthen physical and psychic stamina. Visualizing techniques let us realize and acquire anything we see in the mind's eye. When two or more people visualize together, it's a sure thing for them to get whatever they want. I'm sure you can see what a wonder and powerful method this is for world betterment. Universal peace, abolishment of world hunger and the easing away of violence are all directly available to individual as well as small and large group consciousness."

"The possibilities sound fantastic!" he quipped. "But if you've no infrastructure, how are you going to spread the good word?"

"By manifestation as more widespread consciousness takes over. The superiority of the new approach is so self-evident as to be undeniable."

"How do you mean?"

"It gets results wherever we are—on our own at the grass roots level, within the many, many already proliferated churches and among the established institutions of education, government, business and industry where the need for motivational training is especially evident and voraciously expressed."

"And the churches need motivational training?"

"Well in an analogous sort of way. So many people in the churches need what I would call 'experiential results'. They want to be surprised by the unusual, miracles you know!"

"But I thought these were documented?" he protested, not corrected.

"Less than one-tenth of one percent are ever documented, let alone authenticated."

"You mean they're emotional trips?"

"People want to be titillated by good feelings—feelings of what they call spiritual things, the glow of righteousness."

"Are these, 'born agains'?"

"Well yes. Those babies've been our greatest opportunity."

"Babies? Have been?" he groped, sounding confused.

"Yes, they fold at the first whisper of trial. Compare born-agains of even a few years ago with those of today. Have you any tapes of their sessions?"

"I wish I had," he aspired.

"Well, maybe we can help you. Stop over at the tab. We'll go through the index."

"That would be a real help. But could you give me a hint right now, a brief comparative analysis, as an hypothesis of what to look for?"

"It would be more of an explanatory guide, than an hypothesis."

"Sorry!" he apologized. "My terminology should be more accurate."

"Well yes. One can over-simplify for discussions sake. A few years ago, the born-agains—and they've become such a widespread movement—well, they were all speaking in tongues, singing and dancing in the Lord, you know Jesus as they called him. They were all having good feelings, visions about holy things— holy as defined by the so-called Christian Jesus who leads as the 'truth and the life' for them to follow. But today the shift has been towards the 'truth and the light'. Now, some will say, that distinction is subtle. But it is significant. By shifting towards 'light' and visualization, greater and greater crowds of people are becoming attuned to the universal cosmic forces. They are learning to take matters into their own hands. They are actively creating their own reality, a new reality that is positive and not simply fatalistic in accepting just whatever occurs. It is a regeneration of the planet earth for a new 'paradise' of good for all people universally."

"What has this got to do with comparative religion?"

"Not much in a positive way. But in a negative way, it has shown the bankruptcy of traditional religious education. We are able then, by newer motivational techniques, to draw people into a more positive, self-developmental, and individually achievable self-realization of their own power and creativity emerging from within themselves."

"Dr. Vernal, this has been a very clear and cogent presentation. Your insights will go a long way in helping me realize my independent study."

*   *   *

Bill felt himself almost relieved to get away from her. The interview was strongly redolent of the many conversations he'n Julie had had on the occult, Satanism and other residual wizardry. But one thing was sure, the link between the satanic and new age universalism was there, perhaps getting stronger than ever. But then it was conceivable that the link between the occult and everything else was there as well!

Hardly had turned off the tape recording than Edna's voice tore into him. "Sounds like you're no better than the worst of them!"

Bill gasped. His thoughts scrambled in near panic, before chilling together sotto voce—what's he done to merit such a rebuke!

But the possibility of any question was doomed in the face of her distress. "Those people destroyed my ministry and nearly took my life!"

"Whatever for?" he asked in lieu of struggling for justification, or even a more adequate response.

The anguish in voice was evident as she continued. "They been after me and my children ever since Uncle helped me escape from child servitude and find refuge with Mother in New England. They've used the occult, Satanism and any other wizardry they could think of! One thing for sure, the link between satanic and new age universalism is there, getting stronger every day!"

"Well, you know," Bill offered reflectively, "I've heard the worst of the apocalyptic devastation is over. Some maintain the power of the new age antichrist has been broken and we're into an era of the gospel good news."

"My life's my life!" she protested vehemently. "I just come back from the Interior where Uncle got my grandson back…"

"You—with a grandson!" he exclaimed, unabashed in disbelief.

Unintentionally, his surprise apparently broke the ice. Anyway, she smiled and even voiced a quip. "Yes—despite my 'svelte youth'!"

"What I meant, was," he backtracked sheepishly, "how'd that happen?"

"He'd been abducted—on the verge of being abused for their porno trade. Now, they've got Rebecca on the run. It's a toss-up whether her girls will ever have a chance to grow up normally."

"I suppose backlash skirmishes are gonna continue for some while," he ventured, and then quickly acknowledged concern. "That doesn't make the suffering and terror any less real, or that defenses can be neglected!"

24

Bill waited a couple more days before making another advance on his part towards Edna. He could not this soon hint at, much less reveal his own personal agenda.

Contact with such an attractive person had, at least in the beginning, to be an association of professional reciprocity. Nevertheless he was not about to cop out; he had no reason to let himself be disadvantaged in any possible games feminists play.

Instead he would only come out of himself more were it feasible to build upon the pretext of an announcement from Father Thompson. The priest had asked him to brief the young woman and facilitate another presentation by her to the nearby parish assembly.

Just as he was about to enter the outer office of the counseling suite, the door opened before he had put a hand on the knob. He brought body movement to a halt as the glassed shadow of a female materialized in the widening space.

"Why Ann!" he exclaimed, startled. "You're back! I though you had more of a vacation."

"Don't I wish!" she rejoindered. "Or..." she hesitated as a knowing smile appeared on her face, "you want to give me a longer one?"

"Well'a...if it were up to me," he replied lamely. "But so many things happen around here I don't know about any more."

He felt Ann's eyes on him as if they would penetrate his mind like they used to do as a one-time judge-in-his-head. But apparently she was preoccupied enough to let his sour tone pass without direct comment.

Instead, she retorted. "I'll bet you would. That'd make it easier for you'n the young one!" she added with a toss of head inside presumably towards Edna's office.

"Wha'dze that mean?" He almost sputtered defensively, realizing her change of attack had something to do with matters of juicier import.

"Edna and I had a long talk over dinner last night!" She shot the statement at him at him in an apparently deliberate explanation that made little sense.

"Too bad I wasn't there," he grumbled, caring less whether incipient gripe was about to escape his lips.

"You wouldn't have wanted that!"

"No?"

"Oh, come on Bill! We've had enough association together to understand each other better than that!" she declared while turning away.

"Why'a…" he nearly panicked with anxiety. "Ann, let's see if we can do something…"

"Bill, later," she called over her shoulder. "I've gotta run. Lucy's got problems, settling a new lifestyle."

Chagrined at such a finish to the unexpected encounter, Bill re-grouped body movement towards the open driveway. With an effort of will he propelled his feet across the threshold.

Bill could feel the strain in his face. The skin was deadened, forced as if the countenance had been refrigerated after an affair. Cheek muscles crinkled in dismay, tearing at the heart of resolve.

Though saddened and ill at ease, he entered the outer suite and would have hid out behind the closed doors of his own office. But a further challenge was upon him.

Once abreast Edna's open doorway, she looked up and smiled in apparent welcome and appreciation. At her invitation, he hesitated with no immediate cause for refusal. He entered slowly, returned her greeting and sat down. He had a hard time de-grudging moodiness.

Despite himself, the lilt in her voice was compelling. "Ann'n I had a great get-together last night. It's been some time. We were acquainted years ago."

"Oh, I didn't know that," He edged out the words flatly, not expecting any return on a lost incentive for conviviality.

"Once, Ann visited the Interior while I was still ministering. Somehow, her Christian charity got to me."

The sound of her voice was gentle and of interest enough to soften his strained countenance and deflate the sign that had threatened to escape his lips.

"Bill," she continued pensively, "I believe you're confabulated by Ann-dependency. But from what I could learn, the 'co-' to dependency—if it ever was a reciprocal—has been long gone, as well's most else I could think of."

The words penetrated his sensibility and thawed tension. Relief brightened at the possibility of enhanced communication between them.

Talk about the verbal inspiration offered gratuitously by the Spirit moving over the waters springing from his psyche. All at once, his lips found the words to a topic of mutual interest. Or at least, the concern on his part could have been more readily motivated by misplaced remorse and compunction.

Nonplussed over the brief encounter with Ann had left Bill in no mood to communicate as effectively as he might have wanted. Instead of getting to the soul of his anxiety over Edna, he had let himself flake off into unfinished preparations for a lecture she'd been asked to give at Father Thompson's school.

"One'a the next things we gotta do's plan another seminar at Father Thompson's school. It's that experimental place where adults and kids go together."

"I know the location," she assured him, "at least the assembly where you introduced my speech to those same adults."

"Seems like you're already acquainted pretty well with Church problems down here…"

He was about to add, "as well as every other thing around this place"—when the same Spirit came to his rescue. Could he really have entertained such underhanded backlash on her charitable appreciation?

"Problems overlap everywhere," she commented. "But the Interior's less cosmopolitan than Port City, and certainly more vicious in counter-attack."

"By the way, how's Rebecca…and your grandson?"

The look she gave him did not escape his notice. But he couldn't just yet let her clue in on his interest, however "burning" that may be!

"My grandson's is just fine over in New England with Trudy…" Edna paused. However, when Bill did not take the bait, she continued. "Rebecca's gonna make it, I hope."

"Devastation is not any less real under an urban façade. It's the same antichrist legacy carried over from apocalyptic times. Your point's been made about that female bishop and supporter-industrialist, down here previously, but now up in the Interior. Their instigating attacks, and the savagery of others, have been at the core of legalizing every possibly depravity."

"When are we ever gonna be able to get it out of social consciousness and effect a reversal?" Edna asked whether ruefully, or from a need to level their mutual relations.

"We've got to earn our way back," Bill suggested. "The Lord won't let us free-load, even though He's assured us grace sufficient for the need."

Suddenly, without apparent connection, Edna changed the subject—perhaps to hedge interpersonal equilibrium. "By the way, what's the reason of having adults go to school with children. I never did understand Father's explanation that well."

"Actually that seemingly unlikely mix occurs only in the late afternoons twice a week. It is a post-apocalyptic endeavor in continuing education centered around the idea that every child understand, if only vicariously, socio-financial matters. Young adults, early in life, should be enabled to start building a gross capital investment eventually equal to the sum of ten years average earnings. With that kind of a financial resource over and above wages, a comparatively young adult could engage in a socio-cultural or spiritual enterprise for the gratuitous benefit of humanity."

"For such an endeavor to succeed," she began, considering her words carefully, "a new type of personality would have been engendered. I can see that your research into human motivation would have significance."

"Father Thompson seems to think so, as well. He views the adult-child mix as a radical learning milieu. Children are motivated to achieve in discussing adult questions about the relevance of combining catechetical and secular learnings. In the process, adult insight and enlightenment are rekindled by the rapture of juvenile idealism. The return on endeavor is the new personality you mention."

"So why'm I being asked again to speak to such a group?"

"Father thinks the religious experience of a convert, so young and attractive, would add a dimension not otherwise available."

"Even if that 'svelte thing' is a grandmother?" she parried, slyly.

"Well, you know…" Bill shrugged.

"No, I don't!" she evaded adroitly. "If I were to let my feminist inclinations have their way, I'd say the whole shebang is chauvinistic and revolting."

"That sure is talking like it is!" Bill exclaimed, and added carefully. "I'd kinda like to let Father Thompson know that in some way."

"Don't you dare!" she commanded with a slight rise in strength of voice. "With you it's one thing where, strangely enough, I feel comfortable expressing my thoughts. But don't get me wrong; God knows you got enough hang-ups as it is!"

Bill looked at the woman closely before letting himself add with a chuckle. "You are perceptive! It's not often that somebody comes along where pretence doesn't matter all that much."

"You better not put it on—with me anyway!" she ordered. "Anyway, you got the makings of a sense of humor that hopefully will develop in time."

"You are a cool one, aren't you!" Bill exclaimed. "I'd say it's a streak of suicidal fatalism."

Bill sat for a moment in upright silence. Apparently the wheels-in-head were turning. Then, abruptly, she came to the point. "Now that we've broken the name-calling barrier, maybe we can get on with some sort of relationship."

"Whatta you got in mind?"

"That's not for me to force on anybody!"

Bill hung on to a retort and, suppressing the words, remained silent while Edna went on with her thoughts.

"Maybe I'm reverting to Protestant reserve. But I'm suspicious of any personality formation that ignore a sacramental foundation based principally in penance and the Eucharist."

"I don't think Father implies that at all!" Bill objected.

"Perhaps not intentionally. Still he's so busy with so many other things. Has he ever downsized in order to gain time to focus on essentials? No, I don't think so—'delegation' doesn't seem to be in his vocabulary."

"On the contrary, I think he has. He's taken steps to add a deaconate specialization to local seminary training."

"Is that for managerial support, or the pin-point take-over of homily composition and presentation?"

"Need it be either-or?" he posed with probing directness.

"Yes," she emphasized. "If homily preparation does not have primacy over administration, catechetical training—the essence of deaconate homilies—is all too often at odds with the eucharistic charisma of conserving all things for all people all of the time."

"I hope that is not the cop-out it sounds like."

With that, Edna fixed her eyes on him as if she were pushing hard on some nonverbal communication, making a concertedeffort to bring him around to something he could only guess at. Surprisingly, he felt compelled to ask an obviously 'preposterous' question. "You're not suggesting I oughta consider the deaconate?"

"No," she replied immediately as the light of compatibility returned to her eyes. "You've got a lot of work to do getting your imagination under control before considering that kind of mission."

"My imagination! Why've you been so worked up about it? What's that got to do with anything at all?"

"Everything!" she stated conclusively. "Let me see—no, there's no other way than being direct with the likes of you, even brutal if necessary to register on attention! It's that part of a human mind, especially in men, that can confound truth. Once polluted, it fouls up the quality of the validation referent. Instead of objective reality, illusions and delusionary maneuvers incite extrinsic manufacturings, cooked up by subjectivity."

"I can buy that. That's not very brutal!"

She glanced at him, still concerned enough to blurt out. "It's when related to your sex life!"

"Why'a…why'd you want to do that?"

"For you, I'm guessing, it's the essence of your personality."

"For a lotta other people, I'm sure."

"Then, no better place to begin, don't you think?" she asked pointedly.

"Well, yeah…I guess. No hope for the better?" he asked rhetorically, then clarified himself. "Sure, it's addictive inclinations. But how's that apply in the context you're protesting?"

"Men have a hard time keeping lust out of sex even when monogamous. Any wiggle of a female body sends expectation skyrocketing. Soon men are meshed in with the flesh, not as a person, if he ever was! Love making's rarely been perfect; but for males, it's long gone haywire with porn."

"I can't say the way women dress these days is any help either."

"Unfortunately, feminists have bought in to their own self-destruction in desperation over the lack of monogamy. Anyway, it's not as an individual, particularly. It's just the built-in male hang-ups a woman's gotta deal with all the time—macho-bullying that compounds the normal problems of relationships."

"Well, it's kinda in your doing—you raised us!"

Apparently his cue made no connection in her head. She pushed right on. "Marital sex is one thing. But I'm no porno-bimbo, able and eager to wave the magic wand of fantasy-titillation enticing your imagination into whimsical copulation before you ever get inside a real human vagina. Pascal may have been right; but Eve sure suffered over the demands of her body for impregnation and seminal fertilization."

"Like all feminists," he protested, "you're not taking into account male psychology! After arousal, the female's lower anatomy and women's legs become for men the portaled threshold to a long denied edenic surcease."

"If that's the case, then you're guilty of a heinous sin against God's angel with the flaming sword."

"Oh come on Edna, that's sure puritanical! It's got nothing to do with it in that sense."

"No," she contradicted, "it's a sin on two counts. You're masturbating your own narcissism. Then is your abuse of female flesh—an uncharacteristic exploitation of a woman's deepest make-up as a human being with aspirations."

"If that's the case, females have only themselves to blame," he charged. "Every male is raised by, and bonded to a woman. Why don't you nip that sin in the bud and root it out of imagination before it's too late for males to take accord?"

"It's like the wheat among the cockles. You're stuck with them both until the harvest—supposedly when the male's intellect comes into its own, if ever that'll be!"

"No hope for the better," he reacted, then added. "You think my imagination is on sexual overload? You ain't seen nothing without visiting the porno factories—widespread everywhere!"

"You saying I'ma'nnocent! How do you suppose my adhered cult gets all its money to springle-dance around the congregations 'witnessing' to the gobble-de-guks? Practically every household's got its own cottage industry—aborting fetuses for the pin-money in supplying human flesh for the cannibalizing addictions of health-nut and diet aficionados."

"Yeah, I can imagine...I mean 'guess'!" He corrected himself with a wry smile. "Now, it's the info-mag, web-netted for ease of access to spill out all sorts of lurid sensations. Worse still, though, is the weight of domination enforcing its prevalence. Sexual entrepreneurs fan the diseased versions of freedom of speech and liberated choice. Original concepts have been so laundered as to concentrate power and enforce control to the advantage of a few economic overlords."

"One of them," she agreed, "is the cult's female bishop up in the Interior. Way back she had my children abducted to scare me away from counter ministry."

"Don't lose hope. Already you've made inroads to deflect their effectiveness. They're on the defensive, and'll soon be on the ropes."

"Only retrenched! Never to be defeated?" she queried.

"Not as long as, despite themselves, they do the Lord's work of us having a thorn in the flesh."

At that, Edna's shoulders seemed to slump as if her thoughts would curl up with a sometime remembrance. She began to intone a little song:

"We all have secret fears to face,
 our minds and motives to amend.
We seek your truth; we need Your grace,
 Our living Lord and present Friend."

Bill focused attention in surprise. However he held down any undue reaction, asking simply. "What ever brought that on?"

"Oh, it's a hymn from my old songbook as a child."

"I don't get it."

"It's a reaction to your barb-in-the-flesh left by thwarting experiences," she explained. "Nobody wants them; but they're inescapable. Narcissism can't be eradicated with any less thorny motivation—which you oughta consider in your research. Instead, I suspect it's more to our liking to presume a certain convivial familiarity, even a syncopated and watered-down ritual that will pry loose more favorable treatment by a buddy-buddy god."

Bill interrupted, "…like the glad-handing of Yoofnas liberated Catholics trying to get a hedge on divine providence."

"That socialization of the liturgy aims at twisting the little fingers of god and wheedling his 'blessing' on our own way of wanting things done in our lives."

"That surely gives me something to think about!"

"I suppose an apology could be expected. However, even though my manner of speaking may seem peculiar, perhaps offensive, I'm not exactly sorry. Words like these have to be said. In fact, my convictions will come out before long anyway in our association."

"I am glad you spoke up. It's really made my day!" Bill emphasized as convincingly as he thought possible. "It's this kind of give-and-take that shows the real person. I am grateful for your candor."

"Then it's not too late?" she questioned in a conclusive sort of way, adding ruefully. "Anyway, to the here and now."

"What's that mean?" He glanced directly into her eyes, carefully controlling a polite ignorance.

"You know what I mean," she reacted, probing for the agreement in his head. "We're sizing the other up. Each of us knows we're both professionally more than competent."

"So what's the big deal?" he wondered.

"Nobody else I've ever heard of would tolerate taking time to discern inner self-actualization during employment and engagement in the regular ups-and-downs of professional association."

"How could I hold that against you?" he asked, hoping she would catch on to the rhetorical intent of his statement. "My own life's been one long struggle against the 'gimmies', and the ropes of gulliver holding me bosom-buddied in the spirit of Yoofnas pluralistic religion. I should've always been named for Peter Pan sleeping through a foothills thunderstorm."

"That was old Rip Winkle—you got your monikers kinda mixed up."

"So what?" he reacted as if shuffling off to nowhere was an ordinary matter.

An abrupt shift in her attention caught him in surprise. She seemed to be appraising his inner self. Even though her lips moved, comment was release-delayed. Apparently she was momentarily satisfied with the visible evidence of his own integrity.

Then, briefly, she remarked without embarrassment. "They told me about you—but not the innocent guile you're capable of!"

Once again, he steadied himself lest untoward reaction escape critique. Counteracting the inclination, he ventured. "With my kind of attitudes are you sure any interpersonal association with me at all is worth while?"

"I gotta get past too, you know," she came back at him, obviously tongue in cheek. "Maybe not as lurid as yours, but enough for a poor female dependent to work through!"

Bill glanced at her expression. In sudden about-face, he burst into a guffaw, before observing without expecting recrimination. "You're good aren't you! I've seen many a wile!"

"I bet you have, especially with the girls coming on, pelting affection!"

Bill relaxed his grin, becoming cautious out of feat that some daimonic trophism could enmesh the psyche in self-entrapment.

At that point, she lapsed into a knowing smile. "You sure have taken the high road, Bill Scolan!"

He was uncertain to as to how any reaction for, or against that kind of observation might be handled. Instead, he began in an off-handed manner, before stumbling in hesitation. "Well. I've not been that successful...or even experienced with intimate relations. It's been more sex than chastity...or reverence and respect. I want to make certain my loser streak's over, before..."

"Before what?" she filled in, asking the question in somewhat less than a professional voice.

"Well, you know…before anything develops," he replied lamely as if overcome with untoward deference.

She recovered objectivity quickly. "Each of us have had our lumps in life. In fact, the discernment of past experience may need more mutual exploration. Right now, however, let's get on with the business at hand."

"Okay," he agreed, refusing to feel uncomfortable. "Maybe this's far's we can take the matter right now."

"Do I have your 'blessing' then?"

Bill looked at her once again, trying to discern the extent of wry disdain he suspected might lay behind that question. Instead, he smiled, refusing to fall into the impending breach and defend himself as he'd so often done at a disadvantage in the past.

"Blessing or no blessing," he added without compromise, "we got work to do."

25

Bill had been sitting in his office located within the otherwise unoccupied outer suite. It was still too early in the morning for either the staff to arrive, or Ann and Edna.

He had been trying to put some thoughts together of a professional nature. But the attempt had only been sporadically pertinent to the matter at hand.

Finally he had just let his mind go with the drift of inclination, merging with the need to make sense of rapidly developing feelings for Edna. Perhaps he should just relax and allow himself the luxury of fondling those moments of empathy.

Still, having done that with others in the past had not been particularly successful. That kind of immediately gratifying dalliance had precluded attention to matters of longer-term significance such as the benefit to Edna were she to respond to advances.

Like himself, she carried a professional responsibility that could be all time consuming. Unlike him, she had added family and connections that could weigh upon freedom of choice and condition a woman's inclinations in variant directions.

So far, anyway, these reservations had not shaken his growing conviction that she had an interest in him. In fact, he refused to believe himself to be a victim of wishful thinking although, to be sure, external evidence to the contrary was slender indeed.

Suddenly, attention was distracted by the entrance of a shadowy figure into the outer office. Any distinguishable features were blurred from view in a sitting position behind the opaque glass wall.

Bill called out. "Can I help you?"

"Yes," came an assured male voice. The source of the reply stepped over to Bill's open doorway and was revealed in sight, dressed in clerical garb.

"I'm Monsignor Riordan, Edna's uncle," the minister said.

"She's not arrived yet," Bill replied, glancing at his watch. "I expect she'll soon come, and the office staff."

"I thought she was an early riser."

"She know you're coming?" Bill asked.

"Oh yes, We had dinner last night."

That information struck Bill as odd. He'd not heard anything previously of a visit from monsignor—surprise despite contact with Edna yesterday and even the absence of "office talk".

But then, maybe, he was just edgy from the abrupt interruption of a self-assuaging reverie. Hastily, Bill put aside impatience and opened his mouth.

"Well, come on and sit down. She'll be here soon," Bill guessed, and then remembered an otherwise obvious point of etiquette. He got up, extended a hand and presented himself. "I'm Bill Scolan."

"Oh, I might have guessed," the priest responded and, taking the invitation, sat down.

Bill returned to his chair, momentarily nonplussed by the other's intensity of attention. He was struck, intuitively, by the aftermath recollection of what could only have been some discussion of himself last evening.

Scarcely lessening his scrutiny, of an almost surveillance fixity, the clerical person observed with the concentration of an examination. "I understand you've made some significant contributions to Catholic religious life."

"I've tried, Father," Bill replied with a mixture of evasive caution and suspicion. The feeling persisted that he was under assessment for some corner-on-the-market he was apparently supposed to have. In contradiction, he announced with a strain of humor-in-voice. "This diocesan opportunity has been good for me. I can only pray the Cardinal's blessing will continue."

At that, Edna's uncle chuckled. "I can see why others hold you in appreciation!"

"Which other's?" Bill parried, letting a smile escape and play around his mouth—but deeply hoping to himself that the fellow would slip, implicating his niece.

"That, I'm not at liberty," the priest replied elliptically. "However, I can say Father Thompson and I are in agreement."

"Oh him!" Bill shot out the expression but, as abruptly, sought to remedy the unfortunate implications in more positive voice. "He's long been a father-confessor. Without his blessing, I don't think my life would have amounted to much."

"Well," the minister began in reciprocal expansiveness. "I'm sure the Lord will reward a generous humility. It's the start of a transformation into the spiritual life."

That comment touched a longing in Bill, scarcely yet, emerging from the inchoate subconscious. Instead of stumbling over words, revealing the indecisiveness which worldly-wise cracker-heads would exploit, Bill turned to a topic of impending consideration.

"Father Thompson's got me tagged with the deaconate. It's more than a possibility. But my head's not completely adjusted to it."

"Well, for one thing, it's recommended that only married men be ordained to the deaconate…" The monsignor hesitated out of what seemed like indecisive caution.

Once again, that strange sense of being scrutinized interrupted Bill's attention. In fact, he felt helpless to deny the conviction that he had been a subject of conversation at the dinner table last evening.

"Anyway," the monsignor picked up this thought, "that being the case, deacons are desperately needed in the Church today."

"Why so?" Bill queried.

"People nowadays put more trust in witnesses than in educators. Experience counts more than teaching—life and action more than theories. Admittedly though, there is a strength in personal manifestation; it is available to all no matter one's circumstances, state of life or vocation. I must say, personal testimony gets back to the individual responsibility fostered when America was a republic. Ever since then, unfortunately, that role has been mocked away, little by little. Thus today under the UFNAS democracy of the United Federation of North American States the almighty idol of the state crushed what little remains of personal witnessing, once prized in the Republic."

Bill had listened carefully to the monsignor's words. His thoughts reached out to the possibility of relishing an unfolding interpersonal dimension—at least, that seemed the promise. Maybe this was an opportunity, right under his nose so to speak, for the exercise-in-mind with another person of cognitive merit that would counteract the subjectivity of emotional connivance.

If her uncle showed this kind of intellectual acumen, and nimble exploration of idea, there was a good chance that Edna also would relish the quick-witted exchange of ideas even after having reposed on a marriage bed.

Ah ha, so here again was he "counting chickens"! Better get back to the conversational interaction at hand before the cool appraisal of the monsignor had to be encountered again.

Rather than shame himself over verbal deadlock, he turned the tables on self-anxiety and sallied with a jest, "I've always thought of deacons as flunkies to the priesthood, or like the military batman assigned to limey officers."

Edna's uncle chuckled again, "I can see your incisive mind working overtime!"

Ah ha! Bill thought to himself. The fellow surely couldn't have gotten that impression from anywhere else than in conversations with Edna.

Out loud, Bill deflected the topic of conversation. "Be that as it may, Father Thompson's case rests on the point that deacons can get involved with current affairs. Otherwise worldly interest would undermine sacerdotal integrity.

"That is not idle speculation," the priest agreed. "Experience has shown that people lose reverence for the sacred all too easily. Then, with the glad-handing charisma expected by parishioners, priests grow careless themselves and the consecrated nature of their ordination fades. Deacons can deflect some of that pressure to conform, allowing the priest more objectivity and thus spiritual freedom in administering the sacraments to everyone regardless of religious correctness."

"That's a mighty big job to do in personal relations," Bill concluded. "Obviously, remission won't come any time soon. Even the downsizing efforts that traumatized so many victims of the year-2000 computer fiasco were quickly abandoned after the fix-up."

"Downsizing did wake people up," the monsignor countered, "Even though it was all too easy to run from the underlying psycho-spiritual problems. Actually it may take a century or more to undo the havoc wrought by the antichrist loosed in the reformation. The evils have saturated western civilization at all levels and devastated untold millions of souls worldwide. A hundred years is no time at all, a mere spec on a time-line until Jesus comes in his glory—even if He then does do so. Think how long the Father, in mercy and love for humanity, led the patriarchs and prophets in strengthening faith and trust through nearly two millennia before sending his Son to institute the sacraments."

"Sounds like no quick fix," Bill agreed. "I wonder how many of us have the patience to subsist in reducing earning power, dictated by increased involvement with others in socio-political responsibility?"

"You as a deacon could show the way. For example, your modest financial homestead from publishing and investments must surely yield enough income to devote time and energy to…"

"How do you know that?" Bill interrupted, somewhat alarmed over disclosure.

"Without in any way being noisy or inquisitive, Father Thompson has consulted me in reviewing your potential as a front-line candidate in initiating widespread deaconate preparation."

"Well, I guess that's not surprising for the kind of entrepreneur priest he is."

Quickly, Bill intervened within himself to press under control what could still erupt into anxiety over personal disclosure. Of what profit were such immature disturbances to a psyche struggling to maintain adulthood? After all, he had come a long way from the days of solitary in-grown escapement.

"Don't knock it, Bill. You've take a step in resource provisioning that's eventually to be widely available in the population. The Yoofnas congress has just recently passed the legislation bringing together variant half measure towards financial homestead empowerment that were more frustrating than workable."

"So, I'm off the hook as far as yours and Father Thompson's concerns?"

"Far from it. You—and your deacons-to-come," added Monsignor wryly, "are desperately needed to example and mentor the responsible behavior that will maximize this opportunity for the benefit of all."

"Such as?" Bill demanded. "What kind of an 'e.g.' you offering that's got any meat to it at all?"

"Think of all the piled-up religious rights cases that have been flooding Catholic freedom organizations these many years. The cleansing of bigotry—by the 'Kings and Queens of Tolerance' who idolize the state—from an inclusive, pluralistic society will take another hundred years. More specifically, if you will, enormous time commitments will have to be made to grand-jury duty and widespread trial-jury involvement."

"You've gotta be kidding!" Bill scoffed. "That's for busybodies, living off the government anyway."

"Exactly the type of reaction that's got to be turned around, hundred-and-eighty degrees! Populations of hoodwinked people continue to be exploited by the very government that victimizes them. They are helpless to do anything but unknowingly aid-and-abet the officials who subvert the system that's supposed to be the servant of we, the people."

"I don't understand," Bill confessed. "That doesn't sound like the 'system' I was educated in."

"You can be sure of that," the priest asserted. "The Yoofnas—of UFNAS for the United Federation of North American States—was built on the propaganda cleverly carried over by new age liberals from the previous democracy which their counterparts in the last century twisted out of the founding Republic built on Anglo-Saxon common law."

"I thought that was a 'good' thing—socio-culturally speaking?"

"It was until ultra-liberal judges interpreted out the constitution as based on English common law that kings used to supplant Anglo-Saxon civilization."

"That sounds like tweedle-dum'n-dee—or, am I supposed to detect some difference?"

"You are!" the priest stated emphatically. "And so are the vast electorate of the Republic that has been subverted by the pied piper 'marseillasing' the democracy. In the Republic originally founded under Anglo-Saxon common law, we-the-people were the source of empowerment for a limited government necessary for communal service."

"Agreed! That's what we have."

"In practice, no! That fully functioning political life scarcely lasted little beyond the eighteenth century. Prototype new agers were soon at work twisting judicial interpretations referenced under English common law which the English 'communistic' kings employed to break the ancient people's movements and keep centralized control even while hiding behind the nonfunctional face-saving devices of grand-, and trial juries."

"What's so 'bad' about English common law!"

"That's where power and civil rights are derived from the godless State to be dribbled out to the populace. People are a 'thing' of that idol which advantaged governments when they subverted the religious so-called reformers and exploited their antichrist rebellion against the only Church Christ ever founded."

"You know, Father, it's a hard sell to convince people of such truths after new age relativism and the ecumenism's being fostered in the name of the gospel good news."

"So, it's to be expected. Evangelicals and Catholics no longer hold a grudge. They don't have to, even if they were not motivated by the Holy Spirit to pray together in worship and supplication. Though the liberals have turned the Republic into a 'theory' in order to reify 'democracy' to their advantage, all the old empowerment of we-the-people under God exists in reality—once the electorate can be enlivened in jury duty by the example of deacons and others of mature perspective."

Bill was still skeptical. "How will an apparently obvious mere state-of-affairs like jury duty, be so invigorated as to have such powerful implications?"

"The historical and theoretical background can only be explicated by faculty in 'your' seminary for deacons."

"That," exclaimed Bill, "is sure horsing it further ahead than Father Thompson's sense of timing and my preparation readiness!"

"Without projection, where would incentive ever come from?" asked the priest rhetorically. "Anyway be that as it may, the answer to your question lies in the activation of political maturity among those serving on juries. Anything more immediately effective may not be beyond the power of God. But as for human efforts, conjecture is more wishful thinking than speculation."

"Such as?"

"Oh, in dream sequence, you could imagine the Inland Administrator trading in enormous popular support despite his own immoral lifestyle. In an unlikely born-again experience, he could executive-order public school prayer reinstatement and nullify all legalization of intrinsically evil behavior."

"Uncle…!" Bill exclaimed, then abruptly paused in aghast confusion, "…I mean, Father…whatta hope you got for that!"

The monsignor seemed to have scarcely noticed, and continued. "He would be impeached, of course. But he would go down in the history books as one of the few great leaders in western civilization."

"Yeah, well, to the here and now," Bill redirected himself. "How should juries be used?"

"Right now, voter registration lists are widely manipulated to yield carefully controlled non-randomized panels. Such court-selected jurors are hoodwinked and even browbeaten into submission to the judicial subversion of not only the constitution but especially all things Judeo-Christian. Just consider the extent to which inherently evil behavior has been legalized under politically correct law enforcement that disguises vigilante police action."

"No wonder we got such widespread collusion of police and mob savagery!" Bill exclaimed. "I know; to my shame, I been on the receiving end. Why aren't those judges and politicians impeached?"

"Who's informed enough to even identify the problem, let alone ever personally convinced enough to take action? You'd be a sitting duck for the mob police, if not fool-hardy in the absence of like-minded support."

Bill gibed. "Sounds like anybody 'fool-hardy' enough to become a deacon's got his work cut out for years to come!"

"Don't go away disappointed!" exclaimed the monsignor. "Jury duty is only the civic output of spiritually inspired behavioral changes that may take decades to achieve."

"What on earth may those habit patterns be?"

"All across the country hundreds of thousands of potential jurors have to be informed, educated and motivated. It takes courage to critically challenge officious district attorneys and judges, and countermand—nay, even impeach non-constitutional interpretations that benefit or empower no one but the minions of government and the highly placed politicians who have laws passed, or manipulate existing ones to their advantage."

"That's a tall order!" Bill reacted. "Why can't God do the direct thing, instead of letting us stumble along for years on end?"

"Such intervention is possible…but since we got ourselves into this mess— by letting the Republic be subverted—it's the Holy Spirit's way to enliven individuals to take action. After all, we're the ones titillated by the licentious gimmies of an inclusive pluralistic democracy—the piper's gotta be paid his tune, you know!"

"Yeah, well, whatever…" Bill mused. "It's gonna have to be a divine spirit more omniscient and power than the convivial one moving liberated Catholics and Pentecostals to ecstasy and charisma."

"Yes, indeed! No one but the Spirit of Jesus and the Father will enable a minority of one person to thwart and defeat evil authority figures."

"If you ask me," Bill suggested, "it'd take a saint to stand in the breech like that!"

"No doubt about that at all. 'They', the Contrived Barrenhood for example, are already smarting under the backlash of a major defeat. Public funding for the 'right-to-kill' has been cut off. Private donations have already dried up. Abortion is no longer an 'in-thing'. Their credibility has been substantially undermined."

"I'd guess," surmised Bill, "they're just itching to find scapegoats. Still, they can't take on everybody."

"No, but there'll be more than one martyr to the cause of Catholic liberty before the maturity of freedom embedded in Christ's only established Church is assured."

Bill protested. "And that's what you're asking married deacon's to take on?"

Before the monsignor could reply, there was a disruptive sounds as of someone approaching from the outer office.

Abruptly that individual emerged from around the opaque glass partition, demanding in a female voice. "What about that deacon's partner? You plotting her martyrdom as well!"

"Edna," responded Uncle in an explanatory tone. "We could fill in the context that would help ameliorate hasty conclusions!"

"I bet you could!" she retorted with the easy familiarity of a close relative.

As for Bill, he held his mind aside, not daring to be dragged into something that could escalate to his disadvantage.

He was saved from immediate confrontation by the monsignor who spoke to Edna, tongue-in-cheek. "I arrived early. Meanwhile Bill and I've been solving all the world's problems!"

"That indeed would bring on anybody's martyrdom!" Edna quipped.

Then turning to Bill she added more responsively, he thought, to the male ego. "Sorry, a relative of mine's got you all tangled up in Church business."

Bill shrugged lightly, sensing that she would go on with whatever was in her mind anyway.

She did, in justifiable emphasis. "To some, Uncle may appear overzealous. But to God and the Church he's as submissive as a lamb. Few people would have done so much to help me, and others to survive."

"Others, I know, would be eager to help," Bill added, hoping that any softness of voice would not be interpreted. But the experience at inner objectivity was short-lived; a rush of emotion flooded consciousness.

Surprisingly, a taste of resentment piqued his mouth, sending astonishment into recognition. How come jealousy, suspiciously apparent as envy—how could that base subjectivity have taken ahold of him!

Were his feelings for this female no more nobler than the carnal selfishness of a stud nightstanding with a bimbo? How 'pious" could he be, pretending to himself in expectation of a future relationship with this woman?

Still uncertainty persisted. How honorable could he make himself out to be in having gotten all fussed up over an uncle, and a priest at that, welcoming his niece so warmly?

Yet what else could he do, but accept discomfort with a brave face. Admittedly his cool had been threatened, perhaps even made worse by a memory. Had he let himself be undermined in revealing a note of charm remembered from relations with a surrogate mother?

Noticing the "knowing" look between the two of them, Bill glanced at his watch as a distraction away from any further untoward self-disclosure. He made a motion of body, as if to get up and leave, while tendering his departure. "I'm sure you two have a lot to go over, together."

"No, we've not, Bill," Edna disputed the implied reference. "We won't take advantage of personal transparency. In fact, not only should you be informed, you surely could make very worthwhile contributions to our discussion."

Reassured by Edna's words of appreciation, Bill settled back in his chair. He did not respond verbally, but looked at her in quiet patience. Otherwise the erroneous interpretation they'd seemingly expressed nonverbally might resurface in some comment or other that could be more difficult to handle vocally.

26

The tactic of suggesting his own departure from the impromptu office get-together had paid off in the currency of ostensible commiseration. But he was troubled by a suspicion over the personal quality of Edna's concern. After all, she was a competent professional with an effective "bedside" manner.

So was he; and silence were "part and parcel" of any ongoing counseling session. However, on the other hand, Bill felt some pressure to take responsibility in getting the three-way conversation started again.

He did not want to lose rapport with the monsignor whose incisive mind had already proved so beneficial to his own mental outlook. Nor could he afford the appearance of an uncouth silence in the company of such an attractive female companion.

At the end of what seemed like an eternity, Edna broke the impasse. With apparently sincere graciousness, she extended an invitation.

"Uncle, why don't you start off. You and Father Thompson have long been in on the planning. We also, together, have had words on the matter. I'm sure you've already mentioned it to Dr. Scolan."

That did it for Bill! Protesting the inaccurate use of the moniker title "Dr." was an opportunity to capitalize on, and exploit this opening for verbal re-entry. "Edna! How many times do I have to tell you…"

"…Okay, Bill," Edna interrupted, promising. "I won't 'doctor' you again. It's just I want everybody, especially Uncle to appreciate your merits."

"I'm sure they do," Monsignor responded. "He's got a good head on his shoulders. If only he'd get married…!"

The priest paused, noting the glance between the two young people before him. "Anyway, be that as it may, let's get started with the on-again, off-again nature of the project. Father Thompson has agreed to let the deaconate seminary be situated in Inland City. Up there, the internships required of recruits can be especially meaningful in witnessing to the populace."

At that admission by the monsignor, Bill thought he saw another opportunity. It could be an interpersonal tit-for-tat, as well as supply the leverage for cutting the discussion down to size. At the least, it might help in boosting his nervously compromised macho-esteem back into objectivity.

He ventured vocally. "Edna's experience could be very helpful, if persuasion of her were possible."

"She's my niece," Monsignor quipped. "We'll see."

"Uncle," she retorted, "don't twist your thumb on toppa me!"

"Gracious, no," he backtracked with a smile. "I got more respect for your spunk than that!"

"That's more like an uncle should be," she admonished playfully. "Anyway, if Father Thompson's on for it, what's the on for it, what's the off-again?"

"It's a good thing you're still on the voter registration lists for the regional government. Sooner than later, the liberal vigilantes are gonna notice that fact and agitate removal, if not surreptitiously have your name scratched from the record."

"What's the big idea about that?" Bill asked, before glancing at Edna. "I thought you were going to make a career with us, counseling?"

"I want to," she hastened to reply, but then apparently felt obliged to admit to other pressures on her. "But Uncle and Father Thompson have other plans..."

"Yeah!" Bill gibed in oblique precipitation. "Who's running whose life?"

"Nobody but her," the priest affirmed evenly. "It depends on the two of you..."

"You got us paired off, already!" Bill exclaimed hastily, before realizing the improper impact of the remark. Lamely, he tried to make amends. "I mean..."

"It's okay, Bill," she soothed. "I'm sorry, there couldn't have been more advance warning."

"It's not her fault," Uncle graciously admitted. "There's been so much at stake, we've not been able to be as transparent as we might have."

Bill looked hard from one to another, but addressed his aroused concern to the priest. "You're not sure enough about me to take a chance?"

Instead, Edna answered. "That's not it at all, Bill. But knowing the Interior and the brutality of the vigilantes, it's made some of us paranoid."

"That, I too've experienced; I'm sorry," Bill offered, cringing at the thought of having put this female person on the spot. "I didn't mean to be so judgmental."

"Okay, okay!" interposed the priest. "You two can make it up to each other later in your own way. Now, let's get on with the business in hand."

"What's that?" Edna asked, smiling benignly once again.

"To bring you the best advisement under the circumstances."

"How goes those events?" Bill asked carefully, hoping to signal intention of listening cooperatively.

"The Inland Administrator, initially installed in the aftermath of the Yoofnas federation, lived out two terms of appointment. That period of supposed temporary UFNAS reconstruction was turned into power concentration. The outward frame of democracy was, of course, carefully preserved for propagandistic purposes. But under the shell of elections, finally held, he and his henchmen have been favored in every plebiscite since."

"How can that be? Aren't there safeguards, or check and balances?" Bill wondered.

"Easy, under spin control and the compliant liberal media. When Pandora's jar was opened by the courts, all the proactive viruses of the Republic were demonically subverted by the structure of sin. Anti-commandment legislation has been widely emplaced by new age humanists. Inclusive pluralism has become the watchword of inherent evil. Police gangs hound and ferret out any evidence of socially incorrect phobia. To the tune of the Marseilles they tramp down victims and pillory them to death at home, on the streets or in the elimination centers. Even journalists conducting near-innocuous investigations are harried by the vigilantes."

"What are your sources?" Bill asked, skeptically.

"The devils themselves," came the laconic reply.

"What's that mean?" Bill persisted.

"Uncle's been the Inland Bishop's exorcist since transfer," Edna pointed out.

"How can you reveal secrets of confession?"

"Exorcism is a treatment, not a contrite request for divine pardon," The monsignor reacted. ""Exorcism is applied only after psycho-medical referral and the legal sanction of power-of-attorney."

"Do you have psychiatric training?" Bill probed.

"I am a psychiatrist. But that's only a precaution to rule out mental and physical aberrations. Exorcist power is delegated by the bishop. It is a priestly manifestation of the Holy Spirit working through mental and spiritual faculties for the discernment and expulsion of demons possessing a human being."

"Do all priests have it?" Bill persisted.

"Potentially, yes; actually, no. Only in some cases does the Holy Spirit call a priest to that martyrdom. Then, under Episcopal discernment, one or two clergymen may be commissioned in a diocese. The inland region has two exorcists because of the enormity of the evil there."

"Sounds to me like you're calling Edna back to a living martyrdom," Bill challenged.

The words were scarcely uttered, than the implied solicitude sounded over-protective. He'd better watch out, he thought to himself, lest these emotions of concern become increasingly misdirected towards incipient co-dependency.

Apparently, decorum had not been breached. Edna smiled appreciatively and responded easily. "I've been there before and have survived under God's protection. I did have to leave for awhile because my family and that of a close friend were leveraged against me. Now that my girls are away and Rebecca's found employment in a diocesan agency here on the lower mainland, they got nobody to kidnap—except me if they desire."

"Since Uncle's…" Bill blurted out, before catching hesitation at the undue familiarity and presumption of a relationship that did not exist.

"Since when's he become 'yours'!" Edna exclaimed, amused.

"You know what I mean," Bill protested, a trifle testy. "Since 'the man's' said all newspapers are under thought control, you could be spirited away into oblivion!"

"That is a danger which both of you have to reckon with," the priest cautioned.

"Both!" complained. "Are we supposed to be a team, or something?"

"Not unless you marry and are deacon ordained."

The tone of that statement may have been laid-back. But the boldness of import caught Bill, and Edna, by surprise. They lapsed into momentary silence, ill at ease and too nonplussed for verbal recuperation.

Almost at once, Uncle picked up the loose ends. "Sorry for any mystification. Whether you become a deacon or not is up to you. Administration of the seminary does not necessarily entail ordination for you, Bill, personally. However despite Father Thompson's cogent arguments, my bishop does have reservations. Edna's mission, on the other hand, should she too decide to accept is to create situations out in communities where deacon interns could be placed for the experience of witnessing. She's had a great deal of background with that kinda of in-service training for non-Catholic denominations."

"It's 'denomination' in the singular, Uncle, even though many of the evangelicals come from a variety of sects and lifestyle situations."

"You're right, of course," he agreed and then addressed Bill. "So, while your missions are related, each is implemented separately but with differences. Though you may not want to think of yourselves as a team, considerable cooperation is of value."

"That's not what I meant," Bill disputed. "I guess I'm still confused over such an active role for myself after research, counseling and publishing. The only other time of venturesome enterprise—into evil involvement—has never left me as the shame of my life."

"Bill," the monsignor began, "compunction leading to contrition and the sacrament of forgiveness encourages humility. Mortification is the unleavened foundation of a spiritual life. But scruples puff up the ego into a virtual humility—also known as 'inclusive pluralism'—that is suffused with pride. Then almost like a house-that-jack-built all the other vices concatenate throughout the soul, sickening the psyche and polluting inner freedom. The output is demonically leavened with inherent evil."

"You sound like the judges, seated in my head ever since childhood. They've always been after me, impaneled by God knows whom, probing every thought I've ever had like indictment was going out of style—leaving me in as near a convoluted mental state as any handicapped autistic could be. Only recently have those tormentors ever turned tail, slowly releasing some helper inclinations a person could take a little satisfaction in."

Bill had not spoken violently. But the intensity of expression seemed to have left both listeners silent, yet alert—as if the ancient mariner were about toe capture their attention and pied piper a trance.

Of a sudden, Edna exclaimed. "Are you for real! Have you let the sheepskinned angel stir the daimonic waters, taking possession?"

Bill looked at her, disappointed and feeling sheepish beyond chagrin—pained by the natural exasperation to be expected of any human being.

Uncle countered diplomatically. "Edna, that is a perceptive reaction. I'm sure Bill has suffered internally, intensely, from depredations of the devil. Some people have to go through purgation from inner rebellion. Others, like yourself, have had to suffer from the external revolt of savages who trip the Marseilles while persecuting reputations and inflicting terror. Situations may be different; but which is the more brutal and demeaning, it's hard to tell."

Edna came to, in apology. "I'm sorry, Bill, exploding like that. My mother, his sister," pointing to the priest, "imprinted me with the values of a sunny disposition." Then, tongue-in-cheek, she added. "Unfortunately, as you can see, her brother's a real middle-of-the-roader!"

"Thank the Lord!" exclaimed Uncle, "for the family I've had, as well's the remnant that's apparently going to survive me."

These words seemed to have struck his listeners with the eternal silence of human pathos, or so their lack of response appeared. In a moment, though, that brief lull in the priest's comments was replaced by a more up-beat expression.

The monsignor pushed on. "You both—psychologically, culturally, spiritually—it seems, are prepared for the mission God holds out to you. It strikes me that you both, whether in some liaison team or separately, will profit from an association that reveals the hidden intimacies of life. That kind of friendship can be discovered when an individual finds a companion with whom to eat, pray the liturgy of hours, or study scriptures and communicate the secrets experienced in the gospel good news."

That reflection apparently motivated Edna to respond. "Your words remind me of two things—the widespread home-style cenacles of prayer endowed in the legacy of Our Lady of Fatima more'n a hundred years ago. Secondly, it's about the soul-friends whom Kahil Gibran described:

"You were born together; and together
you shall be forevermore.
You shall lie together when white
wings scatter your days in death.
Aye, you shall ever be together in the silent memory of God'."

"So indeed, Edna," Uncle commented, "you've ever been true to mission. You have broken through the barriers of persona and egoism. You could survive together in friendship, even when living far away from each other. It's not anamnesis, but a kind of transported presence—rare, but not unknown—which presupposes objective events and subjective attitudes not present in the natural realm and not demonstrable. It's that kind of telepathic transference and spiritual communion which has kept alive your efforts and nourished the cenacle movement up in the Interior."

"I'd call it prayer—simple, practical supplication," Bill interposed. "But what strikes me as significant are the implications for personality downsizing, as the release—or catharsis necessary for spiritual transformation."

"That," began the monsignor reflectively, "would fit your research-style inner encapsulation that's complementary to Edna's interpersonal communal processing. I'd guess your so-called emancipation from judges in the head is a metaphor for stripping-away in the dark night of the soul. Quasi-character traits are purged which the world prizes as personality charisma, but nonetheless handicap spiritual growth."

"That's the kind of practical investigation Terry Bulensky and associates were working on when I arrived at Leland House. His applications were the electronic holograms being developed for catechetical demonstrations."

The monsignor's eyes began to sparkle with enthusiastic engagement. "That's where scientific and spiritual truth dovetail!"

He was interrupted by Edna rising from her chair and reacting. "I can see you two have gotten into something really exciting to 'introverts of a feather'."

"Edna, don't leave in impatience! These developments can only be brought to fruition through your enterprise in the community."

"I'm not an agitation-activist!" she protested. "But that's not why I'm leaving. I just saw Ann come in. We've got some planning to do before conferencing with Mary."

"Okay, see you later," Uncle concurred.

In the few moments it took Edna to leave, Bill's thoughts temporarily settled on self-observation. He was not surprised to discover inner expectancy mounting at the prospect of being alone again with the sharp mind of a Catholic priest.

The monsignor turned to Bill, and got right in to an explanation. "Father Thompson and I have reviewed Terry's accomplishments. Those psycho-intuitive steps exemplify the gospel good news as taught by various spiritual masters in the communion of saints."

Bill reacted. "In the other words, the wisdom of God can be discerned when human anthropology is purged of inherent hang-ups. It strikes me as interesting that personality has been alchemized down into a few types by new age humanists."

The monsignor seemed to agree. "Their denial of sin and the put-on of a new face for escapism in no way changes human anthropology. They can rationalize forever; but the seven 'deadlies' still motivate the games people play and bloat the charisma of virtual thinking."

"If only we could get half-as-excited about the virtues! That would sickle-down the flowers of narcissus overgrowing the inner pool and, in temperance, settle the psychic suspension aroused by daimonic infatuation."

"That's a hope to be realized in prayer, fasting and almsgiving," recommended the monsignor. "Interpersonal patience is only possible when the individual person hunkers down his awareness to a salted-down attention, divested of all subjectivity—the 'who' has downsized the 'whats' through centrifugal power of will. In all the treatises of values, few virtues have ever been dealt with in a psychologically functional way except that some religious texts place pride and love of money at the root of all evil."

"They're making a pretty broad generalization." Bill replied in an uncertain tone. "But then, neither have I—at least, not philosophically."

"Even in anthropological literature, I've not been able to locate a developmental humanism of virtue—let alone any meaningful treatment of the reverse psychology of impairment."

"I've tackled it," Bill conceded, "in a rough-and-ready way that makes a common sense correlation with the results of counseling practice. The approach stems from the way people actually behave—an anthropology reflecting the structure of reality. Such patterns of thought and action manifest the Judeo-Christian values of grace, prayer, beatitudes, happiness and gifts of the Holy Spirit. That excellence of manner is sustained by a temperament of the lifestyle piety. Nevertheless such reverence is scorned in the media as religiosity and an affront to 'gimmie' pluralism. They say it lacks inclusive conviviality. Anyhow, it needles the minds of liberal Catholics and new age associates like the edge of a virtual razor in an unsteady hand."

"No doubt you've touched on these matters in your publication which I've not had the opportunity to peruse. Maybe, Bill, you could brief me on the fundamentals?"

"Well, there is a taxonomy that may address your inquiry about a developmental humanism. The scale can sound like a 'house-that-jack-built'. Anyway, it starts out with the fact that every human encounters thwarting experiences throughout life regularly, if not daily. Sometimes, in severe regression, individuals may be foiled hourly. In reaction, fear is a constant, driving a person into conceit, sloth or gluttony. But these escape mechanisms bring no relief, and even accelerate addiction. Self-torment lashes out at others in anger and envy which triggers a lust for power, basely catered to by avarice."

"As simplistic as that sounds," the monsignor granted, "it has a great deal of merit in proportioning the virtues to one another within an overall anthropology and a sound humanistic development. In corollary follow-up, fear is only driven out by faith in the providence of a power, higher than oneself. This principle is a fact corroborated by Jesus Christ over and over again. Indeed, it seems strange that religious writers have not given it more careful attention. Nevertheless, faith depends on hope and leads to commitment and dedication which in turns engender patience, trust and humility. Eventually the person becomes sensitive and gentle enough to downsize lifestyle in the practice of detachment and discernment. Obviously, then, it is futile to pick out any one value for edification. While each may be reciprocal, all constitute an integral pattern of behavior that stems from a psychic conditioning, and holds all the virtues in dynamic interface."

Bill reacted by asking. "Is that what these female mentors have been telling me—that women will never be fully liberated until the male imagination has been downsized of porno prosthetics?"

"Essentially, yes. That's an interpersonal version of the psycho-dynamics according to St. John-of-the-Cross. Human souls suffer from addiction until the mind is purged of imaginative dalliance; whereas, reflection on God-given experience is required for personal growth. However, regurgitation for titillation devastates the purity of mind necessary to discern the inherent truth, beauty and goodness of the universe as endowed and sustained by the Creator."

"How did things ever get so fouled up?" Bill mused.

The monsignor paused briefly, pondering—before replying, as if to a conundrum. "The ten commandments are as much the face of God as is the cosmos which rests on the same foundation. But with scientific relativism, whose comeuppance couldn't get beyond the limited perspective of a single universe, fidelity and truth were cut loose from the commandments upon which that universe is built. Moral life was reduced to a battle of wills, resembling the wagnerian cult-o-clasms of teutonic deities. If God indeed have a floating will, allowing choice to fluctuate in any direction, then the cosmos would have shifted from the foundation of divine law upon which it is built and disintegrate. Recently however, with universe after universe unfolding into limitless space, relativity has had to be replaced with invariance. Otherwise, the slightest deviation would have wrecked the entire cosmos. Yet, you can be sure it'll be some time before the hoi polloi are allowed that kind of insight into commandment-deviance by the politically correct and so-called 'Queens and Studs of Tolerance'!"

For a moment, Bill's thoughts churned—bringing a note of levity to the surface. "You know, Father, my mind's beginning to float. Thoughts are bobbing around like a buoy that's been stormed loose from its mooring in a wagnerian sea. I gotta get back to reality or virtual thinking's done me in!"

"That comes from idle theorizing or because extrapolation is impatient—reaching for validation before the subconscious has been weaned from its pablum."

"I take that, it's moments like these when a person turns to Elijah in prayer for any sort of whisper from the entrance to the cranial cave?"

"Indeed! Otherwise, nobody else'll bother to clue you in!"